FOREVER THE MOUNTAINS

Jon R. Johnson

Published by BookLocker.com, Inc., Bradenton, Florida.

Printed in the United States of America.

The characters and events in this book are fictitious. Any similarity to real persons, living or dead, is coincidental and not intended by the author.

BookLocker.com, Inc.
2012

DEDICATION

This novel is dedicated to the memory of my mother, Mrs. Ruby Johnson. Of all my assorted scribblings, this one was her favorite.

FOREWORD

The setting for this story is the summer of 1925 in Sebastian County in west central Arkansas. All people and events are fictional except for two minor characters who appear briefly in Chapter Five. Anyone remotely familiar with the game of baseball should recognize them instantly. All place names are correct except for Burnham, Mount Moriah and Franklin. These places exist, or did exist, but I have changed the names in a probably futile effort to stem local speculation as to who the main characters really were. They weren't anyone, folks. It's just a story.

CHAPTER ONE
Tuesday, July 21

Joe Potts hobbled to the small plank dining table and dumped a fresh pone of cornbread onto a brown ironstone plate. After setting the blistering hot cast iron skillet back onto the stove, he seated himself and began slicing thick slabs of fresh churned butter. After the cornbread was properly greased, he cut slices from a garden fresh Bermuda onion that gleamed brilliant white beneath the paper thin peel and was so moist it almost dripped.

Filling a tall glass with buttermilk he kept cool in a well out back, he was now ready to start on his summer supper of poke salad, pinto beans seasoned with salt pork and sliced tomatoes. Since he generally ate only one meal a day, he made it a substantial one and at least attempted to conform to nutritional rules learned many dim years ago.

He had gotten down only two bites when there came an impatient banging on the front door of his small cabin. Glancing toward the screen door, he recognized Jimmy Andrews, a skinny seventeen year old boy with bright red hair and a pox of freckles. Jimmy was almighty excitable anyway, but now he seemed in more of an uproar than usual. It had to be something important to bring Jimmy all the way across the valley at this time of day. It was suppertime everywhere in the community. Excitable or not, Jimmy liked his vittles as well as any growing boy.

"Come in," called Joe without arising.

Jimmy pulled the screen door open and stuck his head inside. "Joe, somebody's done kilt old man Larkin!" he gushed. "Figured you ought to know!"

Joe slowly laid aside his fork and squeezed down the current mouthful. "When?" he asked quietly.

"Sometime this afternoon, I reckon! He was only found 'bout an hour ago!"

"Where?"

"Out in his pasture. He was workin' on his east fence. Jimmy paused and then added, "They used a shotgun on him, Joe. Twelve gauge most likely. He's tore up somethin' awful."

"Anybody else out there yet?"

"Purt near the whole valley."

"Prob'ly got the whole place tromped to bits," grumbled Joe. "All right, Jimmy, I'll be along shortly. Thanks."

Joe Potts sat without moving for several seconds after the boy was gone. Tom Larkin dead. Well, it came as no surprise, really. If anyone in the Burnham Community was going to get himself murdered, Larkin was the likeliest candidate. Still, Joe would have expected it to happen in Fort Smith or one of the rough mining towns like Franklin or Coal Hill. Certainly, it should not have happened on his own land virtually under the noses of the entire community. Well, there would certainly be no shortage of suspects. Most of the adult population of Sebastian County had reason to hate Tom Larkin.

It bothered Joe some that he was perhaps the last person in Burnham to learn of the murder, that he had been informed almost as an afterthought. No doubt, the scene of the crime had been trashed beyond any usefulness. Yet he would still have to put in an appearance. As constable, he was all that passed for law enforcement in Burnham Township. He wondered idly if the county sheriff in Fort Smith had been informed yet. Probably not, he decided.

Grunting, Potts heaved himself up from the table. Giving a last regretful glance at the meal he would not get to finish, he then hobbled into the tiny bedroom that comprised the remainder of his small, two room cabin. Plopping onto the straw tick mattress, he gazed for a moment at his bare feet; dirty, stained and thickly calloused. During the warmth of summer he seldom bothered with shoes, but this was a murder investigation so perhaps some decorum was called for.

Sighing, he reached under the bed and pulled out a pair of rough, scruffy brogans. The right shoe was two sizes larger than its mate and was lined in strategic places with old, worn-out socks in order to make it fit properly. It was bothersome and expensive to buy two pairs of shoes in order to have one usable pair. Yet that was the only way to accommodate his broken and twisted right foot with any degree of comfort. That was one of the reasons he liked summertime so well. He could usually dispense with shoes altogether.

Unbidden thoughts came to mind. It was twenty-seven years ago today that the accident happened. No, wait, the anniversary was last week; Wednesday of last week. As gray slowly crept its way into his thick, black hair, dates and places seemed to become dimmer and more obscure. A faint, grim smile played across his lips as he recalled the outrage and patriotism that had once surged through an eighteen-year-old boy at the very words, Remember the Maine! The final few months of school were dispensed with as he joined the noisy throng clamoring to take vengeance on the treacherous Spaniards.

But war turned out to be not at all as expected. Far more men had died of dysentery and yellow fever than from lead poisoning. What passed as food made the situation even worse. How often had he howled about the barrels of rotten pork peddled to the government by those determined to make a quick buck off the war and to hell with the men sweating out their lives in the steaming jungle? Every sack of beans had to be laboriously picked through to separate the pebbles that had been mixed in to pad the weight. The grim smile vanished from Joe's face. Even after all these years, such memories still filled him with disgust.

Disgust, too, with the army. In its less than infinite wisdom, tens of thousands of city boys who had never fired a rifle were made into infantrymen while a crack-shot farm boy wound up as a cook. It had not taken Joe long to realize that the army had hardtack for brains.

Then came the accident while fording one of the mucked-up, sucking rivers crisscrossing the Cuban Isle. A wagon wheel cracked and down went a ton and a half of moldy Civil War crackers and putrid pork. Joe, who had been standing and lashing the laboring mules, was tossed overboard and somehow wound up with his right foot entangled in the broken spokes while being pulled inexorably downward.

As thousands of tropical birds cackled and chattered, Joe Potts, army cook, bubbled and gurgled his life away in a fetid Cuban stream. Had it not been for the huge Cherokee serving as his striker, Joe would certainly have drowned that day. Plunging into chest-deep water, the big Indian had somehow lifted the corner of the wagon, allowing Joe to wriggle free.

Fortunate, but strange; almighty strange. The Indian was strong, but not that strong. No man can lift three thousand pounds of dead weight. But odd things can happen when men are scared and excited. Once when an entire farm was being consumed by flames, Joe had watched in awe as a frail shoestring of a man raced from a flaming shed with a full barrel of molasses. Later, when things calmed down, it took three big men to lift it.

Sighing again, he gingerly pulled on the right brogan and laced it as tightly as comfort and reason would allow. Joe Potts, war hero, he thought with not a little bitterness. Now he was an aging, one-time army cook with a mangled foot and a miserly pension that barely paid for his monthly gallon of Tom Larkin's moonshine.

But no more, no more. Tom Larkin now lay riddled with buckshot, and who else could render such miracles with sugar and corn? He paused for a moment, wondering whether he ought to pack his old Army .38 Colt. No, he finally decided. There would likely be no one to arrest and the sight of any kind of gun would do Larkin's widow no good. He shoved the revolver and holster back under the mattress.

Slowly, he pulled open a drawer and took out a cheap, battered tin star that identified him as a constable. Anymore, the position was mostly a joke, one of the obsolete remnants of Anglo-Saxon culture that the modern world had not gotten around to burying. The position had been conferred upon him as a kindness and almost as a charity. His share of the occasional fine money comprised a modest supplement to his meager pension. No one took the badge seriously, least of all himself. Yet he was still an officer of the law. For only the third or fourth time during his twenty years as constable, he pinned on the badge.

The gray mule looked around at him with surprise and perhaps even a bit of suspicion. She had already been fed, watered and curried for the night, and her lame, chunky master seldom went anywhere after dark. Yet there was no mistaking the wool blanket across her back and the old familiar weight of the saddle. She swelled herself just before the cinches tightened, but then the sharp, hickory cane poked into her belly and she exhaled with a gush. The tactic never worked, but the conventions had to be honored.

"Sorry about this, Suzy," apologized Joe while appeasing her with a couple of sugar cubes, "but we got business to attend to."

As he shoved the bit into her mouth, a funny thought struck him. "Suzy," he asked, "what do you think of a fellow who talks to his mule? Ain't forty-five a little young to have most of your plow points busted?"

Suzy flicked an ear and switched her tail, not deigning to answer. Shoving his cane into a special boot, Joe climbed aboard and backed Suzy out of her stall.

The first stars of the evening were just beginning to appear as Joe pointed the mule down the lane that led away from his tiny cabin at the southern base of Backbone Mountain. The Devil's Backbone was the original name, but lately folks had taken to just calling it Backbone Mountain. This was unfortunate in Joe's opinion. He felt the original name better described the shape and disposition of the broken, craggy monster, the first real mountain one encountered when traveling southward up and out of the Arkansas River Valley.

A few miles to the west on the Devil's Backbone, a Civil War battle had been fought. It didn't really amount to much as Civil War battles went, there being only a few dozen casualties on both sides. That many fell every few minutes at Antietam. Still, those who died were just as dead, and it hardly mattered whether it happened during a massive bloodletting in the picturesque Maryland countryside or a forgotten skirmish on a lonely hilltop.

Or a murky Cuban river.

The battle site had been pretty well picked over by several generations of teenage re-enactors, but one could still occasionally find a broken, rusty bayonet or pitted canteen. Soon, though, no traces would be left, for man's rubble was slowly sinking into the earth. As the Indians said, only the mountains lived forever.

He reached State Highway Ten, still a gravel road in this backcountry, and turned east. Goosing Suzy into an easy lope, the fields and pastures rushed past in a neat checkerboard fashion. The cotton was well into the boll stage by now and looked promising, perhaps three quarters of a bale per acre on average. Just opposite Wynn's store was a large pasture speckled with tawny Jersey cows with faces nearly black. Freed from evening milking and the brutal afternoon heat, they ambled along switching their tails, ready to graze beneath the stars.

Far off to the south, the first whippoorwill of the night began to howl its monotonous call, a wild yet curiously comforting sound. Often, one of the vociferous night birds would orate for hours with hardly a pause for breath. They must be the politicians of the bird world, Joe decided.

To the south and running parallel to the Devil's Backbone was a low, wooded hill too rocky and poor to be farmed, too marginal even to be cleared for pasturage. It lacked the bulk and staying power to be regarded as a mountain. Like most men, it began slowly, attained no great heights and soon played out. No one had ever bothered to even attach a name to it. It was simply called the hill.

Beyond this insignificant ridge were a narrow, sparsely settled valley and then another rugged behemoth called Washburn Mountain. South of this mountain was a broken, rambling, heavily timbered canyon named Pine Hollow for a reason even total strangers to the area could usually guess with little difficulty. No one had ever attempted to settle in that crazy maze folded into the Ouachita Mountains; no one seemed to even know who it belonged to, if anyone. Sheer bluffs, tangled briars and stunted timber made it almost impenetrable. Here was the realm of the rabbit, the bobcat and the moonshiner.

Tom Larkin's farm consisted of three hundred acres at the eastern end of the Burnham community just beyond where no name hill played out and east of Highway Ten which had now turned south to attack Washburn Mountain. North of the Larkin place just at the curve of the highway was a large frame structure which served as a Baptist church on Sundays and as a school during the week. Tom Larkin had never set foot inside this building except for the funeral of his mother nearly ten years before. His only child, Billy, had been a sporadic visitor for school purposes until the age of sixteen when the law said his presence was no longer required. Ever since, the Burnham community had seen little of Billy Larkin and did not consider itself overly deprived by his absence.

The Larkin house was a rambling, two story, white frame structure with five gables, three porches and two chimneys. By far the largest residence in Burnham, it could easily accommodate more than two people and had once done so when Samuel Larkin built it back around the turn of the century to provide a common roosting place for his extensive extended family.

When Tom Larkin became master of the house in 1910, he began systematically kicking out various cousins and nephews, eventually working up to siblings. When occupancy was reduced to three, Tom Larkin regarded the project as nearly complete.

Finally, one crisp autumn evening the peacefulness of the valley was shattered by a paroxysm of screams, breaking furniture and gunshots, following which young Billy Larkin took his leave. Master Tom had finally achieved his greatest goal in life.

The front yard was now occupied by nearly two dozen men and boys gathered to discuss the event of the century. Cigarettes glowed orange in the deepening twilight, and every now and then a stream of dirty brown liquid arced out to spatter on the sun-baked ground. Behind the house an old hound howled mournfully, somehow aware of what had happened.

Joe guided Suzy through the maze of hushed conversations and reined up at the front porch where three men were taking turns from a small, silver-colored flask. Gingerly dismounting, he almost stumbled when his bad foot touched the ground. When he recovered, the flask was being thrust under his nose.

"Have a nip, Joe!"

Joe shook his head and pushed it away. "Has the body been brought in yet?" he asked.

"Yep!" replied Harley Simpson, swelling with pride. "Helped cart him in myself. He's in the south bedroom."

Joe sighed loudly. "I wish you'd have left him in the pasture."

All three men looked properly shocked.

"Hell's bells, Joe!" protested Harley "We couldn't just leave him layin' out there! What's got into you, anyway?"

"This ain't like a regular death," explained Joe patiently. "Movin' him could keep us from findin' out who did it. The sheriff ain't gonna like this one little bit." He paused and then asked, "Has anyone called the sheriff?"

The men looked at each other with blank expressions. There were several grunts and shrugs. Shaking his head, Joe pushed past them and swiveled his way up the porch steps. Just as he reached the screen door, he found his way blocked by a heavy, wrinkled woman with a pained countenance.

"Ain't this just awful, Joe!" she complained. "A killin' right here in Burnham! I just don't know what the world's comin' to!"

"Yes, maam, it's just awful," agreed Joe. With some effort, he finally got past her and plunged into a bevy of commiserating females. Waving aside coffee, cake and cookies, he finally made his way to the south bedroom.

A short, wiry man named Ed Peters, the closest thing to a friend Tom Larkin could claim, had already undressed the body and was now bathing the massive chest wound. With his usual consideration, Ed had first put down a section of canvas to keep the mattress from being soiled. He looked up and nodded sadly when Joe stepped into the room.

"Hold up on that for now, Ed. The sheriff and coroner will want to see the body before its cleaned."

Ed first looked surprised, then angry and finally contrite. "I'm sorry, Joe. I never thought of that." He gazed down at his scuffed boots. "I'm sorry," he repeated.

"Forget it, Ed. Can't be helped now. Where are his clothes?"

Ed pointed absently at a bloody pile in the corner.

Joe nodded dully and then stepped up to the body. The wound was messy, incredibly messy. He had seen men killed by Spanish Mausers who didn't look this bad. The center of the chest was a red, pulpy goo with chunks of bone and heart tissue scattered throughout. He could imagine what Larkin's back must look like and was glad he did not have to see it.

Steeling himself, he bent lower to examine the periphery of the wound for powder burns. There were none and that meant the killer must have been at least ten feet away. Yet the lack of scatter indicated a range of less than thirty feet. Tom Larkin was far from trusting. Who would he let get that close with a shotgun?

"Ed, did you help bring the body in?"

"Yes, I did, Joe."

"Was there a gun next to the body?"

"No, but his shotgun was in the back of his wagon."

"Had it been fired?"

Ed hesitated. "Don't reckon anybody checked, Joe. We had other things on our minds."

Joe stepped to the corner and picked up the pair of overalls, its bib shot to bloody tatters. The flannel shirt was already stiff with matted blood and gore. There were no powder burns on either garment. He dropped them back onto the pile and picked up the boots, examining them closely.

"What are you looking for?" asked Ed curiously.

"Nothing. Anything."

The answer made no sense to Ed. Joe next picked up a pair of gloves. They were what would be expected for a heavy job like fencing; heavy thick leather, well worn and well scratched. He narrowed his eyes suspiciously at a streak of dried blood on the back of the left glove. He returned to the body and studied the now thoroughly washed face, noticing a long scratch on the right cheek. It would only be natural to wipe at it with the back of the left hand. Well, barbed wire was mighty scratchy stuff.

"Were these on his hands or in his pockets?"

Ed was caught off guard by the question and had to think a moment. "In his pockets, I believe. Yes, I'm sure of it. They fell out when we lifted the body and Jimmy picked them up. What difference does it make?"

"Probably none," admitted Joe.

He started to turn away from the body but then suddenly froze. His first view had been from the right side, his second from the left. Now he noticed something odd about the left arm. He tried to lift it for a better look, but the limb was already stiff from rigor mortis.

Squatting, he peered closely at the upper part of the arm and noted that the back of it was badly mutilated. Had two shots been fired? He would have to ask about that. It seemed an unlikely wound. Perhaps this injury had occurred when Larkin fell. He stepped back to the pile of clothes and picked up the shirt. There was no doubt about it. The back of the upper left sleeve was shredded and bloody. He dropped it back onto the pile.

"Ed, I'd like for you to stay with the body until I can get the sheriff and coroner out here. But no more washin' on him, hear?"

"All right, Joe."

"And Ed, don't let nobody bother his clothes. They're evidence."

Ed gave him a strange look. "Evidence? Of what?"

"Not sure, but somethin' doesn't fit here. These clothes could be important. The shirt especially."

Ed shrugged. "All right, Joe, anything you say. I figured to be here all night anyway."

Joe paused a moment. "Ed, I reckon you was as close to a friend as Larkin had. Do you know of anybody who was madder at him than usual?"

Ed smiled sadly and shook his head. "Just the usual squabbles. Nothing new I heard about."

"All right. Thanks, Ed. I'll have someone bring you some coffee."

Joe paused at the door for a last look at the dark, drab death room. A kerosene lantern flickered atop a small dresser, filling the chamber with twitching shadows. Tom Larkin, his eyes still open, stared sightlessly at the ceiling, his mouth hanging ajar and his chin slightly askew. Larkin was a large man, six feet two inches and well over two hundred pounds.

But a twelve gauge plays no favorites; it kills strong and weak alike. Tom Larkin had been a noisy, contentious man, but that was all finished now. He was going into the ground with all the other saints and sinners, and now someone else would have the land he had hogged and hoarded.

"But oh Lord, Tom," whispered Joe, "you sure could make some mighty fine squeezins."

Backing out of the room and pulling the door closed, he almost bumped into Reverend Jacob Watson, a large, almost dangerously obese man with a bald head that now glistened with beads of sweat. He was dressed in a soggy brown suit and his once white shirt now smelled faintly. The handkerchief he used to wipe at his brow looked like it would yield a half a pint if wrung tightly. Why are nearly all preachers overweight? wondered Joe. Isn't the body supposed to be a temple? Perhaps, he mused, preachers overate to compensate for all the other vices they were supposed to forego.

Jacob Watson was a hellfire and brimstone wall shaker in the finest Southern Baptist tradition. Often on Sunday mornings, Joe could hear him rattling the rafters from a half a mile away. He often wondered why the Lord's message had to be delivered in a manner that made children cringe and pull at their mothers' skirts.

But there was little hellfire and brimstone in Reverend Watson tonight. In fact, he looked nervous and out of place; certainly, he was not in charge as he would usually be in such a situation. Someone had sent for him and he had dutifully come, but he clearly would have preferred to be elsewhere. To him, Tom Larkin was an unsalvageable sinner who was already sizzling in one of Satan's more torrid spots. Joe also knew that he himself rated only a notch or two higher in Reverend Watson's estimation. Now, though, the preacher looked at him with a helpless expression.

"Mrs. Larkin has asked me to perform the funeral ceremony." This was offered both as information and as a complaint.

A church funeral for Tom Larkin? Joe suspected it was now very noisy somewhere in the spirit world. "I'm sure you'll make a fine talk," he assured Watson.

"How can I?" he complained. "We both know what he was! Everyone knew what he was!"

"It don't matter what he was, Preacher. Tom's done went to his justice, whatever it is. Funerals are for the livin', not the dead. It's always been that way. All you got to do is comfort Mrs. Larkin a mite."

"I can't! Any comforting words would be a lie!"

Joe wondered about that. Perhaps the most comforting words the good widow could hear would be that her late husband was now sizzling and popping like bacon in a hot skillet. Perhaps this was just her way of getting in the last word in a long, simmering dispute. Mrs. Larkin had been a dutiful wife but hardly a loving one. After all, who could possibly love Tom Larkin?

"Well, Preacher, the way I see it, you got three choices. First, you can get up there and lie through your teeth."

"That I absolutely refuse to do!"

"Or you can refuse to do the service."

"I can't do that either!"

"Well, your only other choice is to howl and fume like you usually do and tell ever'body what a bad boy Tom was."

Anger flashed from Watson's eyes and it was only with great effort that he choked back what he really wanted to say. "Perhaps I could make a brief introduction and then allow someone else to deliver the eulogy."

"You mean pass the buck?"

Joe feared the preacher was going to pop a blood vessel. "You, perhaps," Watson finally squeaked.

Joe smiled grimly. "The only good thing I could say about Tom Larkin is that he made mighty fine 'shine."

"That's not funny, Mister Potts!"

"Wasn't meant to be, Preacher. Fact is, lies seem to stick in my craw, too."

"So what can we do?"

"Not we, Preacher. You. This is your tiger and I'll leave you to wrestle with it." As Joe gingerly stepped past him, he could almost feel the angry eyes boring into the back of his head.

There were only about a half a dozen telephones in the Burnham community, but fortunately one of them belonged to Tom Larkin. This grudging concession to modern gadgetry was a natural consequence of Larkin's multifarious business activities. These included not only the production and distribution of moonshine, but also the delivery of timbers to the mines, breeding of fighting cocks and the buying, selling and trading of coon dogs, many of them with cloudy ownership.

As luck would have it, the instrument was currently dominated by Mrs. Harper, a sixty year old widow and full-time busybody who was going ninety words a minute to a neighbor across the valley. Words like terrible and awful were repeated with monotonous frequency. It seemed a very one-sided conversation. Joe fidgeted and ground his teeth. A hand touched his shoulder. He turned and found it belonged to Jimmy Andrews.

"Figured out who done it yet, Joe?"

"It's way too early for that, Jimmy." He paused a moment. "Jimmy, Ed Peters is sitting with the body. Would you mind takin' him some coffee? He likes it with two dips of sugar and just enough cream to change the color a mite."

"Sure, Joe, be glad to."

"And Jimmy, see if you can do somethin' about that howlin' dog. That can't be doin' Mrs. Larkin's nerves any good."

"Okay, Joe."

Mrs. Harper finally concluded her gab session, but was now turning the crank to ring someone else. Joe pulled the earpiece out of her hand. "Sorry, maam," he apologized, "but I need to use this. Official business."

The woman fixed him with an icy stare. "And just who do you think you are, Joe Potts?" It was clear that Mrs. Harper already had a strong opinion on that matter whether or not Joe provided further elucidation.

"I'm the law enforcement officer for this township," he replied while stepping to the mouthpiece and crowding her aside.

"Well, I never!" she exclaimed angrily and stomped away in a huff.

"No, maam, I expect you don't," he muttered to himself. "Not ever."

Jimmy came by and handed him a cup of coffee just the way he liked it, scalding hot and blacker than a banker's heart. He nodded his thanks and promptly scalded his lips.

"Yes?" came an impatient reply from the earpiece.

"Mary, this is Joe Potts. Get me Sheriff Faulkner in Fort Smith."

The annoyed tone subsided. So this wasn't Mrs. Harper again after all. "It may take a while, Joe. It's after office hours. He could be anywhere."

"That's fine, Mary. I'll wait."

It was nearly a half an hour before a grouchy, half slurred voice finally came over the line. "This is Sheriff Faulkner. What is it?"

Joe identified himself and quickly explained the situation.

There was a long pause. "Burnham? Where the hell is that? You sure you got the right county?"

Joe gave directions. There was another long pause at the other end and then a spray of obscenities. "This'll take up the whole damn night! All right, give me a couple hours to get there!" He hesitated.

"Better make that three hours," corrected the sheriff. "It'll take at least an hour to get the coroner sobered up enough to travel." The line went dead with such finality that even the click seemed to register aggravation.

Joe promptly rang Mary again. The answer was instantaneous. Obviously, she had been listening into his conversation with the sheriff. "Mary, get hold of Doc Hudson and tell him what's happened out here. Tell him I'd like him to come out."

"Don't you want to talk to him yourself?"

"That's not necessary. You can fill him in on all the details." He hung up before her protest could singe his ears.

Jimmy Andrews was waiting for him on the front porch with a kerosene lantern. "I figured you'd want to see where we found him."

As Joe laboriously climbed aboard Suzy, Jimmy deftly sprang astride a tall bay gelding. Joe glanced at the boy with envy, remembering long ago days when he, too, had been so full of vinegar.

As he had feared, the south pasture had been trampled beyond any possible usefulness, the knee-high grass crisscrossed with dozens of trails. No doubt, every man and boy in Burnham had already been out here tromping around, spitting tobacco juice and handling evidence.

Joe sighed loudly as Suzy plodded along in the wake of the bay as Jimmy angled across the pasture toward the southeast corner. When the boy finally reined up, Joe handed him a match to light the lantern and then crawled off Suzy. The match flared briefly in the darkness, and when it died it had been replaced by the less gaudy but more constant flicker of the lantern. Jimmy squatted beside a large splotch of dried blood.

"Right here is where he was layin'," he explained needlessly.

Joe dropped to his knees. "How did he lay? On his stomach? His side?"

"On his back. All stretched out like he just laid down to go to sleep."

"Odd way for a man to fall. Maybe somebody turned him over to see if he was really dead." Joe opened his pocketknife and carved a line in the ground, marking the position of the body.

"I guess you used his wagon to haul him in." Jimmy nodded. "Where was it?"

"In the shade of that red oak."

Joe glanced up at the large shape silhouetted against the night sky about forty feet to their right. Then his eyes shifted to the stretch of fence directly in front of them. "Fence don't look too bad along here. Maybe he was done fixin' it."

"No," corrected Jimmy. "The break was down yonder. 'Bout midway between here and the tree."

Joe narrowed his eyes. "You sure?"

"Sure I'm sure, Joe. He hadn't even started on the fence. He was still clearin' away brush so's he could get to it." The boy shook his head with disapproval. "This whole fence line is growed up pretty bad. Whole fence should have been rebuilt years ago."

Joe ignored this belaboring of the obvious. "What the devil was he doin' this far down?" he muttered.

"What was that, Joe?"

"Nothin', nothin'. Where did you find his axe?"

Jimmy looked dumbfounded. "I, I don't remember seein' it," he stammered.

"Was it in the wagon?"

Jimmy thought for a moment. "No, I don't think so. In fact, I'm sure of it!" The boy sprang to his feet and started for the break in the fence. "I'll look for it."

Joe also arose but much more slowly. However, he had taken only a few steps before the tip of his cane struck something that was not the ground. He bent down and scratched through the grass until he found it.

"Never mind, Jimmy!" he called. "I found it. Bring that lantern back here a minute." Joe chewed at his lower lip. "Wonder why he carried the axe all the way down here. He didn't need it right here."

24

Jimmy arrived and held the lantern close. One side of the axe blade was spattered with blood and the handle on the same side contained a couple of buckshot. "I think we got somethin' here, Jimmy."

"What, Joe? What do you mean?"

But Joe only shook his head. He knelt again and made a long slash in the ground to indicate the axe handle and a short cross cut for the blade. After securing the axe to his saddle, he hobbled down to the break in the fence. Dropping to his knees, he wriggled into the matted growth. A tentacle of wild rose slapped across his back and clung in a thousand places. Joe expressed a few deep-seated emotions regarding the noxious plant. This did nothing for his bleeding back but was balm for his scratched disposition. Within moments he backed out, sat on the grass and began to wipe fresh cow manure off his right hand.

"Half suspected this," he muttered. "Those wires ain't broke. They've been cut."

"Cut? But who would cut them?"

"Larkin."

Jimmy shook his head in disbelief. "Why would he cut his own fence?"

Joe smiled grimly. "He had his reasons. Come on, let's get back to the house."

As they rode slowly past a small outbuilding about sixty feet behind the house, they heard a faint whimpering coming from inside. "Thanks for shuttin' up the dogs, Jimmy."

The boy shrugged. "There was just the one."

Joe pulled up sharply. "You sure?"

"Sure I'm sure."

Joe again swung down from the mule and dropped to his knees. After crawling around for a couple of minutes, he struggled back up. "Lots of fresh chewed bones around here for just one dog. Is that old Marty shut up in there?"

Jimmy nodded. "Can't figure why Larkin kept him. He don't seem the kind to keep an animal just for a pet."

Years ago, Marty had had an unfortunate adventure with a bobcat after which he was no longer of any use for breeding purposes. Now he was so old he couldn't keep up with the younger dogs. Marty's days as a working coon dog were far behind him.

"He was still useful for training pups," informed Joe.

The crowd gathered about the Larkin house had begun to dwindle. After all, it was getting late and tomorrow was another workday. One of the few still remaining was a large, hulking young man standing at the edge of the porch and wringing a shaggy straw hat in huge, work-hardened hands. His faded, patched overalls were smeared with sweat and dust and his bare feet were utterly filthy with caked dirt. Joe smiled and waved a greeting before passing into the house. Before he could reach the south bedroom, Jimmy had presented him with another cup of hot coffee.

Ed Peters was sitting in the same chair, an empty cup and saucer on the floor beside him. Joe put the bloody axe on the floor beside the pile of clothes and then pulled up another chair. Ed sighed loudly and shook his head.

"This is the first killin' in Burnham since, well, I don't know when."

"The first since that lynchin' back in the Eighties," remarked Joe, wrinkling his forehead as he recalled old stories. "But that was in Greenwood, so I guess it don't count for Burnham. Guess we ain't had a killin' since the Rebellion." He took a sip from his cup. "Ed, how many dogs you got now?"

"Three."

"Still got old Blue?"

"Sure. Why do you ask?"

"Just wonderin'. Did Tom ever say anything about gettin' out of the dog business?"

"Never said nothin' to me about it."

"Well, he's down to just old Marty now."

Ed looked genuinely surprised. "He had six bitches last week. In fact, he borrowed Blue to breed a couple of 'em." Ed shrugged. "Maybe he sold 'em."

"But why would he bother to breed them first?" Joe took another sip while Ed pondered this latest mystery. "Does Tom have anything left in the basement?"

"About thirty gallons, last I knew of."

Joe chewed his lower lip. "Reckon we best get it out of here. The sheriff will be along shortly and he may take a notion to search the place. If he finds that whiskey, he may use it as an excuse to try to take the whole farm."

Ed's mouth dropped open. "My God, I never thought of that! Where can we put it, Joe?"

"Somewhere on your place?"

Ed shook his head violently. "My old lady would never stand for it!"

It was the answer Joe had hoped for. "There's a small cave back of my place," he suggested innocently.

Ed nodded vigorously. "I know the one! That's just the place! Nobody would ever look there! When do we move it?"

"It'll have to be soon." Joe clapped Ed on the knee. "You just stay here with the body. I'll take care of it. Soon as ever'body's gone, I'll hitch up one of Tom's wagons and get Jimmy to drive it over to my place. You want some more coffee?"

"I'd appreciate it, Joe."

He picked up the empty cup and saucer before leaving the room.

Doctor Walter Hudson was waiting just outside the door. Hudson was a short, slender man in his early sixties with shaggy white hair and a pair of square spectacles perched low on his beak of a nose. The dirty, rumpled condition of his blue suit was ample testimony that this had been a long, hard day.

"Accident at the mine, Doc?"

The astonishment showed on Hudson's face. "How did you know?"

"You still got some coal dust on your shoes."

The doctor looked down self-consciously. "Well, so I do," he admitted. "Yes, there was an accident. A timber snapped out at the Franklin mine and a couple of miners got some busted ribs."

"Anyone killed?"

Thank God, no."

"Have you seen Mrs. Larkin?"

"Yes. I gave her a sedative. One lady is staying with her. The others have gone home." Joe glanced around and saw that the house had become much quieter. "May I see the body now?" asked Hudson.

Joe nodded. "It'd be best not to touch nothin', though, 'til the sheriff and coroner get here." Hudson nodded agreement. Joe stuck his head back into the bedroom. "Ed, Doc's gonna take a look at the body. It's all right."

After the door closed behind Doc Hudson, Joe went looking for Jimmy and found him in the kitchen with a glass of milk and the cookie jar. The boy looked up with embarrassment and brushed crumbs from his chin.

"Reckon all the excitement whetted my appetite," he mumbled.

"Hitch up Tom's wagon," instructed Joe. "Not the one you carted him in on. Get the other one. Bust a bale of hay and strew it in the bed and then bring it around to the back door. And tie that gelding of yours behind it."

"All right, Joe," agreed Jimmy, arising from the table. "What's goin' on?"

"You'll find out soon enough."

The door to the basement was locked and Joe had no idea where the key might be. Muttering a curse, he stepped back and examined the door for a means of entry other than smashing it. Fortunately, the hinges were mounted on his side. He quickly removed the pins and pulled the door away.

"Have to remember to re-hang it before the sheriff gets here," he told himself.

Along one wall of the basement were several shelves. The bottom two supported ten glass jugs, each containing a gallon of liquid clear as water. The next shelf up held only six and the remaining shelves were empty. Upon each jug was a small paper label proclaiming the contents to be ARKANSAS PYZZON. Few moonshiners had the audacity to label their product, but then Tom Larkin was the very best. Was, past tense.

"Damn shame!" muttered Joe.

Every jug was not only corked, but sealed with beeswax and marked with Larkin's skull and crossbones signet ring. This was not a warning about the whiskey. It was a not so subtle hint that other 'shiners should not imitate his trademark.

Joe managed four gallons on the first trip, but it was awkward getting back up the stairs while juggling his cane and more than thirty pounds of whiskey. He almost dropped one and his heart skipped several beats. This stuff's too precious to waste, he scolded himself. That energetic young pup could do most of the toting. Jimmy's eyes almost popped out when he saw the cargo to be hauled.

When the last jug was tucked safely into the hay, Joe turned to the boy. "Park the wagon next to my cabin and put the team in the stable. Then you go straight home. Don't stop back by here. And Jimmy, drive real careful."

Jimmy was grinning ear to ear. "Sure, Joe. You aimin' to keep all this for yourself?"

"Don't worry your head about that. And don't be samplin' the goods. I'll give you a sniff of it later, but tonight ain't the time for such foolishness. And I meant that about goin' straight home. I don't want you around when the sheriff arrives. This is serious business, Jimmy."

The smile vanished. "All right, Joe. Sure."

Jimmy climbed into the wagon and gave the lines a flick. Joe stood and watched as the wagon lumbered around the house and onto the highway. Then he turned and went back into the house. He had a basement door to re-hang.

About an hour later the night stillness was shattered by a growling, coughing Model T Ford. Joe and Doc Hudson stepped out onto the porch just as the ridiculous machine sputtered into silence. The first passenger out was a fifty year old man sporting an enormous gut and clad in a glistening white suit, Stetson and cowboy boots. His cigar tip glowed in the darkness as he turned to help the second man who was clearly drunk.

"Now watch your step, Bobby Dean," the big man cautioned.

The third man out, the driver, was a tall, slender young man in his early twenties and dressed in the khaki uniform of a deputy. Strapped about his waist was an old-time gunbelt that supported a huge .45 Colt Peacemaker. By the looks of it, it had seen some history. The young man stood for a moment stretching out the kinks of travel. Joe hobbled down the steps to greet the trio.

"Is this the Tom Larkin place?" snapped Sheriff Willie Don Faulkner. He didn't even bother to remove the cigar from between his teeth.

"This is the place," confirmed Joe. He introduced himself and Doc Hudson.

"Constable, huh?" drawled Faulkner. The sarcasm was thick enough to slice and drop into a frying pan. The sheriff turned to the drunkard whose mismatched suit was soiled and sweaty. The man smelled strongly of whiskey.

"Come on, Bobby Dean, we got a killin' to clear up." Then he added under his breath, "Dumb bastard prob'ly shot hisself!" Faulkner waddled past with the drunken coroner in tow.

Hudson shook his head in disgust. "How does a man like that get such a position?" he demanded sourly.

"Which one you talkin' about?" asked Joe.

Hudson smiled thinly. "I was referring to the coroner."

"Politics. He's the brother-in-law of the county party boss." He paused and then added, "Faulkner is a first cousin."

The deputy stepped up and offered his hand. "Name's Charles Martin and I'm not kin to any of them."

"You should be proud," complimented Joe. The three men marched into the house behind the first two.

"In here," announced Joe, indicating the south bedroom.

"Who are you?" growled Faulkner when his eyes fell upon Ed Peters.

"He was watchin' the body to make sure nobody bothered it," explained Joe.

"Get out!" snapped Faulkner.

Ed Peters, normally very even-tempered, quickly arose with his fists clenched in anger. Joe stepped in quickly. "It's all right, Ed. Go out to the kitchen and have some more coffee. We'll be finished here shortly."

When Peters was gone, Joe turned to the sheriff. "There's no call to be growlin' and snappin' at ever'body."

Faulkner pointed his cigar threateningly. "You don't be tellin' me what to do, boy! All right, Bobby Dean, get on with it!"

But Bobby Dean was in no condition to get on with anything. In all his years as coroner, this was the first body he had ever had to view outside of funerals. Local doctors and morticians always did whatever had to be done. He merely signed a few documents handed him from time to time by his pretty little niece who burdened the county payroll as his secretary. Now he gazed down at the bloody, mutilated corpse before him and his face was nearly as white as Willie Don's suit.

"Holy Jesus!" he hissed thinly. "This son of a bitch is dead!"

"Brilliant diagnosis, Doctor," remarked Hudson acidly.

"He ain't no doctor, dammit!" snapped Faulkner. "He's a coroner!"

"My mistake," drawled Hudson.

Faulkner stared at the body while chewing his cigar. "Maybe he shot hisself," he suggested. That would at least wrap up this tiresome affair.

"With a wound like that?" demanded Hudson incredulously.

"He could have been pullin' his shotgun out of a wagon barrel first and somethin' caught the trigger."

"Tom Larkin wasn't that dumb," argued Joe. "His shotgun was in the wagon bed, but it hadn't been fired. Anyway, the body was nearly forty feet from the wagon. I doubt Tom walked any forty feet after gettin' a wound like that."

"Death was instantaneous," pronounced Hudson with finality.

Faulkner gave them both a dirty look and took another bite of his cigar. "Why did you let the yokels move the body anyway?" he demanded bitterly.

"That was done before I knew anything about the killin', Sheriff. Anyway, I wouldn't fault these folks too much on that account. They ain't used to murders and crime scenes and the like. It just didn't seem proper to them to leave a dead man layin' out like he was a dog."

Faulkner snorted contemptuously and pointed at the wound with his cigar. "Dig some of that shot out so we'll know what size it was."

"You, you mean me?" gasped the coroner.

Faulkner affected an astonished expression. "Why, no," he replied sweetly. "I meant for Larkin to do it. Hell, yes, I meant you, Bobby Dean. Who did you think I meant?"

"But, but…."

Doctor Hudson nudged the coroner aside and quickly extracted one of the shot. "Double ought," he announced.

"I can see that!" growled Faulkner.

"I'd like to show you somethin' else," said Joe. He half turned the now stiff body to reveal the wounds on the back of the upper left arm.

The sheriff contemplated this a moment before offering a theory. "I guess he threw his arm up when he saw he was about to be shot. Wouldn't do no good, but I reckon it would be a natural thing to do." Faulkner had now abandoned his accidental shooting scenario.

"Tom Larkin wouldn't cringe from the devil hisself," argued Joe. "He'd stare him in the eyes and spit in his face."

Faulkner glared at him with barely concealed annoyance. "You got a better explanation?"

"I think so." He picked up the axe and handed it to the sheriff. "He had this drew back to swing it. It was layin' next to

33

the body. See, there's dried blood on one side of the blade and some shot in the handle."

Faulkner puffed furiously on his cigar. "Maybe," he grunted, thrusting the axe at Deputy Martin. "Doc, how long's he been dead?" He no longer bothered to even acknowledge the coroner.

"Six to eight hours," answered Hudson.

Faulkner pulled out his watch. "Ten o'clock now. That means he was killed between two and four this afternoon."

"He was found at five thirty," offered Joe.

"Who found him?"

"The hired hand. Mrs. Larkin sent him when Tom didn't come in for supper."

"Where is he?"

"On the porch, but it won't do any good to talk to him."

"He'll talk if he knows what's good for him!" growled Faulkner before Joe had a chance to explain. The sheriff stomped from the room. With a sigh, Joe hobbled out after him.

The hulking young man with the lost, puppy-dog expression was still standing in the exact spot he had occupied for the past several hours. Sheriff Faulkner pushed up so close that his enormous belly was actually touching the young man. He looked him up and down for several seconds before finally taking the cigar from his mouth.

"What's your name?" snapped Faulkner.

The young man looked helplessly at Joe. "His name is Mase. That's short for Mason," explained Joe.

"Let him answer!"

"He can't, Sheriff. He's deaf and dumb."

Faulkner whirled on Joe. "What?"

"He can't hear it thunder or cuss the rain."

Faulkner puffed a few more times. "Can he read and write?" Maybe they could communicate with notes.

"Nope," answered Joe. "Or if he can, he's kept it a secret."

"Then how could Larkin tell him what he wanted done?"

"Larkin could make the Indian sign talk. Mase understands that."

Faulkner took the cigar from his mouth and examined the end carefully. "Now don't tell me, let me guess," he intoned dryly. "Larkin was the only one in this whole pissant valley, besides this lunk, of course, who could make the Indian sign talk. Right?"

"You're just as right as rain, Sheriff," confirmed Joe.

Faulkner cursed loudly and hurled the stub of his cigar into the darkness, the glowing tip making an orange arc toward the ground. Joe hobbled down the porch steps and out into the yard until he located the cigar butt lying amid ankle-high, yellowed grass. He carefully ground out the embers with his left boot and then turned to Faulkner.

"We ain't had no rain in more than a month," he explained patiently. "This may be a pissant valley to you, but it's our home. We'd take it kindly if you didn't try to burn it down."

Faulkner waved his arms in exasperation. "I've had enough of this! Doc, make out a death certificate and all the other paper crap we need! Bobby Dean, get your ass out here! We're goin' home!"

"Don't you want to see the scene of the crime, Sheriff?" asked Joe.

"My deputy can look it over tomorrow. Martin, crank some life into this ugly piece of junk so we can get out of here."

Joe watched quietly as the lanky deputy inserted the crank and turned the engine over. The inert beast sprang to life with a rumble. Suzy, tied to a porch post, flicked an ear and glanced over her shoulder with utter contempt. Martin withdrew the crank and straightened up.

"Sure is a noisy thing," remarked Joe.

"I suppose," admitted Martin, "but it's faster than a horse and doesn't tire you nearly as much. They're the coming thing. One day everyone will be driving them."

"Maybe, but I'd like to see you chase someone through the mountains in one." Martin gave him an odd look.

"Potts!"

Joe walked to the passenger side of the vehicle where Faulkner was sticking his head out. "Somethin's been botherin' me ever since you called. It seems like I've heard this name Larkin before. Can you think of any reason why I should?"

Joe shrugged. "Maybe it's because he's one of the biggest moonshiners in the county."

Faulkner's eyes almost popped out. Unlike most county sheriffs, he did not bother to shake down the moonshiners for protection money and therefore did not know them personally. He was reasonably content with the comparatively easy pickings of the Fort Smith bordellos and speakeasies. And there was also his enormous rake-off as county tax collector. The very dangerous undertaking of strong-arming moonshiners could be left to others with more ambition than discretion.

But now there was a curious gleam in Faulkner's eyes. "You ain't funnin' me, boy?" He tried to take a puff from a cigar that was no longer there. "So maybe this here is one of them gangland killins."

It was not difficult to read what passed for thoughts behind those beady eyes. Solving a mafia murder could pave the way to bigger and better things for Sheriff Willie Don Faulkner; the state senate or maybe even the U.S. Congress!

"More likely he was killed by an irate neighbor," suggested Joe.

Faulkner visible deflated and shot Joe an angry glance. He waved to his deputy to be on their way. "Martin will be back tomorrow to run the field investigation. You give him all the help he needs, Potts. You hear me?"

"I hear you, Sheriff."

Joe and Hudson watched the clattering, grunting monster wobble down the highway until it disappeared from sight around a curve. "When you gonna get you one of them contraptions, Doc?"

Hudson snorted loudly. "The day after you swap in old Suzy for one."

"That long, huh? Doc, when you finish up all you have to do here, would you call the funeral home and have them pick up Tom tonight? Ain't no reason Mrs. Larkin has to see the body in the mornin'."

"Sure, Joe." Hudson walked back into the house.

Joe spotted Mase still standing on the porch and still looking lost and unhappy. Joe placed his palms together along one side of his head and closed his eyes to indicate it was time for bed. Mase nodded solemnly and walked slowly away toward his small bedroom in the back of the barn. Joe hobbled over to Suzy and found a sugar cube in his pocket for her.

"What a night, Suzy," he sighed. "What a God awful night!"

As he climbed aboard, he added, "You ought to be thankful for one thing, old girl. At least you don't have to work for a complete jackass like that poor deputy."

Suzy puckered her lips and blew noisily.

"No smart remarks now," chided Joe. He walked her to the edge of the yard and turned onto the highway.

CHAPTER TWO
Wednesday, July 22

When Joe drove into the Larkin yard early the next morning to return the wagon and team borrowed the night before, there were already four wagons and innumerable idlers around the place. One of those was Jimmy Andrews who trotted over as Joe climbed down from the wagon.

"Mind puttin' this rig away for me, Jimmy?"

"Sure, Joe."

Joe untied Suzy from behind the wagon and led her to the same porch post she had occupied the night before. He swiveled his way up the steps and pushed through the front door. Even though it was only seven o'clock in the morning, neighbor women had already contributed a mountain of food that had overflowed the kitchen and now graced several living room chairs and even a part of the floor. This generosity was in spite of the general unpopularity of Tom Larkin.

Also, a veritable horde of distant relatives evicted in years past had returned to gorge and gloat. Bad/good news certainly traveled fast. There was a highly inappropriate air of jocularity throughout the house. Joe suppressed a faint sense of disgust as he condescended to accept a cup of coffee.

"Where is Mrs. Larkin?" he asked of no one in particular.

"In her bedroom," informed a heavyset woman with crossed arms who had planted herself at the foot of the stairs like a Pillar of Hercules. "But she does not wish to see anyone." The informant/guardian was Mrs. Harper whose tone and attitude indicated she had not forgotten Joe's rebuff the night before.

"I'm afraid she's gonna have to, Mrs. Harper. If not me, then the sheriff's deputy. I believe she would prefer to talk to a neighbor instead of a stranger."

"You can't see her now, Joe Potts!" pronounced the woman with Arctic finality.

"Mrs. Harper, you are interferin' with an officer of the law. You can be put in jail for that."

The matron's face turned ashen. "Well, I never!" Yet she stepped aside.

The words, 'Still haven't, eh?' were on the tip of Joe's tongue, but he choked them back. He was in no mood to bait anyone this morning. He hobbled to the top of the stairs and made his way to the second door on the left where he rapped gently while announcing himself. There was a long pause before a faint voice replied, bidding him to enter.

Mrs. Larkin's bedroom was a dark, airless chamber with flowered wallpaper once blue, but now so old it was faded and peeling. In the center of the room stood a single bed with still rumpled sheets, mute testimony that for years the Larkins had maintained separate quarters. In a far corner was a wooden rocking chair now occupied by a frail, gray haired woman burdened with far more wrinkles than was usual for the age of forty-seven.

Joe looked around for another chair, saw there was none and so took the liberty of sitting on the edge of the bed. He grimaced as he extended his right leg. The crippled foot was hurting more than usual today. That meant rain was coming, a blessing to his neighbors but a curse to him. As he studied the ancient face before him, he was vaguely disturbed by the fact that he was only two years behind Mrs. Larkin in years.

"Mrs. Larkin," he began, "I'm truly sorry to disturb you on this day, but I really do need to ask you some questions."

She stopped rocking and fixed him with drained gray eyes. After several seconds she finally replied, "I'll answer your questions, Joe Potts."

Joe fidgeted and glanced at the floor. "Maam, do you recall hearin' a gunshot yesterday afternoon?" She nodded slightly. "How many, maam? Was there just one or more than one?"

"There was just the one."

"Do you remember what time?"

Again she nodded. "It was one forty exactly."

Joe glanced up with surprise. "How can you be so certain of the exact time?"

She glanced away while answering. "I had just put two loaves of bread in the oven. I timed them, of course."

"Of course," he mumbled. This put the shot a bit outside of Doctor Hudson's estimated time of death. "When you heard the shot, did you look outside to see who was shootin' at what?"

She smiled faintly and shook her head. "I thought perhaps Tom was shootin' at a rabbit or crow. The crows have been after the corn somethin' awful this year."

Joe nodded agreement. "One more thing. Ed Peters told me Tom had six, uh, female hounds as of last week. Do you know what became of 'em? They're not here now."

She flushed slightly and turned her head away from him. "Those dogs were Tom's affair," she replied crisply. "I know nothin' about them."

"I see," spoke Joe quietly. Yet Mrs. Larkin would be the one who carried table scraps to the dogs. Wouldn't she have noticed a sudden decrease in the canine population?

"Well, thank you, Mrs. Larkin. I guess that will be all for now. I know this must be hard on you so I won't take up any more of your time." He drew up his right foot and started to arise.

Mrs. Larkin fastened him again with those empty, lifeless eyes. "He was a hard man, Mister Potts," she stated simply.

"Yes, maam, I wouldn't argue that."

"Did you know I have not yet cried for him? Nor do I expect to."

Joe glanced around uncomfortably but made no reply.

"Does that surprise you?" she asked.

"Maam, are you sure you should be tellin' me these things?"

"Who else should I tell them to?" she asked with a sad smile. She folded her hands across her stomach and leaned back in the rocker.

"I was a good wife," she continued. "I did all the things a wife is supposed to do for her husband and I stayed with him all these years because that is what is expected. But I never loved him and I am not sorry he is gone. I regret that the routine of my life has been changed and that unpleasant decisions must now be made. But I do not regret the loss of Tom Larkin."

Joe had become unduly interested in the scuff marks on his shoes.

"Does this make me a suspect?" she suddenly demanded.

"No, maam, not really. You were a suspect from the very first anyway."

Mrs. Larkin smiled almost pleasantly. "You have always been a very straightforward man, Joe Potts. It is a trait you shared with my husband."

How could a barb be inserted so gently? Years of practice, perhaps. A sharp retort to Tom Larkin would likely have drawn an even sharper backhand. Joe arose stiffly and stood with both hands resting on the head of his cane.

"One more thing, Mrs. Larkin. You've kinda put Reverend Watson on the spot by askin' him to conduct the funeral."

She stopped rocking a moment. "Men of God should have to make a few tough decisions now and then. Good for the soul. Keeps 'em humble." She resumed rocking. "I tried for years to get Tom Larkin into church. I have succeeded at last."

Joe hobbled to the door. "An empty triumph, maam."

"At this point in my life, Mister Potts, even empty triumphs are welcome. Good day to you, sir."

"Good day, maam." She was humming hymns as the door closed. Joe paused a moment in the hall. "Tough old biddy," he muttered. But maybe she had to be to live so long with Tom Larkin and still retain her sanity.

The crowd of exiled relatives had become even larger downstairs. The pleasant chatter and clatter of plates made a positive din. Joe had never been remotely friendly with Tom Larkin, but there was something vaguely obscene about this situation. It was like a flock of vultures gathered about a fallen predator. While Larkin lived, none of these people would have dared set foot on his property. Now they were as thick as blowflies around a carcass, and Joe couldn't help noticing that a few pieces of furniture and several knick-knacks were missing. He would be glad to get away from this place.

But there was one more detail to check on first. As he had feared, Mrs. Harper reigned supreme in the kitchen, presiding like some feudal chieftain over the food and dishes. Two other women were engaged full time washing dirty plates. The exiled Larkin clan boasted a vast number, and all had the hearty appetite of freeloaders. Joe made it to the third cabinet door before again being confronted by Mrs. Harper.

"What do you think you're doing, Joe Potts?" she demanded.

"Looking for bread."

"If you wish to be served, you must stand in line like everyone else."

"I'm not here for a meal, Mrs. Harper. I'm looking for bread." Having finally found what he was looking for, he pulled out a large yellow breadbox and removed the lid. There was a third of a loaf, hard on the outside and dry on the inside. "Is this the only bread in the house?"

Mrs. Harper was taken aback. "Of course not! Mrs. Anderson brought six fresh loaves this morning."

"But did Mrs. Larkin have any bread? Other than this, I mean."

"Why, uh, I wouldn't know."

"Then you've only been serving the bread Mrs. Anderson brought?"

"Of course! It is fresh. This other is fit only for toast."

He replaced the lid and put the breadbox back inside the cabinet. So Mrs. Larkin had lied about baking bread yesterday. Why? So she would have a good reason for noting the exact time of the shot? Why one forty? And why had she been so evasive about the dogs? What possible bearing could bread and dogs have to do with the murder of her husband?

Mrs. Harper was demanding an explanation for Joe's sudden interest in bread. The triumphant look in her eyes indicated she now believed she had proof positive that he was traveling the road of life with loose wheels. He ignored her and hobbled past the starving throng. A remote Larkin cousin was testing keys on the basement door. He was going to be mightily disappointed when he finally gained entry. On his way through the living room, Joe spotted a bowl of fruit and snitched a pear for Suzy.

Just as he stepped onto the porch, a chugging Model T pulled into the yard and sputtered into smoky silence. He was pleased there was only one occupant this time and even more pleased that it was not Sheriff Faulkner. He took out his pocketknife and quartered the pear for Suzy who accepted it as though Joe were a vassal offering tribute.

"I was hoping to find you here," announced Deputy Martin as Joe wiped a handful of slobbers on a trouser leg. "The sheriff wants you to help me with the field investigation."

Joe studied the young deputy with interest, taking special note of the huge Peacemaker strapped to his hip. Desperados beware! But perhaps he was being unfair to the youth. He forced himself to reserve judgment until he knew Martin better.

"Is the sheriff plannin' to come down here again hisself?"

"No, he's going to be too busy with the other end of the investigation."

"What other end?"

"Why, contacting federal authorities and the police departments in Kansas City and St. Louis."

Joe stifled a laugh. "Well, you better tell him to check with the Sebastian County Coon Hunters Association while he's at it."

Astonishment registered on the young man's face. There was also a faint blush as though he suspected Joe was poking fun at the sheriff's department. "What do you mean?" he demanded.

"Larkin had six bitch hounds. They're not here now."

"You think he was killed for his hounds?" asked Martin incredulously.

"Or because he took somebody else's. It's a possibility. Coon hunters are mighty serious about their dogs, Deputy. Now I ain't sayin' that was why he was killed, but it's a loose end we need to clear up."

Martin nodded curtly. "I'll mention it to the sheriff, but that's not the sort of thing he wants to hear from me."

"I know, Deputy. He wants to hear about gangsters, moonshiners and hit men. Well, he's gonna be very disappointed. Larkin wasn't killed by no professional. In fact, he wasn't even killed by a stranger. He was killed by somebody he knew well and wasn't a full time enemy. And that, Deputy, narrows the field somethin' considerable."

Deputy Martin seemed mildly offended. Constables were not supposed to be so forward. "You seem to have made several conclusions. Would you mind explaining them?"

Joe seated himself on the edge of the porch while Martin remained standing in the yard. "A professional killer learns somethin' about his victim, and only a fool would have tried to kill Larkin at close range."

"Some fool did," Martin reminded.

Joe nodded. "Amateur luck. A professional would have used a high powered rifle with a scope." He nodded toward the wooded hill to the west. "Most likely from up there."

Martin shifted uncomfortably. Sheriff Faulkner's theory was in trouble. "Why couldn't the killer have been a stranger?"

"Larkin would never have let a stranger get that close, at least not one totin' a shotgun. He would have armed himself. Then we would of found Larkin's gun next to the body instead of in a wagon forty feet away. Prob'ly, though, we would have found the dead stranger. Or maybe not. Larkin would have got rid of the body."

"A body isn't that easy to get rid of," argued Martin. This was apparently just for the sake of argument since it was not really a valid point in this case.

"A body is very easy to get rid of," replied Joe evenly. "If you know what you're doin', that is. There's a whole river of quicksand not too far off. These mountains have hundreds of caves. But the easiest way of all is to feed it to the hogs. They even crunch up the bones and eat them, too."

Deputy Martin was clearly disturbed by this gory enumeration. "Maybe somebody just slipped up on him."

"Nobody ever slipped up on Tom Larkin," countered Joe with finality. "Not ever. He had too many enemies to be that careless."

"You seem to rate this man rather highly."

Joe shook his head. "I disliked him about as much as ever'body else. But I knew his abilities and Larkin was a very dangerous man. And he made the best moonshine I ever drank."

Martin was immediately alert. "Tell me more about that."

"He made about a thousand gallons a year, half in the spring and half in the fall."

"So he wasn't full time."

Joe shook his head. "He had too many irons in the fire for that. Besides, he went for quality rather than quantity, and really good moonshine can only be made at certain times of the year."

"Why is that?"

"Has to do with humidity and temperature."

"I see," mumbled Martin even though he really didn't. "So what did Larkin do with his thousand gallons a year?"

"He kept fifty gallons from each batch. The rest went to someone in Kansas City."

"So he was connected with organized crime!"

"He sold 'em some whiskey. As far as I know, that was his only connection."

"What about the hundred gallons he kept. He surely didn't drink that much himself."

"No. Fact is, he didn't drink at all. He had an ulcer and couldn't."

"So what did he do with it?"

"Some was used to swing business deals his way. Some was used to bribe various officials so he could run his loggin' operation in the national forest. There were a few local sales. Certain customers who had to be kept happy." He paused a moment. "I bought a gallon a month myself."

Martin looked properly shocked. "You, you had dealings with a moonshiner? But you are an officer of the law!"

"So are half the people who sell it in this county."

Martin shook his head in denial. "I cannot believe that!"

"New to this job, ain't you?"

"I joined the force three months ago," replied Martin defensively.

Joe sighed loudly. "Well, I guess you'll find out in due time."

"Find out? Find out what?"

But Joe declined to elaborate. Instead, he gazed up at the sky that had become darker just in the past few minutes. In compliance with the demands of his aching right foot, a heavy bank of clouds was rolling in from the southwest. As they boiled and rumbled, one could feel the temperature dropping.

"If you aim to look over the crime scene, Deputy, you'd best do it right away. We're fixin' to get drenched before the day is out."

"I'm ready when you are."

Joe hopped off the porch and untied Suzy. "I aim to ride, but it wouldn't be a good idea to take that contraption out in that field. A spark might start a fire. That grass ain't wet yet."

"I'll walk."

Martin would stand for a long time with hands on hips while studying the scene, then move to another spot and examine it from a different angle. Several times he shook his head and mumbled something to himself. He took out a notebook and drew a few sketches. Joe peeped over his shoulder once and saw a confusing array of arrows and Xs. Then the young deputy braved the wild roses and blackberries to examine the cut wires. His handful of manure was not as fresh as Joe's the night before. At last he stood up and examined the cornfield just beyond. The rising wind turned it into a rustling sea of yellow-green.

"Does that cornfield belong to the Larkins?"

"Nope. That there is Amos Hanks's property."

Martin chewed his lower lip. "The killer could have slipped in through that corn. Those stalks are higher than a man's head."

"Corn makes a lot of noise when you go to slippin' through it," argued Joe. "Especially after it starts to turn yellow like that is. And another thing. Crows are thick this year. There was likely some in that field. It just wouldn't be possible to come through there without stirrin' 'em up. Tom Larkin would notice somethin' like that and be on his guard."

Martin strode back to where the body had lain. "You say he was on his back?"

Joe nodded. "Unlikely position. I figure he was rolled over to see if he was really dead. That's another reason this wasn't no professional job. Blast a man point-blank in the chest with a scattergun and there just ain't no doubt about it."

Martin sighed loudly. "Well, I can't make much sense of it. Do you have any theories?"

"None worth mentionin'."

"Then let's get back to the house. I would like to question Mrs. Larkin."

"I done talked to her, Deputy."

Martin whirled on him. "You should have waited for me!" he accused.

"Thought she might tell me more than she would a total stranger."

"And what did she tell you?" It was clear from the tone that Deputy Martin was far from pleased.

"A couple of lies."

Martin narrowed his eyes. "I'm listening."

Joe quickly explained about the missing dogs and the bread that had not been baked.

"I believe we should talk to Mrs. Larkin again," Martin decided.

"If you don't mind, Deputy, I'd like to hold off on that for the time bein'."

"Why?"

"I just think we ought to talk to some of the other folks around here first, try to get a better picture of what happened and when. Mrs. Larkin ain't goin' nowhere. We can talk to her again anytime."

"So who would you talk to next?" demanded Martin impatiently.

"Amos Hanks."

"Very well. Do you intend to ride with me or…" He glanced with amusement at the old gray mule. "Or do you intend to provide your own transportation?"

There was no hesitation in Joe's reply. "Suzy's kind of particular about the company she keeps, so I guess I'll have to ride with you."

By the time Joe had stabled Suzy in the Larkin barn the red had finally vanished from Martin's face.

They had to wait patiently at the end of a cotton field until Amos Hanks finished plowing the current row. Hanks was a burly man of medium height in his early fifties, the same age as Larkin, Joe informed Martin while they waited. At last Hanks laid the plow on its side and unlooped the lines from around his back. He removed a faded black hat and mopped his forehead with a soppy red bandana. After glancing contemptuously at Martin for about a half a second, Hanks shifted his gaze to Joe.

"Make this fast, Potts!" he growled. "I aim to get this cotton laid by before the rain hits."

Joe made it fast. "What time did Larkin get killed?"

"Just after three o'clock."

"How can you be so certain?" demanded Martin.

The sour eyes moved back to the deputy. "My little girl, Susan, brings a bucket of water to the field ever' day at three o'clock just like clockwork. That's how I know. We heard the shot right after she went back to the house."

"Just one shot?" asked Joe. Hanks nodded.

"You said we," put in Martin. "Who else heard it?"

"My boy, Luke."

Martin glanced over at another plow being driven several rows over. "Is that him?"

Hanks smirked loudly. "You're just as sharp as a butter knife, ain't you?"

Martin glared angrily. "Now see here…"

Joe cut him off. "Amos, when was the last time Larkin's cows got into your corn?"

The eyes shifted back to Joe. "Day before yesterday. And I told that son of a bitch the next time it happened, he would have some dead cows to haul off. That's the third time this summer and I ain't havin' any more of it. Don't care if he's alive or dead; next time those cows get into my corn, I aim to kill 'em." Hanks looped the lines around his back and picked up the plow.

"Did you see anybody hangin' around the Larkin place yesterday?" called Joe as Hanks whipped the big Percheron into motion.

"Didn't see nothin' but this horse's ass!"

"Mean tempered old cuss!" complained Martin sourly as they watched him move away.

"Livin' so many years next to Larkin, it ain't no wonder," explained Joe.

Martin turned to Joe. "Why would Larkin cut his own fence? That doesn't make any sense to me."

"He was tryin' to force Hanks to share the work and expense of rebuildin' it. That fence's needed to be rebuilt for years."

"But Hanks refused to help?" quizzed Martin. Joe nodded confirmation. "Well, it sounds like Hanks was the unreasonable one."

"Not really. Hanks doesn't own any cattle. The law says Larkin has to fence his cows in. Hanks don't have to fence 'em out. If Larkin's cows didn't tear the fence down now and then on their own, well, he would just help 'em out a little."

"It seems to me Amos Hanks would be a prime suspect."

"Sure does," agreed Joe, "but he's got his boy and girl to alibi him. Besides, he can't shoot for beans, and I doubt he could slip up on Larkin if his life depended on it."

They had reached the front yard where the car was parked. "Shouldn't we talk to the girl?" persisted Martin.

"Not much point. If Hanks was tellin' the truth, she'd only confirm it. And if he's lyin', she'd still back him up. Besides, she does take water to the field ever' day at three just like Hanks said."

Martin cranked the car to life and got behind the wheel. "Where to now?"

"The Andrews place. Next farm on the right."

"One thing I don't understand," said Martin while backing the car onto the road. "Two grown men, neighbors for years, yet they couldn't come to an agreement on a simple matter like a boundary fence."

"Most men could have, but not those two. They been fussin' and cussin' each other for years."

"Why?"

"Ain't really sure. It started back when they were half grown younguns in school. They're both a few years older than me, so I was just a little tyke when it happened. Best I recall, though, it was over a game of marbles."

Martin, his mouth hanging open, turned to face Joe. "Marbles?" he exclaimed.

"Eyes on the road, please!" commanded Joe stiffly. He braced his arms against the front of the car. He didn't trust these silly vehicles one little bit. One could doze off or look away while riding a horse or a mule and not have to worry about landing on one's head in a ditch. But a machine was dumber than a Yankee or a Republican even and might do anything.

"A forty year feud over a game of marbles!" muttered the deputy. "Unbelievable!"

"There's been blood feuds over less. Turn in here."

The Andrews place consisted of a small, four room log cabin presiding over twenty eroded, brushy acres splashed across the north slope of Washburn Mountain. About half the property was given over to crops and a large truck patch with the remainder invested in pasturage for three Guernsey cows.

A couple dozen spotted Dominecker hens had free run of the yard in pursuit of bugs and grasshoppers, while a short distance away a pair of Poland China hogs grunted in contentment at the temporary break in the summer heat. Three peach trees were approaching fruition, while a half a dozen apple trees still built for fall abundance. An enormous post oak stood just west of the house to provide shade from the afternoon sun.

"The lady who lives here is a widow, by the way,' informed Joe as he climbed out of the car. "There's just her and her boy."

The woman who came to the door was in her early forties, slender and with reddish brown hair. In spite of a few wrinkles, she was still attractive and had certainly once been beautiful. She wore a faded blue dress, patched many times and now speckled with dirt from working in the garden. A large bonnet had already been removed, but a grimy sweatband was still in place. She smiled a greeting to the two men and stepped back from the door to let them enter.

"Hello, Laura," said Joe while pulling off his ragged straw hat.

"Joe, you're looking fit," she complimented. "I haven't seen you for a spell."

"Been keepin' busy," he lied. "Laura, this is Deputy Martin. He's lookin' into the Larkin murder."

She sighed loudly. "A terrible thing!" It was the obligatory observation. "Who would have thought there could be a murder right here in Burnham? Oh, would you like some coffee?"

"No, thank you," replied Joe quickly. He sensed that Martin was going to accept and he knew that Laura Andrews could hardly afford sufficient coffee for their own modest needs. "We just want to ask a couple of questions."

"I'll help any way I can." She settled herself upon a crippled and often patched sofa.

"Do you recall hearing a gunshot from the Larkin place yesterday afternoon?" asked Martin.

"Yes, but I thought little of it at the time. You see, the crows have been very bad this year."

"So I've been told," replied Martin dryly. "What time did you hear the shot?"

Her face crinkled in thought. "Well, it was before four o'clock because that's when I come in to start supper."

"How much before four o'clock?" pressed Martin.

She shook her head in exasperation. "Oh, I can't remember! Maybe an hour."

"It couldn't have been around one thirty?" asked Joe.

"Oh, it was much later than that. Like I said, it was just before I came in to start supper."

"Amos Hanks said it was shortly after three," volunteered Joe. Martin gave him a disapproving look.

"That sounds about right, Joe," confirmed Laura. She looked at him with interest. "Why did you ask about one thirty?"

"There's just a little confusion about the time is all. Nothin' important." He paused. "Laura, how many shots did you hear?"

"Just one."

"Did you see any strangers in the community yesterday?" asked Martin. "Or anyone with a shotgun?"

"No one."

"I see. Could I speak with your son, please?"

"Jimmy? You can speak with him, but he wouldn't know anything about it. He was in Greenwood most of the day. He was on his way home when he saw the crowd in Mister Larkin's yard."

"What was Jimmy doin' in Greenwood?" asked Joe, not a little surprised. Saturday was go-to-town day, not Tuesday.

Laura fixed him with a half amused and half saddened gaze. "A man from the army was in town yesterday. He talked to several of the local boys about joining."

A deep frown was etched on Joe's face. "Jimmy never said anything to me about bein' interested in the army."

"You've been known to speak with disapproval of the army, Joe." A wry smile appeared on her face "Especially when you're in your cups, I hear."

Joe suddenly had to scratch his eyebrow, an action that conveniently covered his blush. "I aim to talk to Jimmy about this."

"I wish you would, Joe." Laura suddenly stood up. "Would you gentlemen join us for dinner?"

"We have to go, Laura. We've still got a lot to do."

She smiled thinly. "I understand."

Joe hustled Martin out the door and toward the car but then said, "Wait here. I'll be right back."

He stepped back into the house and closed the door. "How are things goin', Laura?"

"I think we'll make three bales this year and we've had a very good garden. I've only lost two hens to the 'possums and the hogs haven't taken cholera like last year."

Joe nodded. "Glad to hear it, but that ain't exactly what I meant."

She suddenly turned away and began wringing her hands. "It's been a rough year, Joe. Jimmy's about grown and getting itchy. He thinks he's in love, and now he's talking about the army."

She quivered slightly and Joe knew she was choking back a sob. "It's not easy for a woman to raise a son by herself. Poor James died just when Jimmy needed him the most. Eleven is a hard time for a boy to lose his father."

"Any age is a hard time," replied Joe quietly.

She discreetly blew her nose and turned back to him. "I, I don't know what I'll do if Jimmy goes away."

"He can't join for another year without your permission. I mean to talk to him about that anyway. But Laura, you're gonna have to let him go one day."

This last remark she totally ignored. "Tell him about the army, Joe!" she pleaded. "Tell him about how it destroys lives!" She was grasping at the bib of his overalls.

"That's not quite fair, Laura." Was this really he speaking? Making excuses for the army?

"It destroyed our lives, Joe! Yours! Mine!"

"Laura, please." He gently disengaged her hands.

"I was a fool for not waiting for you, Joe! We all knew that silly little war wouldn't last long. But when I heard you got hurt and then took the fever; well, I, I never really expected to see you again."

"That's all in the past, Laura."

She looked down and began wringing her hands again. "I was true to James and would have been true to him no matter how long he lived. But after the influenza took him, I always thought maybe you and me, Joe…"

She looked up suddenly. "Joe?"

He shook his head sadly and looked away. "I'm sorry, Laura; it just couldn't be. I could never be a farmer again. My foot wouldn't take twenty miles a day behind a plow. Besides, I've lived too long by myself and gotten too old to change my ways. We'd be at each other's throats within a week."

"We could at least try." She smiled sweetly. "And you wouldn't have to make your monthly trips to the harlots in Fort Smith anymore."

His eyebrow suddenly needed scratching again.

"No, Laura," he answered gently. "I've got some good memories of what might have been. I don't ever want to take the chance of losin' 'em."

She smiled sadly and stepped back, conceding defeat. "I just want you to know one thing. I love you, Joe Potts. I always loved you."

The brim of his hat was in serious need of twisting. "I have to go, Laura. The deputy's waitin'." He gave her a brotherly peck on the cheek and hurriedly departed.

Martin was futilely trying to wipe some of the road grime from the windshield when Joe hobbled past without a word and piled into the passenger seat. Martin put away the soiled rag and cranked new life back into the machine. He said nothing until they were back on the highway.

"It is poor police procedure to tell one witness what another one said," he accused.

"Can it, Deputy!" growled Joe.

Martin glanced over at him. "You're sweet on her, aren't you?"

"That is none of your damned business!"

Martin shrugged. "We could have stayed for dinner."

"They've got barely enough for theirselves. They shouldn't have to feed a couple of soft butted lawmen."

"So where do we eat dinner?" He paused. "It looked like there was enough food at the Larkins to feed most of the county."

"Somethin' unhealthy about that place," grumbled Joe. "Anyway, I don't eat dinner. You can go wherever you like."

"Is there any place closer than Greenwood to get some food?"

"No restaurant, but there's a store down the road a piece. Just past the mill. They have sandwich stuff."

"I remember passing the place. It'll do."

They drove past the Larkin place, past the church at the curve and then due west for just over a quarter of a mile. Martin began to slow down as they approached the gristmill to their left. Behind the mill was a large, tall frame structure about forty feet by eighty which housed a cotton gin, idle this time of year and it would remain idle for at least two more months.

The store was located alongside the mill at the junction of Highway Ten with a rugged little dirt road that angled away just south of due west. Several horses hitched outside the store bucked and snorted as the clattery machine eased into a vacant spot.

It is a curious fact of life that in every community, no matter how industrious, there are always some who seemingly have nothing better to do than loaf about in a highly visible location. Today, though, the congregation seemed much larger than usual. A few, of course, were old men well beyond the age for intensive labor. Also, the impending rain forced the postponement of some work. For others it was merely an excuse for idleness.

Besides, the event of the century was still fresh and could not be put to rest until it had been thoroughly discussed and dissected to everyone's satisfaction. Or at least until every oddball theory had been aired to the point of nausea.

There were about a dozen men in the store and they all fell silent when the two lawmen entered. There was a small butcher's table in the rear of the store just behind the now dormant pot-bellied stove. Martin made his way there and ordered a sandwich consisting of a thick slab of Bologna and an equally thick slab of cheddar slashed from a giant cheese wheel. A small jar of mustard was situated conveniently nearby.

Joe went to the wooden icebox in the front of the store and took out a bottle of root beer. Popping off the top, he raised it to his lips. The first swallow seemed to rip down some invisible barrier and loosen all tongues.

"You boys 'bout got this all wrapped up?" asked someone.

"Not yet, Ab," drawled Joe. "Half the county is on the suspect list. We're usin' the tax rolls and takin' ever'body in alphabetical order."

There was a chorus of titters and snorts.

"I hear tell the sheriff thinks some of them Kansas City mobsters did it," suggested someone else.

Martin almost choked on his sandwich.

Joe smiled thinly. "Word sure gets around fast, don't it, Deputy?"

"Bah!" spat a frail old man from a rocker equipped with the obligatory spittoon that he now utilized and almost didn't miss. If he were not in his nineties, he had at least attained the senior eighties. He was, consequently, listened to with awe and respect. The village elder now leaned forward and tapped his cane impatiently on the floor in a demand for silence.

"Ye can all set here jawin' 'til the cows come home and it ain't gonna change nuthin'!" he orated in a scratchy voice. "We all know who kilt Tom Larkin, and if any of you whippersnappers had any gumption ye would already be out doin' somethin' about it!"

Martin halted in mid-chew and stood frozen, his ears almost throbbing in anticipation of a revelation that would conveniently wrap up this whole case. But no revelation was forthcoming from the ancient relic who now leaned back in the rocker and worked his toothless gums in great agitation.

"Who do you think the killer is, sir?" Martin was finally forced to ask.

The old man twisted slightly and fixed rheumy, hate-filled eyes upon the deputy. "This killin' and who done it ain't none of your affair, sonny!"

"Sir, if you have information regarding this crime…"

"He thinks the darkies did it," interrupted Joe.

The old man glared angrily at the constable. "I don't think nothin' of the kind, Potts! I know it, by God!"

Several men nodded agreement. "He may be right," spoke someone. "After all, Larkin was a Grand Dragon."

"Shut up, Harley!" hissed another voice. "Can't you see there's a deputy sheriff here?"

"So what?" grumbled Harley. "The sheriff's a Grand Dragon, too."

After a few seconds of awkward silence, someone else remarked, "Them niggers should have been run out of the county years ago."

"They don't bother nobody," argued another voice.

This latest speaker drew the full ire of the ancient sage. "I fought four years to keep them niggers where they belong!" he raged. "Hell fire's too good for any white man who speaks up fer 'em! You just keep away from me from now on, Will Hadley! I got nuthin' to say to the like o' you!"

Will Hadley blushed and moved away from the old man who leaned forward again with both hands wrapped over the head of his cane. "Why ain't you arrested 'em yet, Joe Potts?" he demanded.

Joe took another sip of root beer. "I got no authority to arrest anybody in Mount Moriah."

The old man snorted his contempt. "You just ain't got the guts! Why, if I was a few years younger…"

The old man broke off and became dreamy-eyed thinking about what he would do if he still had his youth. Why, them two darkies would be swinging from tree limbs before the sun went down and their women and pickaninnies loaded up and on their way out of the county once and for all!

Joe set his empty bottle on the counter and dropped a nickel beside it. "Ready to go, Deputy?"

"Just a minute," sputtered Martin with a full mouth.

"I'll wait for you in the car."

Joe glanced at the old man on his way out and smiled faintly; a knowing, mocking smile that made the old man blush. Joe capped it with a wink that almost sent the decrepit old thing into a paroxysm.

A few minutes later Martin came out and cranked the car back to life. "What do you think?" he asked while crawling in.

"About what?"

"Could those Negroes from Mount Moriah be the killers?"

"Not likely. Just like Will said, they don't bother nobody." He glanced at the deputy. "Tell me, do you really think a couple of darkies could waltz the whole length of this valley, slip up on a sly old fox like Larkin, kill him, then get away without anyone noticin' 'em?"

Martin considered this. "Maybe we should talk to them anyway."

"Fine with me. I ain't seen the Claytons in a spell. Take this road here." He indicated the ominous washboard angling away to the southwest.

They bumped and bounced along for a slow, dusty half mile before either man spoke. The reason for this breaking of the silence was an especially cavernous pothole that cracked Martin's forehead against the steering wheel and forced Joe to hang on for dear life to keep from being spilled out.

"Christ!" exclaimed Martin. "What was that?"

"Our county taxes at work."

"Something should be done about that!"

"Bob Evans lives closest to it. I'll see if I can talk him into doin' somethin' about it."

Martin glanced over. "That's not what I meant. I meant the county should do something about it."

"That'll never happen." After a short pause, Joe said, "Deputy, about that old man back at the store. Don't put a whole lot of stock in anything he says."

"Why not? Those other men seemed to respect his opinions. At least most of them did."

"The human critter has picked up some mighty strange notions," lectured Joe. "Just because someone manages to reach a ripe old age, most folks figure he must be chock-full of wisdom. But it ain't always so. A lot of 'em are just chock-full of meanness and lies."

"And you believe that old man is a liar?"

"He's told his lies so often that most folks think they're the gospel truth. But he didn't fight in the Rebellion. He and all his brothers were bushwhackers. They stole from women and old folks while other men did all the actual fightin'." He glanced wryly at Martin. "Maybe that's how he managed to reach such a ripe old age."

A quarter of a mile later Joe suddenly stiffened and grabbed Martin's right arm. "Pull over!" he commanded.

Martin braked to a sudden halt. "What is it?"

Joe nodded toward the field on their right. "The Hamiltons are balin' hay."

"So?"

"Damn it, Deputy, it's fixin' to rain! If that hay gets wet they could lose it" He looked at Martin. "You know what happens if you stack wet hay in a barn?"

The blank look was sufficient testimony that Martin didn't have a clue.

"It can catch fire. All by itself." Joe crawled out of the car. The Claytons will have to wait. I'm gonna help these folks if I can."

"Potts!" called Martin angrily. "We have a murder to solve!"

Joe turned back to the car. "Half a day ain't gonna make no difference. And if we don't have the help of the folks who live around here, we ain't gonna solve nothin'. Show an interest in their problems, and just maybe they'll show an interest in yours."

Martin gritted his teeth and exhaled loudly. "Oh hell!" Then he also crawled out of the car.

The meadow was a beehive of activity. The hay had long since been cut and now a sulky rake with long, curved teeth dragged it into windrows while a bull rake carried it to the baler that remained stationary in the center of the meadow. The baler was powered by a team of mules that, unattended, plodded monotonously in a circle about it. After the bull rake delivered the cut hay, a man with a pitchfork loaded it into the baler while another man on top stomped it down into the chute.

Behind these two stood a man who tied the bales with wire after which they were spewed out the back. The tie man was also responsible for carrying the ejected bales a short distance away so that the whole operation wouldn't grind to a halt due to a mountain of bales piled up behind the machine.

The baling crew simply contracted to bale a particular meadow. Hauling the bales away and stacking them in the barn was the responsibility of the property owner. That was the bottleneck in this instance, for there was only Rufe Hamilton, his brother Zack and Zack's twelve year old son to do the hauling. Rufe's oldest boy was only eight. He tried to help but actually did more getting in the way.

In spite of his bad foot, Joe deftly crawled through the fence and then held the wires apart for Martin who hooked a barb and tore his shirt anyway. This did nothing to improve the deputy's mood. He was still craning his head around to survey the damage when one of the Hamiltons walked up to greet them. He was a tall, emaciated man with a face full of wrinkles topped by a mop of thin, lifeless white hair. He looked at least fifty but was in fact barely thirty.

"That's Rufe Hamilton," whispered Joe. "He owns this place."

"He looks sick."

"He is. He got gassed in the war. Can't hold up too good anymore."

"Joe!" exclaimed Rufe, sticking out a bony paw. "Ain't seen you for a spell."

"Rufe, this is Deputy Charles Martin. He's lookin' into the Larkin murder."

"Heard about that," replied Rufe while shaking his head with the obligatory dismay. "Wish I could help you, but I just don't know nothin' about it."

"Looks like you could use some help, Rufe."

The thin man sighed loudly. "Just ain't no way we're gonna get it all in before the rain hits. It's already startin' to sprinkle a bit."

There was a brilliant flash of lightning far to the west. Everyone in the meadow paused for a moment and gazed in that direction with solemn expressions. The man on the sulky rake turned his team and started for the gate at the west end of the meadow. His job was finished. The windrows were drawn.

"This is a good crew," remarked Rufe. "They busted their butts to beat the rain. Worked right through dinner. They're gonna make it, too. The balin' will be done within the hour." He stared at the small mountain of bales to be hauled away and shook his head again.

"Come on, Deputy!" called Joe.

"But…" Joe caught him by the arm and pulled him toward the fence. "I thought you wanted to help him!" protested Martin.

"I do. That's why we're goin' back to the store." He called over his shoulder. "Be seein' you, Rufe!"

Martin managed to avoid the crater in the road this time, and at Joe's urging drove as fast as he dared back up the country lane.

"Don't kill it!" commanded Joe when they reached the store. "I'll just be a second."

Already the sprinkle was growing heavier. Joe stuck his head inside the door. "Boys," he called, "Rufe Hamilton's got ten tons of hay on the ground!" Then he was gone.

"Let's go!" he said jumping back into the car.

"Where?"

"Back to Rufe's place. We got hay to haul."

As Martin turned the car around, he asked, "Do you think any of them will help?"

"Look!"

Martin glanced back over his shoulder. Two men were staring up at the leaking clouds with mixed expressions of pleasure and distaste. They desperately needed the rain, but it always seemed to come at a bad time for somebody. A third man quickly pushed past the two gawkers, mounted and galloped away. Resignedly, the first two vacated the porch steps and started for their own horses.

"So they are going to help," spoke Martin with perhaps a trace of awe in his voice. He shifted gears and started back down the Mount Moriah Road.

"Of course they're gonna help," replied Joe. "Next time it might be one of them in a jam."

It seemed almost no time before they were back in the meadow. "Ever hauled hay before, Deputy?" asked Joe as he stared at the huge mound of bales.

"Never. I'm a town boy."

Joe leaned his cane against the wagon, seized a bale by the two wire strands and flicked it easily into the bed. "It's done like that."

Martin attempted to emulate the movement, grunted loudly as he became overbalanced and then fell to his knees. Struggling to his feet while spitting out straw, he finally deposited the bale into the rear of the wagon.

"Right!" he growled acidly while examining a bloody finger sliced open by the wire. "Nothing to it!"

"There's kind of a knack to it," admitted Joe, suppressing a smile. He stepped closer and examined the cut finger. "Reckon maybe you ought to wear gloves," he suggested.

A pair materialized from somewhere and Martin pulled them on. They helped some, but he still knew he would have blisters tomorrow. Every now and then he would glance over at Joe who, hardly moving from his tracks, would load three bales to his one. And he did it so effortlessly! For the first time, the deputy noticed the huge forearms and bulging biceps. What did a cripple do to keep himself so enormously strong?

And at long last the wagon was loaded. Martin flopped panting onto the ground and mopped his brow with an already soaked sleeve. He noticed with disgust that he had lost a button. He heard a rumble and looked up to see two more wagons arriving. Back on the road still heading for the west gate were three others. Riding as passengers on the five wagons were most of the store loafers.

"I'll be damned!" he muttered.

There was a hand on his shoulder. "Pile on, Deputy," invited Joe, indicating the loaded wagon. "Now comes the hard part."

"The hard part?" mumbled Martin with dismay.

"Now we have to toss it up into the barn loft."

It seemed to take forever, and the longer it took the heavier the bales became. Martin suddenly realized this was more than just growing exhaustion. As the load went down, they had to throw the bales further and further. Already, his arms, back and even his legs were one gigantic ache. He didn't believe he could possibly finish, but fortunately he was not put to the ultimate test. Several men strode into the barn and both he and Joe, the weakling and the cripple, were shunted aside by the reinforcements. The job was quickly completed.

"Okay, move this one out!" shouted someone.

Joe glanced at Martin who was bent over with hands on knees. "Ready to go, Deputy?"

He nodded weakly and crawled onto the seat beside Joe albeit without enthusiasm.

On the way back to the meadow they met two more wagons, each bearing a ton of hay and rocking precariously in the growing wind. The men on board waved noisy greetings as Joe guided Rufe's empty wagon past. When they arrived back at the meadow another loaded wagon was pulling away, and Will Hadley was lashing down the load on yet another.

The bull rake, Joe noted, was also now gone. The balers were almost finished and the once huge stack had now diminished by considerably more than half. Rufe just might win this race after all. If the rain would only hold off for another thirty minutes! Will Hadley stepped away from his wagon and looked first at Joe and then at the bedraggled deputy.

"Why don't you two drive my wagon to the barn," he suggested. "Me and my boys will load this one."

Joe glanced at Martin. "That all right with you?"

That question was utterly needless!

On the way back to the barn they met first one and then a second empty wagon bouncing noisily back to the meadow. Joe eased behind a load still waiting to get inside the barn and crawled down from the wagon. Martin more or less collapsed off the seat. Rufe and Zack Junior had now been shunted aside and stood amid a cluster of men watching others work. Indeed, there were so many present there was not room for all to work at once.

The air inside the barn was thick with stirred up dust and floating straw. Someone told a ribald joke and all laughed with good spirits. There was an almost giddy feeling of joy and camaraderie. A wagon was emptied and replaced by a loaded one. Men relieved each other so the work could continue at breakneck speed. Another loaded wagon pulled up behind the one Joe had just parked.

Just as the final bale was tossed into the loft, there came a brutal crash of thunder and the sky opened. Almost as one, all gazed up at the furious metallic roar on the tin roof above. Only an occasional drop found its way into the snug, dry barn. The wind increased several fold and became a demonic howl. Mules stomped nervously, flicked their ears and cringed from the storm that could not reach them. Everyone stood mesmerized, staring up at the metal roof as though some enraged monster were attempting to gain admittance.

The spell was finally broken when a thin, nasal voice sang out, "All right then, dammit, rain!"

There was a chorus of snickers.

A sun darkened man in a yellow slicker raced into the dry sanctum, looked at all the faces about him and then advanced to

Rufe Hamilton to present his bill. Rufe produced a black, ragged wallet and counted out the money. Disappointingly little remained after the bill was paid. The man in the yellow slicker again looked from face to face and then turned back to Rufe.

"You got some mighty fine neighbors, Mister Hamilton."

Rufe nodded curtly and broke into a wide grin. Stepping to the corncrib, he took out a two gallon jug still nearly half full. "These ain't the best squeezins, boys, but I reckon they'll do in a pinch."

Joe noticed Martin stiffen beside him. Leaning close to the deputy, he whispered harshly, "Not a word! Not a single word!"

When the jug came to Joe, he tipped it up and took a long pull and then handed it to Martin. The deputy hesitated, noticing that every eye was on him. With a sigh, he finally tipped the jug up and took a tiny sip. Joe quickly seized the jug from him before the coughing fit struck. Eager hands were suddenly slapping Martin on the back until he finally raised a hand to acknowledge that the cure had worked. The jug completed its first round and began another. Outside, the storm raged, abated and then struck again with renewed fury.

An hour later it broke. The roar on the roof diminished to single, distinguishable pelts. In the west, rays of sunlight began to pierce the boiling mass of black clouds. In a tall, dripping cottonwood nearby, a nervy mockingbird trilled arrogantly his survival of the elements. One by one, Rufe's neighbors began departing, leaving him with a filled barn and a nearly empty jug. Holding it to his ear, he shook it and listened to the tiny slosh inside. With a shrug, he took another pull and then handed it to Joe who ended its misery.

At last only three of them were left; the cripple, the warrior with lungs permanently scarred by German gas and a young deputy sheriff who's every muscle ached with annoying persistence. Joe led the way out of the stuffy barn and into the storm cleansed air outside. Dead, yellowed grass was already showing signs of new life. As the afternoon sun emerged triumphant, the dripping trees and bushes sparkled with an almost agonizing intensity. For a few days the countryside would be beautiful. Then the heat and dust would inevitably crush out the new vigor. Joe pulled a corncob pipe from his bib pocket and began to load up.

"Makin' much headway, Joe?" asked Rufe.

"Not much," he admitted while tamping the bowl.

Rufe had to study his cornfield for a while. "Talked to Billy Larkin yet?" he finally asked.

Joe glanced up at him quickly, but then returned his attention to the pipe and popped a match into fiery life with a thumbnail. "Ain't seen hide nor hair of Billy for nigh on to a year." He took another puff. "Any reason I ought to talk to him, Rufe?"

Rufe shrugged. "He's been in the area recently. I hear he was over to see Floyd Neely last weekend."

"What about?"

"You'll have to ask Billy. Or Floyd."

When they were back in the car, Martin asked, "Are we going to see this Floyd Neely now?"

Joe considered a moment and then shook his head. "It's been a long day, Deputy. I'm hungry and I just don't believe I could abide Floyd on an empty stomach. We'll pay him a visit after the funeral tomorrow."

Martin nodded agreement. "All I want now is a long bath. After that hay business, I'm not fit to be seen in public anyway." He glanced accusingly at Joe. "I tore my shirt getting through that fence."

Joe smiled faintly. "I saw, but it was worth it."

"Do you know how much these shirts cost?" asked Martin hotly.

"No, but I'll tell you somethin', Deputy. You ain't a complete foreigner to these folks no more. That could wind up bein' worth a lot more to you than a whole crate of shirts."

Martin considered that a moment. "Maybe," he conceded grudgingly. "Where do you want me to let you out?"

"Larkin's place. I left Suzy there and I've been a little ill at ease about her all day. Larkin has some mighty sticky-fingered relations."

After a hot supper of bacon, beans and cornbread, Joe stepped outside his cabin to enjoy the clean, fresh night air. A million tiny specks of fire blazed fiercely, partitioned by the meandering richness of the Milky Way. Orion with bow poised crept stealthily across the night sky in search of celestial game.

After resisting the temptation for all of five minutes, Joe broke into one of Larkin's jugs of ARKANSAS PYZZON. After a few swallows of the smooth fierceness, the stars seemed even brighter and clearer.

He wondered idly where Billy Larkin was tonight.

CHAPTER THREE
Thursday, July 23

Before he had even gotten to the church, the all too unfamiliar suit and tie were driving Joe to distraction as he unconsciously pulled and tugged at the alien creature constricting his throat. The weather did not help the situation either. Yesterday's storm had been followed by the obligatory sauna with the temperature in the high nineties by ten o'clock. The heavily starched white shirt had already been transformed into a sticky, scratchy plaster. The worst punishment of hell Joe could imagine would be an eternal summer Sunday sitting rigidly at attention in starched stiffness while listening to Reverend Watson deliver a noisy, interminable tirade whose central theme was 'I told you so'.

Behind the wheel of the chugging automobile was Deputy Martin, who for the moment had swapped his khakis and badge in favor of the mandatory black uniform for funerals. He, too, looked stiff and uncomfortable, but this was not due to his attire. Joe had noticed earlier that Martin's every movement seemed to be accomplished with sheer agony. The previous day's hay hauling had taken a severe toll. Even so, the deputy still did not look like a creature from an alien planet which was exactly how Joe felt.

"You're not used to wearing a suit, are you?" observed Martin absently. Joe's misery was a perverse balm to the deputy's aching muscles.

Joe's immediate reply was a grunt of disgust. This suit, his only one, was ten years old and had been worn to exactly twelve funerals and nine weddings. At the weddings there was always a reception afterward and usually a surreptitious jug to soften the suffering. Funerals promised only the eventual relief of shedding such ridiculous attire in favor of something less civilized.

Martin turned off the highway and onto the bare ground surrounding the large frame structure that doubled as both church and schoolhouse. It was an odd looking building about forty feet by eighty on an east-west axis. It had neither doors nor windows in either the east or west ends. To atone for this, the entire north wall was a solid row of tall windows. At the southwest and southeast corners were small porches that gave access to tiny cloakrooms. A single massive chimney serviced the entire building whenever it needed to be so serviced which it certainly did not on this day.

Extending between the cloakrooms was a long, narrow classroom separate from the main hall that was well illuminated from a solid bank of windows along the south wall. The classroom had now devolved into a dusty repository for odds and ends seldom used.

Inside the main hall near the south wall was located a small stage on which stood a lectern used by either the teacher or preacher as the occasion decreed. Facing this were the students' desks, and flush against the north wall was a single row of church pews. To the left of the stage was a small, treadle-powered organ from which now emanated appropriately somber music. In front of the stage on this day was a table bearing a rough pine coffin. Half of the lid had been removed so the body could be viewed.

There was a large, hushed crowd composed of neighbors most of whom had never been very neighborly with Tom Larkin. But funerals are for the living, not the dead. These people were in attendance for the sake of Mrs. Larkin who was, in fact, the only Larkin present. None of the other relatives dared attend for fear of missing out on some impromptu division of the spoils. Beside Mrs. Larkin sat Mase, hulking and awkward in a black suit several sizes too small. Joe led Martin to one of the pews in back.

After about ten minutes that seemed more like ten hours, Reverend Watson walked tiredly to the lectern on the stage. No doubt, he had spent a night of turmoil deciding how to play this one. At his second impatient signal, the organ finally fell silent. With this covering sound gone, feet could be heard shuffling on the hardwood floor while every starched collar rattled with the slightest movement. There were several muted coughs and one gargantuan sneeze before silence finally reigned supreme. Reverend Watson laid aside for the moment his ragged, well-thumbed King James Bible and took from his pocket a single sheet of paper.

"We are here today…" His voice cracked and he was forced to clear his throat and start over.

"We are here today to pay our respects to Thomas Edward Larkin, a lifelong resident of the Burnham community. Mister Larkin was born April 14, 1873 and passed from this life July 21, 1925. His age was fifty two years, three months and seven days. He is survived by his widow, Dorothy Gibson Larkin; one son, William Allen Larkin; and two brothers, Andrew Jackson and George Wilbert Larkin, both residents of Fort Smith, Arkansas."

Joe could hardly suppress a snort of derision at this piece of information. Residents of Fort Smith, indeed! In fact, the two brothers shared the same address; to wit, a dilapidated shack in Coke Hill, a flood-prone, riverfront shantytown wherein resided a majority of the county's bums, winos, pickpockets, burglars, thugs and trolls. No doubt, those two had already wrecked Larkin's basement in search of the highly prized ARKANSAS PYZZON. It was just as well that the current stock had been removed. Had they found it, the two brothers would probably have already drunk themselves to death.

Reverend Watson put away the piece of paper and leaned forward, gripping the sides of the lectern tightly. Here at last was his moment of truth. Gazing out at the sea of faces, he was more than half tempted to launch into a noisy condemnation of Thomas Edward Larkin and all his kind, consigning them to the lower environs of Hades and good riddance! That would be the honest thing to do.

But it would not be proper. It would be horribly offensive to the widow and could make no possible difference to the deceased. His eyes rested a moment on the stern visage of Mrs. Larkin and he was suddenly struck by the wild thought that such an outburst might not be so offensive to her after all.

The congregation was becoming restless and he knew he could delay no longer. Straightening and rubbing a sweaty palm across his glistening pate, he put the tirade from his mind and summoned forth his most confidential manner.

"Thomas Larkin was not a member of this church or of any other church that I know of. But that is none of our concern. We have no way of knowing what lies inside a man's heart or what terms, if any, he has come to with his Maker. It is not for us to pass judgment on Thomas Larkin or any other man. All we can do is seek the road to righteousness and beg for God's mercy in the name of his son, Jesus Christ."

The eulogy now evolved into a sermon albeit much tamer than was Reverend Watson's wont. With the subject now in the more comfortable realm of generalities rather than the probable fate of one particular blighted soul, the congregation relaxed and breathed a bit easier. Hand-held fans bearing images of the Crucifixion began to flutter. Eyes wandered and feet shuffled. One old man nodded off. With commendable Christian mercy, Reverend Watson made his delivery short, concluding naturally enough with an impassioned prayer in which Larkin's name was not once mentioned.

Immediately after Amen, Reverend Watson gathered his tattered Bible and page of notes and retired from the field of battle. From the front row of desks arose an adolescent girl, the pride of the community due to her somewhat better than average singing voice. Clad in a navy blue dress of some crisp, rattling material and balanced precariously upon a pair of white high heels, she waddled awkwardly to the stage and opened a hymnal. With a nod to the organist, she launched into a nasal rendition of the obscure hymn, 'Prepare To Meet Thy God', her eyes glued to the page of unfamiliar words. People shifted uncomfortably and exchanged nervous glances, for this song was a harangue at an inveterate sinner to change his ways before it was too late. In Larkin's case, of course, it was now far too late.

"This seems hardly appropriate," whispered Martin to Joe. "Why do you suppose Reverend Watson chose it?"

"He didn't. Mrs. Larkin did."

Martin's face registered astonishment. "A strange woman," he muttered.

At the end came the traditional viewing of the body. Mrs. Larkin went first, hurrying past the coffin with hardly a glance and then out the door to be driven home by Mase. She spoke not a word to anyone. The rest of the congregation proceeded in a slow, ragged line, ultimately spilling out the southwest door.

Outside the building, clusters formed as pipes were lit, cigarettes rolled and plugs bit into. Joe stationed himself on the tiny porch and made sure people kept moving so the passageway would not become blocked by gossipers. Finally, the pall bearers emerged with their burden and made their way to the horse-drawn hearse waiting nearby. The last person out of the building was Reverend Watson who emerged mopping his sweaty brow and looking decidedly uncomfortable.

"A good service, Preacher," complimented Joe. "I was wonderin' how you would handle it."

Watson's reply was a grunt of displeasure.

"Fact is," continued Joe, "if you preached like that more often, why, I might even show up for a service now and then."

Watson shot him an angry glance. "It was a wishy-washy service, Potts, and now I feel tainted."

Joe suppressed a smile. That was a common reaction by most who had any dealings with Larkin. "Welcome to the world, Preacher."

Joe stepped off the porch and went in search of Laura and Jimmy Andrews. They were waiting patiently by their wagon as he had asked. Laura was clad in a dark green taffeta that Joe knew was the only fine dress she owned. Jimmy stood next to her, looking awkward and ungainly in a black suit too short in the sleeves and legs, too pinched in the shoulders and considerably oversized in the waist. It had clearly belonged to his father.

"Hello, Laura. You're lookin' fine today." She smiled sweetly as Joe nodded a greeting to Jimmy.

"I might say the same," she replied. "That suit looks as good on you as when you first got it."

"You're a mighty poor liar, maam."

She laughed gaily. "I suppose that's what being civil is all about. Filling each other with nonsense."

Joe fiddled self-consciously with his cane. "Laura, would you mind drivin' yourself home? I'd like to borrow Jimmy for a bit."

"Not at all, but it's almost dinnertime."

"I'll try to scrounge some vittles for him."

"All right, Joe."

She allowed herself to be helped into the wagon seat, a polite gesture on Joe's part that was totally unnecessary. Laura

Andrews was perfectly capable of boarding a wagon without any assistance. Indeed, it was a maneuver she could accomplish far more easily than Joe.

As the wagon clattered away, Joe turned to Jimmy. "Hope you don't mind ridin' in the deputy's automobile."

"No, sir!" The eyes were as large as saucers. "Where we goin', Joe?" It required a strong act of will on Jimmy's part to keep from bounding away toward the vehicle, leaving Joe to hobble along alone.

"My place first. I want to change clothes."

Joe made no effort to speak to Jimmy during the short trip. It would not have been possible anyway for the boy's attention was now focused solely on the machine. Perched in the middle of the back seat and leaning forward between the two men, his eyes took in every movement Martin made while his mouth ran non-stop, emitting a constant stream of questions. How fast would it go? How much did it cost? How hard was it to drive? Martin patiently answered each question.

Joe sat quietly on the passenger side, staring moodily out across the countryside. It was approaching noon and the sun was making some progress at burning away the morning mugginess.

When they reached the small cabin Joe immediately alit and started inside, but Jimmy lingered to study the automobile more closely while Martin stood by as answer man. Joe cast a contemptuous glance over his shoulder.

"When you two get done admirin' that modern marvel, you can come in and get some grub." He was already shedding portions of the suit before he reached the front door.

By the time the other two finally came in, Joe had already changed into a pair of bib overalls minus shirt and shoes. Martin unconsciously let his eyes drift down to the crippled foot, but then quickly looked away. Joe pretended not to notice and busied himself setting the table. A breadbox containing a half a loaf only hours away from petrifaction was accompanied by a platter heaped with thick slices of smoked ham.

"There's butter or mustard if you like. Sorry, nothin' to drink but well water or cold coffee."

"You got Larkin's…."

"Don't talk with your mouth full, Jimmy!" scolded Joe. The boy blushed and took the hint.

Martin looked from one to the other. "Larkin's what?" he asked quietly.

Jimmy lowered his eyes while Joe looked appropriately sour. "Larkin's whiskey!" he snapped. "Twenty six gallons."

Martin froze in mid-chew. "You removed it from the house?" The answer was a curt nod. "Why?"

"I was afraid the sheriff would search the place and find it. Then he might try to seize the farm and turn it over to some of his freeloadin' relatives. He's done it before."

Martin did not reply for a long time. "It was evidence," he pronounced quietly.

"So now you know it was there and the killer didn't take it." Joe stomped over to the door and stood staring out.

"Aren't you going to eat?" asked Martin.

"Joe only eats one meal a day," informed Jimmy.

"Less fuss and bother that way," grumbled Joe still with his back to them. He suddenly whirled and hobbled back to the table. "Jimmy, what's this about you wantin' to join the army?"

Jimmy blushed and put down his sandwich. "Ma told you?"

"She did. It has her considerable upset." He paused and then asked, "Why didn't you talk to me about it?"

The boy shifted uncomfortably. "Because I knew what you'd say."

"Did you?" He dropped into a chair and drummed his fingers on the table.

"The army ain't necessarily a bad life, Jimmy," he lectured. "It don't pay that much, but it does pay and they feed you regular. More than one poor boy has made a better life for hisself by puttin' on the uniform. But, Jimmy, you got to think about more than just yourself. With you gone, your mother will be all alone. Who will take care of her?"

"I could send her my pay. Most of it anyway."

"You and me both know she wouldn't spend it."

Jimmy leaped from his chair and turned away, running a hand through his thick red hair. "And how am I supposed to take care of her on a twenty acre hillside farm? That dirt is so poor it won't hardly grow respectable weeds."

"The world's changin', Jimmy. There's jobs to be had in Fort Smith."

"Yeah, makin' chairs for two bits an hour!" He whirled to face Joe again. "And don't you even mention the mines! I ain't goin' under the ground to breathe black dust and wait for one of their rotten timbers to snap or get blowed up by gas!"

"I'm not tellin' you what to do, Jimmy. I just want you to think things through because your decision is gonna affect more than just yourself."

After a few more seconds of finger drumming, he spoke again. "No matter what you decide to do, Jimmy, I advise you to put it off for a year. Finish your schoolin' and get your diploma."

"I been goin' to school since I was six, Joe. What difference will one more year make?"

"Likely none," he admitted. "But folks are strange, Jimmy. They set a lot of store by that piece of paper that says you stayed the course."

"He's giving you good advice, Jimmy," agreed Martin. "If you quit school now, you'll regret it for the rest of your life."

Jimmy looked down and shrugged his shoulders. "That's what the sergeant said, too. Anyway, I can't join until I'm eighteen unless Ma agrees to it and I know she won't" He dropped back into his chair but did not finish his sandwich.

"Jimmy, there's somethin' else I want to ask you about," continued Joe. "Have you heard any talk about Billy Larkin bein' back in the area?"

Jimmy nodded without looking up. "I heard the Jackson boys talkin' about him. He's supposed to be sparkin' Floyd Neely's daughter."

"Which one?"

"Wanda."

"How old is she now?"

"Sixteen, I think."

Joe shook his head. "Billy sure likes 'em young." He arose suddenly. "Deputy, let's go see Floyd!"

"Can I come, too?" asked Jimmy eagerly.

"Don't you have chores to do?"

"Fields are too wet to plow."

Joe shrugged. "It's all right with me if Deputy Martin don't mind." He glanced slyly at Jimmy. "I don't suppose you've got eyes on Wanda, too?"

"Not me!" protested the boy blushing. "Sally Carter is my girl. I just want to ride in the car some more."

"It's all right with me," agreed Martin. "Just let me change back into my uniform."

As Martin began to peel off his suit, Jimmy went to the chair where the deputy had draped his uniform when changing clothes earlier that morning. The boy squatted in order to better view the leather gunbelt and big .45 caliber Colt revolver. The walnut grips were stained and worn from years of handling.

"Boy, that's an old one!" exclaimed Jimmy.

"It belonged to my father. He was a deputy for Judge Isaac Parker for about ten years."

"Bein' a lawman must run in the family," remarked Joe.

"Can I look at it?" asked Jimmy.

"Yes, but be careful. It's loaded." As Martin watched the boy test the feel of the weapon, he asked, "Ever fired a revolver before?"

"Joe's let me shoot his a few times. It's a .38."

"Army issue," explained Joe. "They may still be lookin' for it."

"You ever shot anybody, Mister Martin?"

"No, and I'm thankful."

"Joe shot a man once."

"That was in the army, Jimmy, and ever'body was shootin' at that sniper. I don't know that I was the one that killed him."

"Shooting a man is serious business, Jimmy," explained Martin. "It's not something you do lightly."

"Did your father ever shoot anybody?"

It was a long time before Martin answered. "Yes, he did. He once had to kill a man who was crazy drunk. It set heavy on his mind until the day he died."

Jimmy gazed intently at the revolver as though it possessed some magical quality for having killed a human being. "Not with that," Martin added with a sad smile. "He used a shotgun." He paused for a moment. "He threw it into the river the next day."

Jimmy replaced the revolver in its holster. "I'm ready," announced Martin, strapping on the weapon.

After turning onto the highway, Joe suggested, "No need goin' all the way back to the store to get to the Mount Moriah Road. This lane up ahead cuts right through to it."

Martin started to make the turn, but then slammed to a halt. "It looks kind of rough," he remarked doubtfully. "It doesn't save that much time."

"Store'll be full of loafers about now. I'd just as soon not have them speculatin' on where we're goin'."

Martin shrugged and turned onto the tree-lined lane. Joe twisted in his seat to face Jimmy, "How is Sally?"

"Still in Oklahoma."

"Her aunt doin' any better?"

"About the same, Mrs. Carter says. I was over to visit them on Sunday."

"Seems a little strange to me," mused Joe, "sendin' a sixteen year old girl to see after a sick woman. Why didn't the Carters bring the woman to stay with them?"

"They said she was too sick to travel."

Martin turned onto the Mount Moriah Road and there was silence for a half a mile. "How does Sally like Oklahoma?" asked Joe.

"All right, I guess."

"Doesn't she say in her letters?" There then ensued a quarter of a mile of silence. "Have you had any letters from her, Jimmy?" Joe asked quietly at last.

"I guess she's been awful busy!" blurted the boy, looking away.

Joe turned back to the front. "Road intersects just ahead," he told Martin. "Turn left."

The new road made a sweeping curve back to the east to follow the southern base of no-name hill. "Jimmy, I'm sorry I pried into your affairs," apologized Joe. "It was none of my business."

Jimmy was clasping and unclasping his hands. "I've wrote her five times, but she won't write back!"

"What do her parents say?"

"They say she's real busy. Or maybe the letters got lost in the mail. They don't know."

"Would you like me to speak to them?"

The boy shrugged hopelessly. "If you like. I figure she's found a new boyfriend."

There was little point trying to respond to this speculation since he could neither confirm nor deny. "Neely place is the next one on the left."

They pulled into a weed-infested yard littered with an assortment of odds and ends including several hundred rusty tin cans. At one corner of this feral greensward squatted a set of crushed bedsprings from which grew a battalion of poke salad stalks now going to seed. At the geographic center of the yard, hulking in glorious splendor, sat an archaic sofa, broken springs protruding and its upholstery ripped to shreds. Upon this prized possession of the Neely clan were perched an emaciated yellow cat and three chickens.

The manor of this estate was constructed of odds and ends of scrap lumber assembled in no particular order, but as the mood struck the architect. A small portion of this structure had been painted white, a smaller portion green and most of it never painted at all. The roof was partly of wood shingles, partly rusty sheet iron and all of it leaky. Fewer than half the windows boasted glass, but all were adorned with burlap curtains. A small vegetable garden had received only passing attention, and consequently the food-bearing plants were being gradually overrun by swarming masses of weeds. Off to the left was a crooked, collapsing barn swamped in a sea of ten feet tall Johnson grass.

Joe tapped on the doorframe even though the front door stood wide open, allowing free access to swarms of houseflies. It seemed to Joe that about as many were departing as were entering which must be a commentary of some kind. From inside came the sounds of babes bawling, pans clattering and streams of profanity; a vast amount of profanity from a profusion of voices both young and old.

At last a frail woman with hollow cheeks and dull eyes came to the door. She was clad in a loose-fitting dress pieced together from flour sacks with little attention to various brands and colors. This wondrous garment, however, failed to conceal the bulge at her middle, a bulge that had reappeared with dreary frequency about every other year for the past sixteen. Nearby stood a teenage girl who possessed a similar abdominal bulge. A horde of dirty infants tottered or crawled about the floor.

"What do you want?" demanded the woman sharply.

"Maam, my name is…."

"I know who you are, Joe Potts! What do you want with us?"

He introduced Deputy Martin. "Maam, we'd like to talk to Floyd."

"He ain't here!"

"When will he be back?"

"Don't know!" She started to turn away.

"Maam, this ain't a social call. It's official business. You're gonna have to talk to us one way or another."

She whirled to face him again, her eyes snapping with anger. "You wouldn't be so high and mighty if Floyd wuz here!"

"No, maam," agreed Joe blandly. "Has Billy Larkin been here?"

The sudden question took the woman by surprise and her eyes widened slightly, but then quickly returned to normal. "Ain't seen him!" The girl, however, had almost jumped at the mention of Billy's name.

"Folks are sayin' Billy was here last weekend," pressed Joe.

"Maybe he seen Floyd! I ain't seen him!"

Joe rubbed his chin reflectively. "How many dogs has Floyd got now?" he suddenly asked.

The woman was again taken by surprise and this time answered honestly before she caught herself. "None." Her face immediately twisted with rage. "I got no more time to talk to you, Joe Potts!"

"That's fine, maam. I'd like to look around a bit if you don't mind."

"Reckon I can't stop you!" She stomped away into the dim recesses of Floyd Neely's castle.

"Good day, maam," spoke Joe to the emptiness. "It's been a pleasure." He turned away and put his hat back on.

Martin followed Joe to the back of the house, wading mud and weeds as their trouser legs became soaked and covered with hundreds of tiny burs. Joe halted at a pen in which the weeds had recently been broken and trampled. He squatted and examined the ground closely, poking at some lumps with a stick.

"Dog droppins," he remarked. "Lucky the rain didn't wash 'em all away." He picked up a bone. "Fresh chewed."

Martin bent down and confirmed the judgment. "You believe Billy took his father's dogs and brought them here." It was more of a statement than a question.

"And it's a damn cinch that Billy didn't take 'em while Tom was still alive." He struggled to his feet and slipped the bone into a pocket. "We really need to have a chat with that boy."

Joe stopped again at the front door and called the woman back. He did not remove his hat this time and he did not call her maam. "When Floyd gets back, you tell him to come see me right away."

"And if he don't?"

"He's gonna have to talk to the law and I'll only give him two days to come in on his own. After that, I'll get a warrant and come after him. Two days, Mrs. Neely, or he'll be lodgin' with the county for a spell."

Her eyes widened perceptibly, but there was still a trace of rebellion there. "You don't scare me none, Joe Potts!"

He tipped his hat and smiled mockingly. "No, Maam, I reckon I don't. I reckon you're just too damned stupid to get scared. Good day again, Mrs. Neely." He turned and started for the car.

As they pulled onto the road, Joe remarked, "If I get half an excuse, I aim to arrest both Neelys."

Martin looked at him with surprise. "I can understand you wanting to arrest Floyd. He may be an accomplice to murder. But why his wife?"

"Because they ain't fit parents. If I could send both of 'em down to the state pea farm for a spell, maybe those younguns could be got into decent homes. As it is, they're just gonna grow into more Floyd Neelys and brood sows."

It was a half a mile before Martin spoke again. "Your motive is sound, Joe, but it's a dangerous practice to start taking people's children away from them. The next thing you know, the government will be stepping in because the parents don't go to the right church or they vote for the wrong political party."

Joe studied Martin with new interest. "I've thought about that, Deputy. Why do you think I ain't already sent Floyd away? God knows I could nail him on a dozen petty charges. None of 'em too serious, but lumped together, enough to get him a few years."

"And now you're going to do it?" asked Martin quietly.

Joe considered the proposition for a long time. "This will be the first chance I've ever had to nail 'em both. I just ain't sure I can resist the temptation."

Martin looked over at him and Joe thought he saw something in the deputy's eyes that could have been disappointment. Joe looked away again and concentrated on the countryside flowing past, feeling as bleak as an orphaned puppy.

They were approaching the road that would take them back to Burnham. Martin slowed and started to make the turn, but Joe suddenly said, "No! Keep goin' straight."

Martin gave the wheel a sharp jerk and stayed on the same road. "Where are we going?"

"Where we started yesterday. To see the Claytons."

They topped a low rise and dropped into a magnificent little valley where the mountains curved and tumbled upon one another. A lazy, tree-lined creek wormed its way through the gay, green confusion in search of an outlet. The land that fell gently away from them was speckled with neat fields and pastures still glistening from yesterday's rain. Small, prim farmhouses invariably painted white were scattered here and there and always reinforced by proud, regal barns. Herds of Jersey cows grazed upon fields of clover or else lay beneath shade trees while munching their cuds with haughty detachment.

At Joe's direction, Martin pulled in at a house marginally larger than the others in the valley, mainly for the fact that it consisted of two stories. "This is where the colored folks live?" he asked a little surprised.

Joe smiled faintly and nodded. "Quite a story behind 'em. Care to hear it?"

"Yes, I would."

"Two brothers and their families live here. The place came down to them from their grandpappy. He had been the slave of a man named Clayton. After the Rebellion he took his master's last name. The original Clayton, the white one, had been a Confederate officer. You remember the old man back at the store, the one I told you was a bushwhacker?"

Martin nodded.

"Clayton hanged his two brothers for all the robbin' they'd been doin'. That old man escaped the same fate just by the skin of his teeth. So he don't have much use for anybody named Clayton, white or black.

"Anyway," continued Joe, "after the war, all but one of Clayton's slaves left him. Then the carpetbaggers came and started stealin' ever'thing in sight. Well, old man Clayton didn't have no younguns of his own and no relations worth shootin', so he up signed the whole place over to his ex-slave. Since the colored vote was keepin' the Republicans in power, they left the Claytons alone after that. And that's how a couple of darkies come to own one of the best farms in the county."

As an afterthought, he added, "Their names is Howard and Samuel. Howard is all right, but Samuel is kinda moody. About half mean, too."

"Mean enough to kill someone?"

"If pushed, yes."

By this time the car had been surrounded by an army of dusky, noisy children ranging in age from five to the teens. Every knob and protrusion on the vehicle had to be felt and examined and debated. On the porch appeared a tall, gangly man in his late thirties who was already taking on tinges of gray above the ears.

Coming around the corner of the house was another black man a few years older, a little shorter, but more powerfully built. He carried a pitchfork that he casually spun in work-hardened hands. Martin realized without being told that the latter was Samuel and that a pitchfork could have more than one use.

Both black men visibly tensed at the sight of Martin's uniform and badge, but relaxed somewhat when they recognized Joe. Howard forced a smile and stepped down from the porch to greet them, extending a bony, calloused paw as he approached. Samuel maintained not only his detachment but also a loose grip on the pitchfork.

"Hello Howard, Samuel," greeted Joe.

"Hello, Missa Joe," answered Howard eagerly. "What can we do fo' you?"

Joe introduced Martin. "We're lookin' into the killin' of Tom Larkin," he explained.

Howard adopted an appropriately somber expression even though there was no doubt that he, for one, would not miss Tom Larkin one little bit. "Yessa, we heerd 'bout dat. Awful! Just awful to think that a man would be shot down right on his own place. Things like dat, dey happen in de big city. Not here 'mong us country folk."

"Well, it happened, Howard, and now we have to find out who did it."

"Do you think we killed him?" demanded Samuel almost belligerently.

"There's some who think that," admitted Joe.

"Oh no, we didn't have nothin' to do with no killin'!" exclaimed Howard frantically.

"Hesh up, Howard!" snapped Samuel. "What do you think, Potts?" He pointedly did not use the word mister.

Joe met the angry gaze without flinching. "I don't think you killed him, Samuel."

"Why?"

"Because he's dead and you're alive. Larkin would never have let a colored man get that close to him with a shotgun."

Samuel considered this a moment and then leaned the pitchfork against the house. "Why did you come here?" he asked.

"Mainly to give you a warnin'."

"About what?"

"The weekend's comin' up. Men are gonna get likkered up and somethin' could happen. You've got relations in Fort Smith. This might be a really good time to visit 'em."

"So we could come back to find our place burned to the ground?"

"At least send your wives and children away."

Samuel seemed to consider this. "Maybe," he conceded. "But I'll tell you one thing, Potts. There ain't gonna be no lynchin'. They may shoot me down; they may burn the house down around me. But they ain't gonna have no live nigga to hang and there just may be a few dead white men to tote away"

"I believe you, Samuel." He paused and then added. "Look, we're gonna put out the word that we're lookin' for Billy Larkin. That might slow up the hotheads some."

"You mean Billy kilt his own Pa!" exclaimed Howard, genuinely shocked at the idea of patricide.

"He might have, Howard. There's some evidence against him." He looked back at Samuel. "I just wanted to let you two know how things stand."

Samuel nodded but did not speak his appreciation. "What about you, Deputy?" he suddenly demanded. "You ain't said nothin'. Do you think we did the killin'?" The 'we', of course, meant just Samuel. Clearly, Howard was not capable of killing anyone.

It was Martin's turn to meet the harsh gaze and he, too, did so without flinching. "I don't know, Samuel. Right now I'm willing to trust to Constable Potts's judgment. But until I know for sure who did it, I'm not ruling anybody out."

"I 'spect the sheriff would just love to hang this on a nigga."

Joe broke in before Martin could reply. "Give the sheriff some credit, Samuel," he pronounced with good humor. "He's got greater ambition than that." This remark not only mystified both black men, but also earned him a nasty glance from Martin.

"We'll be goin' now," concluded Joe. "Howard, take care of yourself. Samuel, keep your powder dry."

When they were back in the car, Martin said, "Surly fellow. And you as much as encouraged him to fight a mob."

"He didn't need no encouragement from me."

"The smartest thing to have done was take them into protective custody," asserted Martin.

"Easier said than done. And I ain't sure that would have been the right thing anyway."

Martin looked at him with surprise. "If there is a lynch mob, he could die."

"Yes," agreed Joe solemnly. "But if we took them in, it would like we suspected them of murder, and you can be sure this place wouldn't be standin' come Monday mornin'."

He paused. "Besides, I ain't sure a man should be discouraged from fightin' for what's his, even if it gets him killed. Do that, then we might as well turn the whole damn country over to the riff-raff."

"Point taken," admitted Martin with a sigh. "Where to now?"

"Home, I guess." He glanced toward the back seat. "I expect this has been a borin' trip for you, Jimmy."

The boy shrugged. "You reckon they got cars in the army, Joe?"

Joe faced back to the front and stared glumly out the window. "I expect," he answered sourly.

After turning back onto the road to Burnham, they passed a large cornfield on the left most of which would end up being bottled. This piece of information Joe kept to himself. Suddenly, a single crow, no doubt startled by the noisy car engine, rose up out of the field and lumbered awkwardly toward a large cottonwood. Just as it approached the tree, he was attacked by two tiny, gray specks. The crow squawked in terror and turned back the way it had come. But the two assailants refused to break off the attack and continued to dab at the crow's head.

"Look, Joe!" exclaimed Jimmy excitedly. "A pair of scissortails are after him!"

Joe twisted around to see past Martin's head. Sure enough, two of the tiny, long-tailed birds were assaulting the crow with a vengeance. The crow was far larger than both attackers put together, but was utterly helpless as its enemies swooped and darted, using their nine inch tail feathers as rudders. The attack was well coordinated, first one side and then the other, never giving the victim a moment's respite or one iota of mercy. The one-sided aerial combat was headed their way.

"Those scissortails likely have a nest in that cottonwood," remarked Joe. "If the damn fool would get back down in that corn, he would lose them. Must be a young one that don't know no better."

Martin was becoming interested in the fight, and as a result, the car was weaving crazily from one side of the road to the other. "Pull over before you kill us all!" admonished Joe.

"I just saw black feathers fall," spoke Jimmy.

"You got sharp eyes, boy," replied Joe.

The crow suddenly plummeted into the cornfield right next to the road. The gray specks circled angrily for a few seconds, and then finally peeled away back in the direction of the cottonwood. The crow, however, did not reappear. A slight rustling could be heard among the yellowing cornstalks.

"Toot the horn, Deputy," commanded Joe. Martin complied. Nothing happened.

"That should have roused him out of there," said Joe. "I think they blinded him."

"They what?" exclaimed Martin.

"They may have pecked his eyes out," explained Joe impatiently. "Come on, Jimmy, let's see if we can find him."

Martin waited at the edge of the road while the other two stomped around in a muddy cornfield looking for a blind crow. At last Jimmy found him and waded back to the fence, his undersized suit now thoroughly soaked. He was holding the crow upside down in one hand with both wings pinned back to keep from being thrashed. The entire head was a bloody pulp, the black beak ajar as the bird continued to pant from fright and exhaustion.

"Good Lord!" exclaimed Martin. "I've never heard of such a thing!"

"Scissortails have a real hatred for crows," lectured Joe. "Crows raid the nests of other birds and eat the babies, you know. That pair likely thought this fellow was after their happy home." He glanced at Martin with a twinkle in his eye. "I reckon somebody ought to have took 'em into protective custody."

"The crow was the one who needed protective custody," corrected Martin. "You're going to kill it, aren't you?"

"Why?"

The deputy looked at him with genuine shock. "Why? Because that's the humane thing to do."

Joe studied the crow with interest. "You know, if it was left to nature, this fellow would starve to death. Or, if he's lucky, get tore to pieces by coyotes or hounds." He glanced back at Martin. "You think we ought to be meddlin' with Mother Nature?"

"We already have. It was this automobile that scared him toward those little monsters."

"Good point," admitted Joe.

"Joe, why don't we keep him?" suggested Jimmy. "I hear tell if you catch a crow young enough and split his tongue, you can teach him to talk."

"I expect it might not set too well with your ma if I sent you home with a blind crow. She likely wouldn't talk to me for a year." He winked at Jimmy. "Besides, you think the army would let you keep him as a pet?"

Jimmy blushed deeply.

Joe took the crow from him. "No, I reckon we best do the humane thing, Jimmy."

He seized the bird tightly about the neck with his right hand and made a rapid clockwise swing. He then tossed the lifeless, thrashing body into the ditch and wiped his hand on his overall bib.

"Ever seen a cockfight, Deputy?"

"No!" replied Martin with distaste.

"Funny thing," mused Joe. "Most people I know, even those who'll set and watch a pair of roosters peck and flog each other to pieces, would have killed that critter to end its misery. The human animal sure is a strange cuss."

Martin wore a bright red blush for a good half mile.

The presence in Burnham of an automobile, even for a few days, was an event so noteworthy that it would undoubtedly be discussed for months, perhaps even years. However, the sudden appearance of a second was unique to the point of being scandalous.

But as Martin inched up the lane to Joe's cabin, right there big as life was a flashy green Packard with a glistening brass horn and rubber mud flaps. Such ostentation and decadent gaudiness could only be the whim of someone possessing far more wealth than was Christian. Jimmy's eyes almost rolled out of his head, and his recent infatuation with the county's Model

T evaporated like an early morning dew savaged by a summer sun.

"Joe, you got company!" exclaimed the boy needlessly.

From the shade of a large oak arose a short, slender man who in spite of the summer heat wore a light gray suit. His hair was a thin, wispy blond, but this he soon covered with a dark blue fedora with brim bent low in front. The man was in his late twenties and exuded supreme self-confidence. There was a conspicuous bulge beneath his left arm.

As he ambled toward them, brushing grass and twigs from his trousers, his hands seemed to glisten in the sunlight. The reason soon became clear. On his left hand were two enormous rings, one emerald and the other jade. On his right was an eye-popping diamond. A sedate turquoise seemed to get lost amid all this flash and pomp. Ignoring both the deputy and Jimmy, the man walked directly to Joe and extended his glowing right hand.

"My name is Willis Cox.," he announced.

Joe stared at the man's hand a moment, but made no move to accept it. "Afraid I might singe my ugly paw if I touch all that fire," he drawled at last.

Cox smiled thinly and withdrew his hand. "May I assume you remember me?"

Joe nodded. "I remember whippin' the snot out of you for stealin' the Widow Farley's chickens." He glanced toward the Packard. "You've moved up in the world, Willis."

Again the man flashed the thin smile. "I learned two lessons from you, Joe. I learned there's safer and more valuable game in this world than chickens, and I learned to not ever, ever get caught."

"What brings you back to this neck of the woods, Willis?"

"I need to talk to you, Joe." He cut his eyes toward Martin. "Alone."

JON R. JOHNSON

Joe turned to Martin. "You mind takin' Jimmy home?"

Martin shrugged and turned back to the car. Jimmy, his eyes still glued to the Packard, followed reluctantly. He stumbled several times as he tried to look in one direction while walking in another. At last they were gone, but Willis refused to speak until the Ford was completely out of sight.

"You still work for the Kansas City Syndicate?" asked Joe.

"I do, and that's why I'm here. What the hell's goin' on, Joe?"

He shrugged. "Tom Larkin was murdered. We still don't know who did it. Or why."

"This is gettin' ticklish, Joe. This hick sheriff's rattlin' everybody's chains. He's even talked to the G-men. We hate losin' Larkin. His stuff brought top dollar even though there wasn't much of it. But we hate the noise Faulkner is makin' even more."

"I thought you boys had a stock solution for problems like that."

Cox made a face and shook his head in agitation. "Only as a last resort. We prefer to settle our problems with a little less, ah, noise. At least when we can." He paused. "You really don't have any idea who did it?"

"I'm pretty sure you boys didn't have nothin' to do with it. The killlin' was too sloppy for that."

"Well, I'm glad somebody believes in us."

"Not a good choice of words, Willis."

The gangster ignored the slight. "Any other ideas?"

"Right now, Billy Larkin is our best lead."

Cox looked doubtful. "Billy doesn't have the guts for somethin' like that."

"I agree, but he was home the day of the killin'. If I can catch him and squeeze hard enough, maybe somethin' will pop out."

"Look, Joe, we want this cleared up, and the sooner the better. Catch who did it and there's five grand in it for you."

This induced a noticeable lifting of the eyebrows. "That's a lot of money. Why don't you boys just buy off Faulkner?"

"He's ambitious. We can't trust him to stay bought. Joe, no matter who takes the credit for it, if this guy gets caught, it'll be your doin'."

"You seem to have a lot of faith in a hick constable."

"I remember how you trapped a chicken thief sixteen years ago. And how it only took you a week to find Jeff Cook's coon dogs even though they were already in another state."

"I had a little help on that one."

"But you knew where to go to get that help. That's half the job right there. There ain't nobody else in this county who could track an elephant across a snowfield."

This was not a point Joe cared to dispute. "Willis, I aim to catch whoever did it if I can. But as for your money, I don't want it."

Cox reacted to this very much as would a Baptist preacher to a blatant profession of atheism. "Good God, Joe! Why not?"

"I have my reasons. I doubt you'd understand any of 'em. But since I sure wouldn't want you boys feelin' obligated, you can give the money to Reverend Jack Fuller."

Willis now looked doubly shocked. "You want us to give it to a preacher? Joe, you never struck me as the religious sort."

"I ain't, Willis. But Fuller runs a shelter and soup kitchen on the north side of Fort Smith. He could put the money to good use." With a wink, he added, "Maybe he can even patch up a few of the lives ruined by your demon rum."

"Very funny! All right, your Reverend Fuller will get the money. If you wrap this thing up."

"If I wrap it up."

Cox crawled behind the wheel of his Packard. Joe came over and leaned against the door. "Tell me, Willis, how many chickens would it take to buy one of these things?"

"A hell of a lot more than the Widow Farley had. I'll keep in touch."

Then he was gone, careening recklessly down the rough, rutted lane, slinging mud and gravel. Willis Cox lived in a fast, furious world. If he broke his car, he would buy another even bigger and better. This was the beginning of the throwaway world.

Shaking his head, Joe hobbled into his cabin to see if anything had been pilfered. He knew beforehand, however, that he would find everything untouched. These people had a curious morality all their own. They were from a different planet.

He retrieved the current jug of ARKANSAS PYZZON and treated himself to a healthy slug, sighing with masochistic pleasure at the burning inside his empty belly. He began to think about supper and wondered if the deputy would stay for a bite to eat.

The deputy. He ought to start calling Martin by his name, he decided. They had been working together two days now. The young man should be more than just a badge with a number.

Ten minutes later, Martin rumbled up in his no longer quite so glamorous Ford. For some odd reason, Joe found himself liking the black, square contraption a little better. Martin came to the door, hesitated uncertainly and then finally knocked on the doorframe.

"Hell, Charlie, you don't have to knock. You're almost part of the family by now."

Martin gave a start at being addressed by his first name. He stepped inside and said, "Jimmy's home now. His mother was a little upset that he got his suit wet."

Joe smiled faintly. "I knew there was some reason I didn't want to go along. Stay for supper?"

Martin shuffled self-consciously. "Guess I better not. The sheriff will be waiting to hear what we found out today."

Joe shrugged. "Suit yourself."

Martin turned to leave, but then paused at the door. "You didn't have to kill that crow on my account. I had no objection to Jimmy keeping it as a pet."

"Wild things ought to be free. Even crows. If they can't be free, they ought to be dead."

"That's a rather extreme position."

"That's what they told old Patrick Henry, too."

Martin smiled faintly "So you meant to kill it all along." Joe nodded. "Well, I'll be going now."

When Martin was almost to the car Joe hobbled to the door and called to him, "Charlie, no need you makin' a round trip from Fort Smith ever' day. Pack some clothes tomorrow. You can bed down here."

Martin smiled and waved to him. Joe turned back inside and began putting together his supper. From outside he heard a metallic clank of the crank being inserted and then the rumble of the engine turning over. A few minutes later the popping machine had receded beyond hearing.

But it took a lot longer than for the Packard.

After supper, Joe wrote a long letter to an old army buddy now living in Oklahoma.

CHAPTER FOUR
Friday, July 24

Martin glanced toward the passenger seat where Joe lolled comfortably, clad only in an old patched pair of overalls and a ragged straw hat that should have been cremated years ago. The ever-present cane rested lightly between his knees while a strand of wild oats danced wildly from his teeth. After two days of riding in the Model T, he no longer sat like a spring about to pop. He was an old hand.

"I expected you would dress a little better to visit a businessman," remarked Martin with a little irritation.

"You ain't seen the business he's in. Turn right at this next road."

Highway Ten had carried them halfway to Greenwood, but now they turned north onto a narrow washboard of a road bounded on both sides by cow pastures. This pitted, pockmarked ribbon was nature's grudging concession to man's often frivolous need to get from one place to another. Well, they could have their path, but it would not be pleasant. Martin downshifted to temper the violence of the bounces.

"One thing I'm not clear on," remarked the deputy. "You say Larkin sold timbers to the mines, but there is little timber on his farm. Where did he get it?"

"Same place as ever'body else. The national forest."

"Is that allowed?"

"If you have a permit. Larkin had one."

"How does one get a permit?"

"Bribery." Martin gave him a sharp glance. "Charlie, you can make a lot of friends with a few gallons of prime 'shine," explained Joe.

Martin assumed an appropriately sour expression for a quarter of a mile. "That damned stuff is corrupting the whole country!" he grumbled.

"That's a fact. Road ends at this cemetery. Take a right."

Long before making the turn, a dull roar had begun that could be heard even above the car engine. The further they went, the louder it became and the air began to be filled with a thin, inky dust. At last they topped a low rise and spread out below them was a noisy, smoky outpost of hell, an operating room of man's brutal surgery to extract black rocks from the bowels of the earth.

There were towers and conveyors and weird shaped buildings that all presumably served some purpose. Functional labels like washer and tipple were utterly alien to Martin. The whole bizarre layout was punctuated in various places by enormous mounds of varying shades of black. A line of railroad hopper cars waited patiently, still empty this early in the day.

Spreading out from this madness was a large, dingy settlement where people pretended to live normally. There were no actual colors; only a dark, universal grunginess. A church steeple, once briefly white, now possessed its own grimy coat of coal dust. People came and went, apparently oblivious of the black fog. For nearly as far as the eye could see, the earth and all living things were stained a dismal brown.

"This is the Franklin mine!" shouted Joe in order to be heard. "It's one of the biggest in the county. Larkin provided most of their timbers."

"What a madhouse!" exclaimed Martin. "Where do I park?"

"By that green building."

"What green building? They're all black."

"Well, it used to be green. Here, on the left."

Martin whipped in beside two other automobiles and killed the engine. He followed Joe into a small building that, sure

JON R. JOHNSON

enough, had once been green. This was some kind of office, apparently the nerve center of the inferno going on outside. A large wooden desk, unoccupied at the moment, squatted in the center of the room and supported an impressive heap of dirty, smudged papers. A half filled coffee cup with a cigarette butt in it sat precariously close to the edge of the desk. It was a long way down and the tiled floor was very hard. A misstep would be fatal.

Back in one corner beneath a shelf housing an army of bulky ledgers was a second desk. A thin, hatchet-faced young man with shaggy black hair and horn-rimmed glasses glanced up at them a moment and then returned his attention to the current ledger. True to his lofty position as a bookkeeper, he wore a business suit, appropriately black, and an expression of smug superiority. As all the world knew, or should know, bookkeepers were the elite of clerkdom and thus entitled to look down upon lesser mortals.

"Where is Mister Wellman?" asked Joe.

"He's not here," replied the young man without looking up.

"I can see that. When will he be back?"

"He's inspecting some tunnels. I don't know when he'll be back."

"Go get him."

At last the young man looked up again. From his expression one might have assumed that Joe possessed at least three heads, all of them mounted backwards. "You must be joking!" exclaimed the bookkeeper.

"I am not. This is police business. Go get him."

"I do not go into the mine!" pronounced the young man with great conviction. "Not ever!"

"You should. That mine is what pays your way in the world. You should take more interest in it."

"You will just have to wait," he spoke with finality. He returned to his ledger.

Joe sat down in the squeaky swivel chair behind the first desk and stretched out his right leg. "Let's see," he mused, "you'd be Henry Adams, wouldn't you? Seems we've met somewhere before. Now where was it?"

Joe screwed up his face with feigned concentration. Within seconds he exploded into a wide grin. "Now I remember! It was at Bonnie's in Fort Smith. You always ask for that fourteen year old colored girl." He assumed his very best dirty old man leer. "You reckon that's what your church deacons would call a mortal sin?"

Henry swung around in his own swivel chair and was gripping the arms so tightly that his knuckles were white. His face had turned pasty while his quivering lower lip was drooping far in the direction of his lap.

"Why don't you go get Mister Wellman?" suggested Joe quietly.

Henry bolted for the door, but Martin caught him by the arm and swung him around. The clerk, almost bumping his nose on Martin's badge, looked up wildly, his baby blue eyes appearing as tiny islands in a sea of chalk.

"This concerns a murder investigation," explained Martin roughly. "It is so important that we see Mister Wellman that I want you to go down and find him yourself. Don't send someone else." Pausing, he then added ominously, "Or I won't like it!"

A shrill squeak escaped from Henry which was all he could muster in the way of a groan. Martin shoved him roughly out the door and then walked over and helped himself to Henry's chair. Joe gazed at him with considerable amusement.

"You likely caused poor Henry to ruin a perfectly good pair of Fruit-of-the-Looms. Why the second scare?"

"I don't like snooty clerks either. Do you have that kind of dirt on everybody in the county?"

"Purt' near, Charlie; purt' near."

"That can work both ways, you know. You had to be in that place yourself to see him."

Joe leaned back with both hands laced behind his head. "It only works if you give a damn about what folks think."

"And you don't?"

Joe pondered a moment. "I guess in one way I'm like ever'body else. I'd rather have folks think highly of me. But I'm not about to put on an act to make sure they do. I won't be a slave to public opinion."

"No," agreed Martin dryly, "I'd already gathered that." His eyes wandered to the coffeepot atop a small stove in the back of the room. "Do you think Mister Wellman would mind if I helped myself?"

"Go ahead if you don't mind coffee that tastes like coal."

Martin's expression indicated that he thought Joe was kidding. At the first sip his face twisted with revulsion. He put the cup down and moved well away from it. He stopped in front of a map of the whole county and studied it with interest.

"What are all these squiggles?" he asked.

"Mine tunnels," answered Joe. "That map is supposed to show every mine tunnel in Sebastian County along with its depth."

"Supposed to?"

"Most companies plat and register all their tunnels. That's so ever'body will know where they are. But there's outlaw tunnels, too, some of 'em goin' back twenty or thirty years. They're a serious problem."

"How so?"

"They all fill with water eventually after they stop bein' used. Then another company comes along and tunnels into it, not knowin' it's there. Then you got some drowned miners."

"Why weren't they plotted like these?"

"Because someone was takin' coal where they didn't have the mineral rights."

"In other words, they were stealing."

"Yep! That's really the world's oldest profession, you know."

Martin reoccupied Henry's chair. "You're a cynic, Joe."

Joe smiled thinly and swung around to stare out the one small, dingy window.

Thirty minutes later the door opened and in stepped a thin, middle-aged black man. His hat was black, his clothes were black and his face was black; the only exception to this visage of ebony were the whites of his eyes and that made him look like a refugee from a minstrel show. He was trailed by a crestfallen bookkeeper who was if anything even blacker. Joe and Charlie exchanged surreptitious smiles.

The first man stepped to the back of the room and unzipped a pair of coveralls that he dropped into an inky pile. He instantly assumed a more human visage. After filling a bowl of water and scrubbing his face into a florid paleness, the transformation was complete. The dejected Henry looked on with dismay. He had been too flustered to think of borrowing a pair of coveralls. His neat suit was hopelessly soiled.

"Henry, wash your face!" ordered Wellman. "You look awful."

Henry tried, but the result was a lurid smearing that made him look even worse. The mine superintendent sighed loudly. "Go home and get cleaned up. I'll expect you back by noon."

"Yes, sir," he squeaked. Henry retired, not happily but with considerable relief.

Wellman glanced into his coffee cup, made a face and then dumped the mess out the door. After refilling the cup, he plunked into his swivel chair and fixed Joe with a sour look. "I hope you have a good reason for costing me a half day of bookkeeping."

"The best reason, Paul. A murder investigation."

"Larkin," he spoke with a sigh. Then in spite of himself, he broke into a smile. "I'd sure like to know what you said to Henry. I didn't think any power on earth could make him go down into the tunnels."

"If I told you, I couldn't use it again."

"And you'll use it again, won't you?"

"If the need ever arises."

Wellman shook his head in good humor. "All right, how can I help you?"

Joe first introduced Martin and then got down to business. "I know you're quite a coon hunter, Paul. Larkin had six bitch hounds and we're pretty sure Billy Larkin took 'em."

"You think Billy killed his father?"

"We're not certain, but it's a possibility."

Wellman shook his head doubtfully. "I don't think Billy had it in him to go after an old he-bear like Tom Larkin."

"You never can tell, Paul. Anyway, I was wonderin' if you knew about anybody suddenly havin' some new bitch hounds."

"I can ask around, Joe. But to be honest, the people I know wouldn't have any dealings with the likes of Billy Larkin."

"No, but Billy has dealins with some of the union men, and I know your company has spies among 'em."

Wellman looked startled. "That's something you're not supposed to know, Joe!" he complained.

"We gonna stand on ceremony, Paul?"

Wellman sighed and shook his head. "All right, I'll have our boys see what they can find out." He gave Joe another sour look. "You'd blackmail your own mother to get Larkin's killer, wouldn't you?"

Joe smiled thinly. "I don't like this sort of thing happenin' right under my nose. Kinda hurts my pride."

"I can see your point. Anything else?"

"Yep. Where were you Tuesday afternoon, Paul?"

Wellman had to look astonished before he could look offended. "What are you getting at, Joe?" he growled.

"Just this. I know the Franklin mine's havin' trouble payin' its bills. Breakin' that last strike cost you a bundle. Larkin hadn't been paid for his last three shipments and was gettin' ready to sue. Maybe somebody figured it would be easier to deal with a distressed widow woman."

Wellman was sitting stiffly in his chair. "That's crazy, Joe! Larkin was our main source of timbers. This is going to cause no end of trouble."

"That won't wash, Paul. Larkin was an absentee owner of the timber company. The business is still a goin' concern with or without him. In fact, the Franklin mine could be in a good position to take it over." He paused. "Tuesday afternoon, Paul."

Wellman was straining to keep himself under control. "I was right here, just like always," he replied tightly.

"The whole afternoon?"

"Yes." Then his face fell. "No," he added weakly. "I had to go into Greenwood to see Phil Cooper at the bank."

"When did you go?"

"Just after the noon break."

"When did you get back?"

Wellman blushed deeply. "Right before the end of the day shift."

"You spent three hours with Mister Cooper?"

Wellman looked positively sick. "I, I had other business as well."

"I know you've got a mistress, Paul, but isn't Wednesday your usual day with her?"

Wellman glanced wildly at Martin and then back to Joe. "Damn it!" he hissed.

"Charlie can be trusted," assured Joe. "He's an upright man." Then he grinned maliciously, "But he'll have to get over that if he wants to be a decent county Mountie."

"I think I have a master teacher," remarked Martin dryly.

"I think so, too," agreed Wellman. "All right, Joe, I was with her part of the afternoon. About two hours as best I recall."

"You're a durable man, Paul," drawled Joe. "I'll have to check that out, you know."

"I know, and that will likely finish it between us."

"Well, you know the one about the dog that got the tip of his tail lopped off by a freight train."

Wellman groaned loudly. "Please!"

Joe suddenly arose. "Time to go. Charlie, thank Mister Wellman for the fine coffee."

"Thank you for the fine coffee."

Wellman muttered something that is almost never heard in Sunday School. He followed them outside and stood beside the passenger door while Martin turned the crank. "Joe, I always had a suspicion you could be a hard case if the need arose."

"Only as hard as folks force me to be, Paul." They drove away, leaving Paul Wellman standing outside his grimy, once upon a time green office.

Charley was now quite ready to depart the dreary hamlet of Franklin forever, but Joe had other ideas. He directed the deputy down a muddy, rutted street and then another. After wending their way deeper into the jumbled company town, Joe at last pointed toward a shotgun building about thirty feet by seventy that in a practical concession to reality had been painted black.

A large sign above the door stated in bold red letters, Social Club. Martin started to get out, but Joe shook his head.

"You best wait out here, Charlie." To emphasize the point, Joe removed his constable badge and slipped it into a pocket. He crawled out of the car, leaving behind an unhappy and fidgeting deputy.

Joe stepped into the so-called social club and stood for a few moments beside the door until his eyes adjusted to the dim interior. It was hot and stuffy inside the windowless, nearly airless building. The only ventilation was provided by a couple of ceiling fans that served mainly to roil and evenly distribute the acrid aromas of sweat, cigarette smoke and cheap whiskey. A few forty-watt light bulbs produced a modicum of illumination, and through the haze Joe could see that even this early in the morning there were a few customers. All faces turned toward him and there was no mistaking the hostile expressions. An outsider had entered the inner sanctum.

To the right was a rough plank bar running perhaps half the length of the building. Here were seated about a half a dozen sullen miners. Ex-miners, rather. The recent strike had left them with no secure niche in the scheme of things. A burly bartender looked equally sour. The remainder of the building was occupied by tables, only two being currently in use. The one nearest the door hosted three large men wearing the same monotonous scowl.

So that there could be no possible mistake regarding the sentiments of this establishment, the wall opposite the bar was graced by an enormous poster of the dour-faced John L. Lewis, President of the United Mine Workers and kingmaker of the C.I.O. Smaller pictures of the same bitter visage speckled other available space. On the wall behind the bar were snapshots of various mines and clipped newspaper accounts of strikes, riots, cave-ins and explosions. Like all such places, this tavern was a comfortable retreat to engage in nostalgia and fond reminiscences.

At a table near the rear of the building sat one man alone. He was enormous, powerfully built and with a thick shock of appropriately black hair. A long, ugly scar ran along his left cheek. Joe waved and the man returned the gesture by hoisting a whiskey bottle still more than half full. The acknowledgment constituted permission to enter the den.

Joe headed straight for the table of wolf-king Jackie Prentiss, thrice charged with manslaughter and once convicted, an event that represented a seven year gap in his life. Prentiss not only owned the Social Club, but was also president of the U.M.W. local. However, he no longer labored below the ground. He had discovered a surface mine.

"Been a long time, Jackie," remarked Joe as he sat down.

"You still pretendin' to be some kind of lawman?"

"Still pretendin'." He glanced at the bottle. "May I?" Prentiss shoved the bottle toward him and Joe took a sip. "Billy Larkin's stuff if I ain't mistakin'." Prentiss nodded confirmation. "Had a shipment from him lately?"

"Two months ago."

"His stuff's nearly as good as his old man's. Good teacher, I reckon."

"What brings you here, Joe?"

"Seen Billy lately?"

"I just told you. Two months ago." Prentiss took a swig. "What do you want Billy for?"

"He may have killed his old man."

"Not likely. He ain't got the nerve for it."

Joe leaned back, folded his hands over his belly and sighed loudly. "You know, folks keep tellin' me that. If they tell me often enough, I might start to believe it. Then I'll have to look somewhere else for my killer."

"What are you gettin' at?"

"Just this. Larkin supplied timbers. A mine can't operate without timbers. The Franklin is the biggest non-union mine in the county."

"Larkin isn't their only supplier."

"But he's the biggest. Or was. With him dead and under pretty strange circumstances at that, other suppliers may get a bit leery of doin' business with the Franklin."

"Out with it, Joe."

"Where were you Tuesday afternoon?"

"Right here. I have at least a hundred witnesses."

"They'd also swear you was jugglin' ten bobcats at the time."

"Maybe I was," he replied deadpan.

"Well, if any man could actually do that, I guess my money would be on you, Jackie."

"I didn't kill Larkin."

"You've killed before."

"A company goon swingin' a two-by-four studded with sixteen penny nails."

"Resultin' in a slanted opinion of non-union mines."

"If I wanted to stop the supply of timbers, I wouldn't have to kill Larkin. Just burn his sawmill."

"An idea you've toyed with, I expect."

"Yes."

Their eyes locked for several seconds in a mutual stare. Joe finally leaned forward and took another drink from the bottle.

"Jackie, you're one of the few men I'll take just on his word. You've always played it open and square, even with the mine owners you hate. So I'm gonna play it square with you. I don't think you had anything to do with Larkin's murder. But I can't say the same for some of the characters who hang around this place. If I ever so much as suspect you're coverin' up for any of these yo-yos, I'll be all over you like flies on a privy."

For the first time, the big man's lips curled into a one-sided smile. "I never knew you were so fond of Larkin, Joe."

"I wasn't."

"You're just sore because your favorite source of corn squeezins is shut off."

"I'm sore because he was killed in Burnham. If he'd got his throat slit in some speakeasy, I wouldn't really give a damn, corn squeezins or no corn squeezins. But not in Burnham. I won't let this go 'til I get whoever done it no matter how long it takes."

Prentiss sighed and shook his head. "Always beware of a man driven. I won't stand in your way, Joe. And I don't intend to risk my freedom protectin' some other dumb son of a bitch."

Joe nodded. "One more thing you ought to know. Sheriff Faulkner's tryin' to make this a syndicate thing."

"Jackass!" There was no inflection in the word. It was just a simple statement of fact that somehow managed to convey several tons of contempt.

Joe did not dispute the commentary. "That'll dead-end on him and he'll have to look somewhere else. There's a good chance his eyes will fall on you."

"Not likely. Too many union votes in this county."

"Maybe. But there's also some mighty rich men who'd like to see you have free lodgin' the rest of your life."

"He ain't smart enough to run a frame."

"No, but we got us a prosecutor who's smart enough to stack a jury."

Prentiss toyed with the bottle. "I'll keep that in mind," he replied quietly.

Joe picked up his cane and started to rise. "Jackie, it was good seein' you again."

"Come fall, I'd like to buy a couple haunches of venison."

"I'll put your name on the list."

As Joe neared the door, the three men at the table arose and formed a line to block his way. "I know you!" growled one. "You're some kind of half-assed lawman! Lawmen ain't got no business bein' in here!"

"Boys, let's not have any trouble. I already done what I came to do. All I want to do now is to leave quietly."

The spokesman grinned viciously. "You're gonna leave all right, and you're gonna be mighty quiet when you do."

The three men came at him in a rush, but the fight was to end much more quickly than they had anticipated. The tip of the cane flew up, solidly striking the first man in the groin. He dropped to the floor and curled up in a ball while making squeaky, whimpering sounds much like a child's squeeze toy.

At the same time, Joe raised his left arm to block a roundhouse right from the man in the center. Then the cane punched forward in a sharp, vicious jab to the solar plexus. There came a gush of exhaled breath so powerful it almost blew Joe's hat off. This man, too, curled up on the floor.

The third man backed away for a moment and stared dumbly at his fallen comrades. One-on-one was not quite his idea of great fun. He wavered a moment, undecided whether to continue the rumble or flee. But flee from a crippled man? Whatever tiny element of pride he still possessed asserted itself at the very instant his hand brushed a bottle on the bar. He snatched it, smashed it and advanced slowly, waving the jagged end menacingly.

The cane lashed again, smashing the broken bottle from his hand. As the man stared at his numb and bleeding hand, the hook of the cane snaked around his forearm while the shaft locked behind his wrist. Suddenly his whole arm was being violently twisted, every joint somehow locked. Thrown off balance, he tumbled heavily to the floor. As he tried to rise, the cane flew again, striking him across the nose. There was a crunching sound and blood squirted halfway across the room. Slapping both hands to his face, the man fell back on his rump while squealing and bleeding heavily. Joe had not once moved from his tacks.

The front door flew open and there stood Martin with his revolver drawn. He looked faintly puzzled for there seemed no obvious target at which to point his weapon. It wavered and then slowly sagged as he stared with open astonishment at the three casualties on the floor.

"I thought I heard a fight in here," he mumbled.

"Just a slight misunderstandin'," replied Joe. "He turned and gazed with annoyance at Prentiss. "You could have called 'em off," he accused.

The big man shrugged. "They've been a bit troublesome of late. They needed a lesson. You've saved me the fuss of doin' it myself."

Joe again started for the door. "Come on, Charlie, let's get out of here. And put that thing away before you hurt somebody."

When the two lawmen were gone, Prentiss slowly arose and walked over to the three would-be bullies now struggling to hands and knees. Shaking his huge head with mock disappointment, he drawled, "You boys ought to be ashamed of yourselves, lettin' a cripple beat up on you that way." He then quietly returned to his table and bottle.

Martin cranked up the Ford and then crawled behind the wheel. "Where to?" he grumbled.

"Back to Burnham, I guess. I'm all done here."

"I should think so!"

Joe glanced at him, but said nothing. In fact, neither man spoke again until they were well clear of the worst of the noise and dust. As they bounced past the cemetery, Martin gave Joe another sour glance.

"Sometimes I think you're not as crippled as you let on," he complained.

"Bein' crippled is mostly a state of mind, Charlie. We all gotta make do with what we got, and some just have more to make do with." After a moment he added, "There's ways of bein' crippled that can't be seen, too."

Martin looked over at him again, but now Joe seemed concerned only with a large pasture populated with Guernsey cows. After turning back onto Highway Ten, Martin spoke again.

"I still haven't talked to Mrs. Larkin."

"I know," sighed Joe. "I reckon it's time to pay her another visit. You want to eat first?"

"I can wait."

"Then we might as well get this over with."

When they reached the north slope of Backbone Mountain, Martin had to stop and put the car into reverse. The slope on this side was too steep to accommodate the gravity feed of the fuel supply to the engine. Joe sat lost in thought as he stared vacantly down-slope while Martin backed slowly and carefully up the mountain, the straining engine sputtering and protesting every foot of the way. Finally attaining the top of the crest, Martin now turned the vehicle around to complete the trip.

Incredibly, Larkin's house was now nearly empty even though the master was less than three days dead. A dozen wagons were piled high with furniture, farm equipment, canned goods and various odds and ends. Someone was even hauling the new crop of hay out of the barn. Joe was struck with the thought that it did not take long for vultures to strip a carcass.

Mrs. Larkin was either unable to halt the plundering or else had no desire to do so. Oddly, Joe suspected that the latter might be the case. As he hobbled across the porch he was almost knocked down by a husky woman, something the three bar bullies had not come close to doing. She rushed past with a box of silverware under one arm and holding a lamp in the other. Martin tipped his hat, but she did not even acknowledge the polite gesture.

Just inside the door they were confronted by a pig-eyed fat man dressed in patched overalls. "Are you Joe Potts!" he demanded, ignoring the deputy.

"I am."

"Did you take some whiskey from this place Tuesday night?"

"I did."

The fat man blinked stupidly for a moment, clearly surprised by the frank admission. "I want it back!" he snapped at last. The man certainly was not lacking for gall to demand the return of illegal whisky from law officers.

"No," answered Joe simply.

There was some more stupid blinking. "I've got friends!" he threatened. "We can find where you live!"

"Yes, I expect you can," admitted Joe in a quietly dangerous tone of voice. "In fact, if you like, I'll even draw you a map to my place. But neighbor, if you come sneakin' around, right there is where they'll bury you. You and ever' one of your two-bit white trash friends."

The thick, greasy mouth dropped open. "You can't talk to me that way!" he whined.

Joe pushed the man roughly aside and started up the stairs with Martin right behind him.

Mrs. Larkin was sitting in her rocking chair and staring out the window at the wagons laden with the items that had made this house into a semblance of a home. For a moment, Joe was struck by the wild thought that she had not budged from this very spot since he had last visited her two days before. That, of course, was ridiculous. She had, after all, attended the funeral. She rocked gently, a thin, sad smile upon her face and her bony, arthritic hands concealed by an ancient red shawl.

"Mrs. Larkin," spoke Joe gently.

She stopped rocking and turned her head to see who had spoken. Nodding to Joe, she turned back to the window and resumed her rocking.

"Mrs. Larkin, this is Deputy Charles Martin. We have some questions we'd like you to answer."

"Why do you keep pestering me, Joe Potts? I told you everything on Wednesday."

"No maam, I'm afraid you didn't." The rocking halted again and she turned cold eyes upon him. But the matronly stare was futile. "Maam," continued Joe, "I don't think you baked no bread on Tuesday. You used that as an excuse to make up a phony time for the gunshot."

"I suppose you can prove that?"

"Not likely, but I think I can prove that Billy was here that day." The old woman averted her eyes. "That's why you made up that time for the gunshot, ain't it? Because you knew Billy had an alibi for then."

She was again staring out the window, but no longer at the wagons. Her eyes were now fastened on something no one else could see. "Billy didn't kill Tom," she stated simply.

"Where was Billy before he came here?"

"He stopped by the John Carter place to get a drink of water and pass the time of day."

"What time did he get here?"

"About two thirty."

"And Tom was killed about an hour later?" She nodded reluctantly. "Did you see who did it?"

"No." She paused, but now that she was finally talking she seemed to want to get it all out.

"I had fixed Billy a bite to eat. We both heard the shot but didn't think much of it at the time. Crows have been bad this year. But later, I looked outside and Tom was layin' out in the middle of the pasture. That didn't seem right." She hesitated.

"Go on."

"I asked Billy to go see about him."

"And?"

"He refused." Her eyes dropped to her lap. "Billy was mortally afraid of his pa."

"So you went, didn't you, Mrs. Larkin?" She nodded weakly. "How long was this after you heard the shot?"

"I don't know. Fifteen, maybe twenty minutes. He, he was still warm."

"But the killer was gone?"

Again she nodded weakly. "Billy laughed when I told him. It was a mean laugh, the laugh of the devil. I know he hated his pa and I couldn't really blame him for that. But he should have had enough respect for me not to laugh."

"He took the dogs when he left?"

She nodded confirmation. "He wouldn't have had the nerve to take them while Tom was still alive. But the dogs ain't all he took."

"What else, Mrs. Larkin?"

"He took what he come for in the first place, money. He tore the house apart until he found Tom's moneybox. There was close to two thousand dollars in it."

She looked up with an indescribable hurt in her eyes. "He wouldn't leave me any of it. Said I had enough with the business and the farm." Again the sad eyes dropped. "I know nothing of Tom's business other than he was having trouble getting money from that mine." She hesitated. "All I have now is about ten dollars in my purse."

"After all he did, why did you lie for him, Mrs. Larkin?" asked Martin.

"He's still my son. And, and…." She dabbed a handkerchief at her eyes. "I don't think I could bear the scandal if folks thought that Billy killed his pa."

Joe toyed with his ragged straw hat. "Maam, why are you lettin' all these people take your things? Say the word and I'll put a stop to it."

The thin smile reappeared. "No need, Joe Potts. Ed Peters done made the same offer." She shook her head sadly. "Leave 'em be. I don't want those things anymore. They're just bad memories. The new owner can bring his own furnishings."

"You're sellin' the place?"

"I done talked to Mister Cooper at the Greenwood bank. He's gonna take care of everything. The business, too. Soon as everything's sold, I'm movin' in with my sister in Booneville."

"I see. What about Mase?"

She puckered her lips. "I've worried some about that. He ain't got no folks. At least none that want him." She looked up at them. "Did you know Tom bought him? Just like a slave. For fifty dollars."

"I didn't know that,' replied Joe honestly.

"Mase couldn't tell nobody. Likely didn't even know he'd been sold. Anyway, I think he was happy here, as happy as he could have been anywhere else. I fed him good and Tom never beat him. Tom never beat animals 'less'n they needed it. Mase never did 'cause he was a good worker."

"Well, I guess he can stay here for the time bein'. The place will need a caretaker 'til the new owner gets here." Joe hesitated. "Maam, why don't you reconsider sellin' the place? Sell the sawmill but keep the farm."

She looked at him with surprise. "Whatever for?"

"Maam, this county's got more orphans than it knows what to do with." He ignored the sharp look from Martin. "This is a big house. You could take in a whole passel of 'em."

She shook her head resolutely. "I couldn't take on all that responsibility by myself."

"You wouldn't be by yourself. You'd have Mase to help you."

"Him?"

Joe nodded. "He ain't really as dumb as most folks think. He knows ever'thing there is to know about runnin' a farm. And you know all there is to know about runnin' a home. The two of you could do a bunch of younguns a lot of good."

"I, I don't know," she replied hesitantly. "This place has such bad memories."

"Memories are in the mind, Mrs. Larkin, not in places or things. You'll still have those bad memories whether you're here or in Booneville. But this is a chance to add a few good memories to the collection."

He paused before adding the clincher. "And to give a few poor youngens maybe their only chance for a proper Christian upbringin'."

Immediately a gleam came into her eyes. "I, I suppose there could be no harm in givin' it a try."

Joe suppressed a triumphant smile. "You want me to make those folks put ever'thing back?"

She shook her head. "I can refurnish the house with what I get from the mill." She frowned. "But you could call Mister Cooper for me. I don't even want to go downstairs until that rabble is gone."

Joe quickly arose. "I'll take care of it, Mrs. Larkin."

He almost stumbled hurrying down the stairs. "Charlie, round up ever'body from outside!" he ordered. "Those down at the barn, too. Tell 'em we've found Tom's hidden gold. Then get out of their way so you don't get trampled."

Grudgingly, Charlie complied. Soon the living room was jammed with about three dozen greedy relatives, eyes wide and gleaming at visions of bulging burlap bags crammed full of gold coins. The room buzzed as men exchanged speculations and suspicious glances. Joe had to bang his cane on the wall several times before he finally got their attention.

"There's been some changes made," he explained. "All farm equipment and foodstuffs are to be returned immediately." Of this latter category there was little left anyway since most of it had already been consumed.

Joe's announcement induced several seconds of stunned silence. "You can't do that!" exclaimed someone at last.

"That's right! Tom promised me his breakin' plow!"

"What about the gold?" demanded someone who refused to be distracted from the main issue. There were several echoes of, "That's right!"

"There is no gold!" This almost caused a riot for the mob was now convinced they were to be cheated of their just due. Joe immediately whipped the cane upward, a movement that commanded immediate silence.

"There is no gold!" he repeated. "Now I want all you men to go out and stand beside your wagons. I'll inspect them and anything I say should stay, stays!"

"What right have you...."

Joe cut him off. "As an officer of the law, I can impound this whole place and ever'thing on it 'til I complete my investigation. I guarantee you, that could take a very long time." He paused to let this sink in.

"The only reason I'm gonna let you keep anything," he continued, "is because Mrs. Larkin wants all the household stuff removed. You women clear this house of ever'thing you ain't already stole and get it on the porch. Divide it up and be quick about it. Ever' damn one of you is gonna be out of Burnham by sundown."

"Now see here...."

"If I hear any more grumbles I'll keep it all."

"Shut up, Oscar!" commanded a rustic Amazon.

Joe tapped Mase on the shoulder and beckoned him with a finger. Outside, the first wagon yielded the prized breaking plow. Joe pointed to Mase, then to the plow and finally at the ground. The idea was communicated. Beaming proudly, Mase hoisted the plow from the wagon, his huge muscles bulging at the weight. A corn planter, two shovels and a splitting axe soon followed. Out of the corner of his eye, Joe spotted one man easing his wagon toward the road.

"Charlie, go shoot that feller," he commanded casually.

The driver heard, yelped loudly and spilled out of the wagon so fast he didn't even secure the lines or set the brake. The team plodded mindlessly on toward the road. Mase bolted forward, caught the team and led it back to the house. The woman on the passenger side was furiously explaining something to him, perhaps unaware that the big farmhand was surrounded by a world of silence.

Joe mused wistfully that deafness could have its advantages. Most talk, after all, was merely verbal garbage. He stepped forward and inspected this wagon with such a vengeance that it was almost empty by the time he finished.

The inspection and unloading took the better part of an hour. At the end of that time the front yard was littered with plows, planters, harrows, harnesses; all the items necessary to operate a farm.

Joe then turned his attention to the porch that was now nearly bare. Two women, however, were arguing noisily over a large blue vase. Joe stepped between them, raised his cane and smashed the disputed item to smithereens. Then he turned to one of the women.

"Pick up half of it!" he commanded

"But, but it's worthless now!" she complained, her face still registering astonishment that anyone would do such a thing.

"Pick up half or you won't carry nothin' away from this place!"

Her eyes burning with rage and humiliation, she dropped to her knees and began picking up shards. Joe turned to the second woman who was discreetly backing away.

"You pick up the rest of it!" She hesitated a moment, sighed and also dropped to her knees. Significantly, several other minor squabbles were quickly resolved.

"The wisdom of Solomon," drawled Martin acidly.

"I've always wanted to do that," quipped Joe. "Do me a favor, Charlie. Go make sure those fellers restack all that hay in the barn instead of just throwin' it on the ground like they're doin' right now." He winked. "You should know how it's supposed to be done by now. You have my permission to shoot them if you need to."

"I'm sure that would make it perfectly legal," replied Martin dryly.

"Thanks, Charlie. You're a pal." He turned and hobbled back into the house to call a banker.

When he stepped back onto the porch several minutes later, most of the wagons were gone. Two more were just pulling onto the highway while one man was still securing his now greatly diminished load. Martin was returning from the barn where he had clarified a few minor facts of life for some of the Larkin kin. The hay was now being restacked properly.

"You sure haven't made any friends today," remarked the deputy.

"Some folks ain't worth havin' as friends, Charlie."

The one man still in the yard overheard this remark and glanced up sharply. He quickly finished tying off his load, climbed onto the wagon seat and lashed his mules furiously as though all this was somehow their fault. Only Mase was now left standing amid all the scattered farm equipment. It would take him the rest of the day to put everything back in its proper place, but the prospect did not seem to bother him greatly. He stood there beaming proudly, just glad to have everything back.

"You had no call to do this," spoke Martin.

"A farm is nothin' without the tools to work it."

Martin considered this for some time. "You're not going to bring orphans here. You're going to take the Neely children and turn them over to Mrs. Larkin."

Joe slowly nodded.

"There's one thing you haven't taken into account. What if Mrs. Larkin is lying to you again? What if she killed her husband? Perhaps she and Billy were in on it together. Have you ever thought of that?"

"I've thought of it, Charlie. But she ain't lyin' this time. She didn't kill her husband 'cause it ain't the Christian thing to do. And Billy didn't kill his pa 'cause he ain't got the guts for it."

"Others may not see it that way."

"Likely not. But a lawman has to learn to judge people, Charlie. You have to look at more'n just the evidence. Most times there ain't enough evidence to sneeze at. So you got to be able to look at people and know what's inside 'em, know what they can and can't do. A thousand people could have killed Larkin, but only one actually did it. You got to know which trails to sniff and which to ignore. You got to follow the boar coon and not the chipmunk."

"Are we going to see John Carter now?"

Joe considered a moment and shook his head. "It's been a long day. Tomorrow's soon enough. When the last of the hay is restacked and the last of the Larkins out of here, we'll go home and get somethin' to eat."

*****

After finishing their supper, Joe pulled out the current jug of ARKANSAS PYZZON and filled two tumblers. He pushed one toward Martin who stared at it quizzically but did not pick it up. Joe raised his eyebrows as though some minor heresy had been committed.

"You don't drink?"

"Seldom." Martin shifted uncomfortably in his chair. "It hardly seems proper for a lawman to drink since it is illegal," he explained.

"Hell, Charlie, if we only did what was proper, life would be so borin' it would hardly be worth livin'." Martin smiled grimly and took a small sip. Then he took a huge gulp. "Hey, take it easy!" warned Joe "This stuff can waylay you."

"This is very good!" exclaimed the deputy. "Smooth. I've never tasted better, not even the bonded stuff."

"This was made by a master." Joe stretched out on the rickety sofa while Martin remained at the table and refilled his glass from the jug. "Remember that feller who was here yesterday? The one in that ugly green machine?"

"The Packard? What about him?"

"He's with the Kansas City Syndicate. He offered me five thousand dollars if I catch the killer."

Despite the deputy's previous comment about the smoothness of the whiskey, he now became choked on it. It was nearly a minute before he regained control and Joe was becoming concerned.

"Five thousand dollars?" squeaked the red-faced deputy. "Why?"

"Faulkner's gettin' to be a pest and they want this settled."
He paused. "I turned it down."

This shock was almost too much. "Five thousand dollars?
And you turned it down? Joe, you could retire on five thousand
dollars!"

"I already take life way too easy. Retirement would kill
me."

"But five thousand dollars!" Martin had to take another
gulp. "Think of the things you could buy with that much
money! You could build a bigger house! Buy some decent
clothes!"

"Did it ever occur to you, Charley, that I might not want
those things?"

"Not want them? But why not?"

Joe sat up and handed his glass over for a refill. "Somethin'
I've noticed, Charlie. Folks who have all those nice things
spend most of their time stewin' about 'em, or tryin' to get 'em
fixed when they break, or maybe worryin' about somebody
tryin' to steal 'em. Me, I got about all I need and ain't much of
it even worth stealin'. Ain't got a lot of worries neither like all
the folks who are so caught up in this money thing."

"Money makes the world go round."

"So who wants to go in circles?" This caused Martin to
smile. "The way I look at it, Charlie, if a man ain't got nothin' I
want, then he can't own or control me."

Martin shook his head. "Life isn't that simple, Joe. If that
man has a gun he can own you."

"A man with a gun can kill you just like a bear or a rabid
skunk can kill you. But he can't ever own you, not unless you
surrender yourself to him. Most people sell their freedom,
Charlie, whether it's for a few more years of life or a green
Packard. It's all the same."

Martin considered this a moment. "You're a strange man, Joe," he concluded at last.

"So I've been told more times than I care to count." Joe finished a half a glass at one time. "You're kind of a strange one, too, Charlie."

"How do you mean?"

"The way you talk. You use words the way they're meant to be used. You never say ain't. You've had some education, Charlie."

"Two years of college," he admitted.

"Couldn't you do better than deputy sheriff? I know that some do pretty good takin' protection money from moonshiners, but you ain't turned that way."

"I have always wanted to follow a career in law enforcement."

"Footsteps of the old man, eh?"

Martin shrugged. "Partly, I guess. Mostly, though, I want to get the profession out of the hands of men like Faulkner. I want it returned to what it used to be."

"Used to be?" asked Joe with raised eyebrows. "We may have more gadgets now, but human nature ain't changed much since Cain did in his kid brother. There's always been Faulkners in law enforcement. There always will be."

"My father wasn't like that!" protested Martin heatedly.

"I'm sure he wasn't. But for ever' one like your father, there's a whole passel of Faulkners. Positions of power always attract thieves and starry-eyed fools."

"And which am I?" asked Martin coolly.

Joe suddenly realized that a well lubricated tongue had led him into a trap. "You're not a thief, Charlie, and I reckon you're not a fool neither. I spoke out of turn. Usin' such big labels can get a man in trouble."

He emptied his glass and handed it to Martin. "Mind pourin' me another refill? Takes quite a bit of the stuff to wash down such a big mouthful of crow."

Charlie had to concentrate carefully on the task for the world seemed to be wobbling a bit.

"Why do you carry that old Peacemaker?" asked Joe. "There's better guns made now."

"Why do you keep that old thing?" responded Martin quickly. He had nodded toward an ancient Kentucky rifle hanging on the wall.

Joe smiled fondly. "My grandpappy carried that in the war."

"Which one? Revolution or 1812?"

Joe feigned a hurt expression. "Do I really look that old?"

It was Charlie's turn to grunt an apology.

"Actually," continued Joe, "up to a hundred yards it is still the most accurate rifle in the world." Martin gazed at him skeptically, wondering if he was being primed for a 'whopper'.

"I'll tell you what my old grandpappy could do," asserted Joe, warming to the subject. "He could stick an axe handle in the ground, shoot the edge of the blade, split the lead ball and bust two clay targets with just one shot."

That required another refill to wash down properly. "Of course, your grandfather is dead," remarked Charlie cynically.

"Twenty odd years now. He tried to teach me the trick, but I wasn't as good as him. I can only manage about half the time."

"Perhaps you'd demonstrate," challenged Martin.

Joe gazed at the bottle and then at his glass. "Too much joy juice," he concluded. "Maybe tomorrow, Charlie."

"Riiiiight!" Martin drained the last of the jug into his glass. "All gone," he pronounced thickly.

Joe arose woozily from the couch. "Hell, Charlie, we still got twenty five gallons to go!"

CHAPTER FIVE
Saturday, July 25

Even though it was nearly nine o'clock in the morning, there was no response to the insistent pounding on the door. At last, Jimmy Andrews pushed his way into the cabin. The first sight that greeted his eyes was Deputy Martin sprawled lifeless on the sofa. He had one shoe on and one off, his shirt was missing and the gunbelt housing the precious Colt Peacemaker was down around his ankles. His service cap lay upside down on the floor near one end of the sofa and contained the majority of the shards from a tumbler along with a dead mouse. Jimmy could hardly wait to ask someone about that unusual combination.

On the table sat one empty jug and beside it was a second still half alive. A tumbler lay on its side. Jimmy tiptoed through the assorted litter and wreckage on the floor and made his way to the table. He sniffed the still active jug and then tipped it to his lips. Gasping and coughing, he placed it back onto the table.

A low moan emanated from the second room of the cabin. Jimmy wiped his mouth with the back of a hand and walked to the door. Joe was sprawled face down on the straw tick mattress. One suspender of his overalls was flipped over his back, but that was all he had managed in the way of undressing.

"Joe," called Jimmy softly.

"Shut up, Jimmy! Fire up the stove and put on some coffee. Double strength. Don't talk to me again 'til it's done." Jimmy discreetly withdrew.

For the next thirty minutes Joe drifted in and out of consciousness, reality mingling with an alcoholic fog. A jaybird squawked raucously outside. There was a metallic clanking from the cook stove. Why was a jaybird chucking stove-wood into the firebox? He jerked his head up with a start, attempted to assemble these odd bits of information, then grumbled loudly and lay back down. His crippled right foot was throbbing. A hangover in your foot? Then he recalled. Sometime the night before there had been a mad scramble for a mouse. Why? The reason escaped him for the moment. A pang shot through his head, not unlike a splitting mall thumping into a block of red oak. Now that was more like it.

Jimmy arrived with an ironstone mug steaming wildly in the heavy morning air. "The deputy ain't up yet," he remarked. Joe sat up and accepted the inky panacea.

"Well, it's high time he was. A white lightnin' hangover is a real adventure. I wouldn't want him to miss a minute of it." He sipped the coffee and yelped. "Christ, Jimmy! Why didn't you tell me it was hot?"

"I figured you knew."

Joe blew on it and took a more cautious sip. "Why did you make it double strength?"

"Because you told me to."

Joe muttered something under his breath. "Get some for Charlie."

Martin opened his eyes and the first thing he saw was a spider walking on the ceiling. For a moment he was struck by the wild, disorienting thought that he was lying on the ceiling and staring down at the floor. He had to close his eyes again. When he opened them the second time the spider had moved a good six inches and there was no longer any danger that it would fall up and hit him. Wait a minute; that couldn't be right! He gave his eyes a third try. This time smoke drifted across his vision.

Fire! He sat up wildly, an action that forced him to pause and check to make sure his head was still attached. An insistent pounding assured him that it was. He looked up to see a skinny, redheaded kid holding a steaming mug of something. There was a superior little smirk on the boy's lips that communicated better than any words, you hurt and I don't, ha ha! Martin accepted the mug, and just like Joe he scorched his lips.

Joe appeared in the doorway. "Good Lord! What happened in here?"

Charlie closed his eyes tightly for a moment. It did no good. The little man inside his skull with the vices on his eyeballs refused to let up.

"Mouse safari," he replied at last.

Joe considered this solemnly a moment, and then hobbled to the table and plopped into a chair to examine the mess before him. Charlie removed the gunbelt from around his feet and placed it neatly on the floor next to his hat. He then lifted the deceased mouse by its tail.

"Want to have it mounted?" Joe asked.

Martin snorted in derision and misery.

"Who killed it?" quizzed Jimmy.

"Joe did."

Joe nodded approvingly and then asked, "How?"

"Threw my glass at it. I doubt Walter Johnson ever made a better pitch."

Joe put his elbows on the table and massaged his temples while groaning softly.

"Why do you guys drink this stuff if it makes you feel so bad the next day?" asked Jimmy.

"That's a good question, Jimmy," replied Joe. He took another delicate sip from his cup. "Charlie, answer it for him."

Martin looked up suddenly. "What? Me?" He realized he was still holding the dead mouse and put it back into his hat. He thought about that a moment, then remove it and placed it on the floor.

"It's liquid courage, Jimmy," he explained at last. "A man has to have it before he sets out to kill a mouse."

"Charlie, you're just a natural born comedian," drawled Joe.

"Joe, you gonna be able to umpire today's game?"

He looked up at Jimmy with a stunned expression. "That's right, today's Saturday, isn't it? Damn! It slipped my mind."

"We're playin' the team from Lucas," continued Jimmy. "The reason I come over was to borrow some tape to re-tape the bat handle. They say Lucas is supposed to have a real good pitcher."

Charlie arose and helped himself to another cup of coffee. "I have a feeling this means no interviews today."

"Not 'til after the game. That could take 'til four o'clock. Sorry, Charlie."

Martin found his shirt wadded into a compact ball behind the sofa. He shook it out and found it be a limp, soggy mass of stains and wrinkles.

"No matter," he sighed. "I couldn't see anyone looking like this." He pulled on the soiled shirt. "I guess I'll head back to Fort Smith."

Then he plopped back onto the sofa. "Just as soon as I get my head straight."

"What's the rush? You got some kind of weekend duty?"

"No, but I have a social life."

"Oh, who is she?"

Martin smiled faintly. "I'm not sure I should tell you. I wouldn't want you making an entry about us in your little black book."

Joe drained his cup. "Hell, Charlie, what makes you think you're worth spyin' on anyway? I figure you for the ice cream social type. That ain't very interestin'."

Charlie rubbed his eyes and yawned. "By the way, I still want to see you do that trick where you split the rifle ball and break two targets with one shot."

"Sure. Jimmy, you mind settin' ever'thing up?" The eager expression on the boy's face indicated he didn't mind at all. "Hand me my muzzle loader and riggin' before you go."

Martin gazed at him with surprise. "You intend to do it right now?"

"No time like the present." He winked. "If I miss, I got a good excuse."

Jimmy brought the rifle, powder horn and leather ammunition pouch. He then rushed outside to set up the targets. Martin came over to the table and examined the weapon with interest. It was well worn, but had also been well cared for. The Roman nose stock dated it from the latter days of the Kentucky rifle era. At a glance, he identified it as about a .45 caliber.

"Never was really sure why these guns are called Kentuckies," pronounced Joe. "Nearly all 'em was made in Pennsylvania." He oiled a patch and swabbed out the barrel.

"This here is a John Johnston with a Pennebecker barrel," he continued. "It was made in Pittsburg. Don't ask me what year. My grandpappy got it when he was a boy."

He tested the hammer, then held the weapon up and squinted as he examined the nipple where the cap fitted. This also dated the rifle as a latter era product for all the early Kentuckies had been flintlocks. Satisfied with the condition of the weapon, Joe placed the butt on the floor between his feet.

Opening the ammunition pouch, he took out a small, shallow metal cup with a wooden handle. Removing the wooden peg from the powder horn with his teeth, he filled the cup with the fine black grains, being careful not to spill any or run the cup over. Eyeballing the cup to make certain it was perfectly level, he re-pegged the powder horn and carefully emptied the cup into the barrel.

"I've got a powder flask that pre-measures the charge, but I don't trust it for precision shootin' like this is gonna be. The secret of this trick is to have ever'thing just exact. Just the right amount of powder, not too much or too little. You only use balls made from the same mold and always make sure it's pure lead; no impurities or it might not split true."

He oiled a small, square patch and placed it over the end of the barrel, being careful to get it perfectly centered. Reaching into a heavy, lumpy sack, he took out a small gray ball. He examined it with one eye, but then rejected it for some unstated reason.

On the third try he found one to his liking. He placed it carefully on the patch and rammed it home with an even, fluid motion. Replacing the ramrod in its slot, he showed just as much care in selecting a cap. However, he did not place it on the nipple just yet, but slipped it into a pocket instead. He arose unsteadily, cane in the right hand and rifle in the left.

"Well, Charlie, are you ready to be astonished?"

Martin arose and followed him outside.

Years ago, Joe had constructed a special platform just for this trick. It included a notch that would accept a standard axe handle and keep it perfectly centered. At the rear corners were two upright posts that now supported small pieces of tin about six inches square. Jimmy had set up the platform just east of the cabin on a stretch of land that had been graded and plumbed to make certain it was perfectly level. Joe halted about thirty paces away.

"Jimmy, is that axe sharp?" he asked

"Sharp enough I could shave with it."

Joe shook his head in mock dismay. "Jimmy, no matter how hard you try, you'll never be able to scrape them freckles off." No one seemed to notice the boy's glowing blush.

Joe raised the rifle and tilted it slightly upward, then cocked the hammer and slipped on the cap. Fitting the butt to his shoulder, he slowly lowered the muzzle to bring it in line with the target. The sharp explosion took everyone but Joe by surprise. A thin wisp of slate gray smoke slowly drifted away.

Oh Lord, but this whole ill-conceived escapade had been a terrible mistake! Joe felt as though a concrete block had been dropped right onto his head from some impossibly high point, completely undoing all the beneficial effects of Jimmy's double strength coffee. Wincing in pain, he glanced over at Charlie who had clamped his eyes tightly closed and was holding both hands to his temples. Both men stood like this for some time, unable to speak or move. At last Jimmy raced back with the two pieces of tin.

"Joe, you did it!" he exclaimed. "You got both targets dead center! I never seen you do it better!"

Joe finally recovered sufficiently to examine the two targets and then nudged Charlie. "Wanna see me do it again?"

Martin still had not opened his eyes. "Uh uh!" he squeaked. He then turned and wobbled back to the cabin, having never even looked at the two skewered targets.

Joe again looked at the targets. He could not have measured and drilled more perfectly centered holes. "My grandpappy never told me the real secret to this trick," he muttered. "You gotta do it when you have a hangover." Shaking his head, he turned and followed Martin back to the precious coffee.

An hour later Martin cranked up the Ford and eased away, muttering curses at every rut and pothole. Joe watched from the doorway until he was out of sight and then turned to Jimmy.

"Tape's in that top left drawer. Come back and wake me just before game time." He hobbled back into his bedroom and closed the door.

*****

By one o'clock that afternoon, Art Jackson's east pasture had been converted into a baseball field. Straw-filled burlap bags served as bases and two tall sassafras saplings had been chopped down and eyeballed in as foul posts. A worn-out disk blade represented home plate. About forty people were lined along Highway Ten to watch the festivities. A few bottles and flasks passed discreetly from hand to hand.

A dozen teenage boys and three adults from Lucas watched the Burnham team whip the ball around the infield. Both teams were dressed alike, being clad in ragged overalls or patched denim blue jeans. But this made no difference. Anyone you didn't recognize was the enemy.

"Play ball!" called Joe from behind the pitcher's mound.

It was not really a mound at all, just a designated spot that seemed to be the center of the diamond. Joe immediately regretted raising his voice. A second pot of coffee and two more hours of sleep had gotten the pain in his head down to a barely noticeable ache. Now it returned with full force.

A husky, six foot Burnham youth named Les Collins stepped to the mound and took a couple of warm-up tosses. "I'm ready," he then announced. Joe waved to the first batter to step to the plate.

A skinny Lucas boy watched the first pitch blaze across the middle of the plate and thump into the catcher's mitt. "Strike one!" bawled Joe.

On the second pitch the batter topped the ball and sent it skittering through a fresh cow pile, after which a loudly cursing shortstop fielded it and pegged it to an equally disgusted first baseman.

The next batter fanned on the fourth pitch. The third hit it a mile high but only fifty feet out. After running in circles for what seemed five minutes, the third baseman finally caught it and grinned triumphantly as he flipped the still slick ball to Joe. There was some good-natured razzing as one team ran out and the other in.

A lanky, black haired youth who looked to be about fourteen took the mound for Lucas. The Burnham players looked at each other and grinned. This was Lucas's mighty pitcher? The boy whipped in his first warm-up toss. It was almost as fast as Collins's best fastball. A showoff, thought the Burnham players and spectators alike. The kid was showing his best stuff in his warm-up to impress everybody.

The second warm-up throw blazed in and this one was even faster than Collins. Warm-up or not, this kid definitely had something on the ball. He was faster than Collins. The Lucas pitcher hiked up his ragged trousers.

"I'm ready," he announced.

"Batter up!" called Joe.

The Burnham shortstop of manure ball fame stepped in. The ball was thrown. The batter stared. The other Burnham players stared. The spectators stared. Even Joe stared. The kid hadn't been showing off during his warm-up at all. The speed of his fastball was unbelievable. The Lucas catcher, knocked onto his rump by the force of the pitch, straggled to his feet and threw the ball back.

"What was it, Ump?" demanded the pitcher arrogantly, a tiny smirk playing across his lips.

"Strike one!" called Joe while shaking his head in disbelief.

Another pitch, this time even faster. "Strike two!"

"Hell's bells!" wailed the batter. "You gotta see it to hit it!"

"You think that's fast?" snapped the pitcher. "You ain't seen nothin' yet! I don't get really fast 'til the third or fourth inning!"

The shortstop glared at him angrily, but an angry glare is no substitute for a fast bat. He took a mighty swing at the third pitch but to no avail. The catcher was already sitting on his rump before the hitter got the bat around. The pitcher put his hands on his hips, leaned back and laughed loudly. The batter took three steps toward him, but Joe raised his cane and pointed at him sharply.

"We'll have none of that!" he commanded. "Back to the bench!" He tapped the pitcher on the shoulder. "I ain't seen nothin' that tickled my funny bone!"

There was something about the tone of voice, something in those eyes. The pitcher choked off the mocking laughter. "Sure, Ump."

It took only six more pitches to register two more strikeouts. This time when the teams changed sides the bantering was not so good-natured. Joe scanned the spectators and noted no smiles. Also, the bottles and flasks were changing hands much more frequently. It was going to be a long afternoon, he realized grimly, and his head was hurting like crazy. Les Collins signaled that he was ready.

The first Lucas batter, the clean-up hitter, was the pitcher. Collins narrowed his eyes and fired in his fastest pitch. The batter took it for strike one, grinned and shook his head in disparagement. Collins was seething by the time the catcher returned the ball. Joe noted the warning signs.

"Easy now," he cautioned.

Les threw twice as hard, but for some reason the pitch wasn't as fast as his first one. The batter swung, there was a sharp crack that Joe felt in the very center of his brain and a line drive shot over the shortstop's head. As two outfielders converged, the ball dropped and took a low trajectory hop between them.

There was no wall to stop the bounding ball. It was a footrace, but the outcome was never in doubt. The runner crossed the plate long before the ball made it back to the infield. But instead of running directly to the bench, the Lucas player stood atop the plate and thumbed his nose at the Burnham pitcher.

Les Collins gave a violent start. "That smart alec little bastard!" he snarled. "Next time he comes up I'll take his head off!"

"No, you won't!" snapped Joe. "Somebody could get killed that way! I won't have it! I'll stop the game first!"

"We're not gonna take this kind of crap, Joe!" Les grumbled.

"I know; I know. I'll talk to him when he gets back out here."

After the rocky start, Collins managed to retire the side without incident, giving up only one scratch single. This time there was no banter at all as the teams changed sides; only silent, bitter glares. When the Lucas pitcher reached the mound, Joe was holding the ball. The boy reached out his hand for it, but Joe shook his head. The pitcher raised his eyebrows questioningly.

"Let's get some ground rules straight right now just so there's no mistake. The smart stuff stops. One more time and you're out of here. Understand?"

"Just tryin' to make the game interestin'," replied the boy with a shrug.

"I don't like interestin' games. I like 'em to be just as borin' as hell."

"Sure, Ump, I gotcha. They can't take it."

"Just pitch and keep your mouth shut!"

Smirking, the boy pretended to zip his lip and reached for the ball. Beginning to seethe a bit himself, Joe gave it to him.

But the boy didn't keep the ball for long, only nine pitches. In fact, nine pitches were all he made in any inning. Burnham couldn't even manage a foul ball, and as the afternoon wore on the mood of players and spectators alike grew uglier.

Meanwhile, Collins lost his concentration and began to give up hits. After five innings the score was four to nothing. But at least there were no more provocations. Then came the bottom of the sixth. The Lucas pitcher walked to the mound, took one look at the first batter and threw down the ball in disgust.

"These monkeys can't hit me!" he announced loudly enough to be heard in neighboring counties. "My little brother can beat these guys! Paul, get out here and finish up!"

So saying, he walked off the field. The Burnham players were so stunned that no one could react to the insult before the opposing pitcher was back on the bench. Then they were given the greatest insult of all. A twelve year old boy, a slightly smaller version of the previous terror, raced eagerly to the mound. The Burnham batter backed away from the plate.

"We ain't gonna bat against him! He's just a kid!"

"What's the matter?" screamed a shrill voice from the Lucas bench. "Scared?"

Joe hobbled halfway to home plate. "Get back up there and bat! There ain't no age limits! He's their pitcher now!" Then he turned to the Lucas bench and shouted to the adults.

"And keep his mouth shut! If you don't, I swear to God I'll have him tied and gagged! And there won't be no shortage of volunteers to do it, neither!" There was a murmur of agreement from the spectators.

But the new pitcher was no improvement from the Burnham point of view. Once again, the side struck out on nine pitches. The jubilant Lucas players raced in to take their next turn at bat, but they were to be disappointed. Les Collins remained on the bench while the rest of his team took the field.

At long last the Burnham pitcher slowly arose, stuck his glove in his hip pocket and just walked away. The other Burnham players exchanged quick glances. Then the first baseman walked away. One by one, the other players deserted the field. Shaking his head, Joe hobbled over to the Lucas bench. The first pitcher grinned maliciously at him.

"Sissies! They just couldn't take it!"

"They can take gettin' beat," corrected Joe. "They're just an average team. They get beat about half the time. What they can't take is havin' their noses rubbed in it."

He paused a moment. "Young man, you've got a million dollar arm, but I wouldn't give two bits for your brain. You ain't gonna be a kid much longer. Unless, you learn to rein yourself in a mite, you're gonna lead a mighty adventurous life."

He then hobbled over to the three adults at the end of the bench. "I would strongly advise you not to waste any time gettin' out of Burnham."

One of the men made a nodding reply. "We're used to that kind of advice. We don't even have to be told anymore."

Joe glanced toward the Lucas pitcher. "Can't you do anything about him?"

"Not a thing. We've tried. He just threatens to join some other team."

"If it was up to me, I'd tell him to go right ahead. It's just a game. It ain't worth that kind of ill will. What's his name, anyway?"

"Jay Hanna Dean."

"Well, I suspect we'll be hearin' it again one day."

"You think he'll make it to the big leagues?"

"Nope. I expect to read about his murder long before that." He tipped his hat and hobbled away.

But they would all hear of him again someday and not about his murder, either. Jay Hanna Dean would make it not only to the big leagues but all the way to the Hall of Fame. Just nine years later, Dizzy Dean and his brother Paul would win forty-nine games between them and lead the St. Louis Cardinals to a World Series victory over the Detroit Tigers.

As Joe struggled through the barbed wire fence, Ed Peters, half drunk and very angry, strode over to meet him. "Somebody ought to horsewhip that smart mouth kid!" he asserted.

"Somebody ought to," agreed Joe. But it won't be any of us. Not in Burnham."

"Well, it's a damn sorry way to be!"

"Forget it, Ed. It's just a game."

Hardly mollified, Ed shuffled away and joined a group of men that included most of the store loafers. If Ed Peters, one of the most easygoing men in Burnham, was so enraged, Joe could well imagine what the mood of the others must be. It did not bode well for the Lucas team.

Joe climbed aboard Suzy and rode over to the two wagons where the visiting team was loading up for the long trip home. At Joe's approach the boys fell silent and the adults looked apprehensive. He suspected that the Lucas team had had to fight its way out of more than one town. Baseball games often degenerated into brawls and it seldom took much provocation. Joe prided himself that such had never occurred in Burnham, at least not since he had been umpiring.

"Thought I'd tag along with you fellers as far as Washburn Mountain," he volunteered. "I have some lawman business over in that end of the valley anyway."

"You're a lawman?" asked one of the Lucas men with surprise.

"Constable."

"Well, we appreciate the company."

At first the Lucas boys were reticent in the presence of a lawman, especially one from a community they had just drubbed. But they began to warm to him when he complimented their play. Then he started giving batting tips and they listened with rapt attention. He got a laugh when he remarked that he couldn't tell them much about their fielding since he didn't get to see any. But the ice completely melted when he started talking about Aaron Ward, the starting second baseman for the New York Yankees who had grown up in nearby Booneville.

"You, you know Aaron Ward?" asked one starry-eyed boy.

"Yep. He was playin' in one of the first games I ever umped. Booneville against Abbott." He leaned over and whispered confidentially. "Had to call him out on strikes his first time up."

"You called Aaron Ward out on strikes?" The tone was one of disbelief.

"He sure didn't like it much, but do you know what?"

"What?" This was a noisy chorus that caused Suzy to flick an ear in annoyance.

"He didn't let it get to him. He didn't get mad or cuss or stomp or anything. He kept hisself under control. Played a real good game, too." He glanced meaningfully at young Jay Dean. "And today he's in the big leagues."

Joe suddenly reined up. "Boys, this is as far as I go. Have a good trip home. Hope to see you play again someday."

Against someone else in some other place, he added silently.

There was a unanimous chorus of noisy good-byes and the waving continued until the wagon disappeared around a curve. He pulled Suzy around and started back downhill. At the foot of the mountain he turned into a small neat yard and rode up to the farmhouse. He swung down off Suzy and tied her to a porch post.

Mrs. Carter, a worried-looking, frazzled woman in her early forties met him at the front door. She pulled a stray strand of hair from her face with a flour-covered hand, leaving a white smudge on her sweaty forehead. Both hands immediately went to wringing a stained and frayed yellow apron. Shy, fourteen year old Elaine, just stumbling into womanhood, peered uncertainly from behind her.

Joe tipped his hat. "Good day, Mrs. Carter; Elaine."

"Joe Potts! What brings you out this way?" The voice was very strained.

"I need to speak to John, maam."

"He's feelin' poorly, I'm afraid. He's abed."

Joe raised his eyebrows with surprise. "I still need to see him, Mrs. Carter."

She looked around uncertainly. "I, I suppose it's all right." She led Joe to the bedroom door albeit without enthusiasm.

With the shades pulled and the door closed, the room was nearly as dark as night. Joe stuck his head inside, sending a narrow beam of light into the room and across the bed. John Carter had a quilt pulled up to his chin and was gripping it tightly. A quilt on a July afternoon? This could be serious. Suddenly, Carter bolted into a sitting position and looked about wildly.

"Who is it?" he demanded. "Who's there? Mary, is that you?"

"It's Joe Potts, John." The man gave a visible start. "I need to talk to you."

Carter flopped back down. "Can't talk now," he mumbled. "Can't talk now."

Joe hesitated a moment and then closed the door. He turned and almost bumped into Mrs. Carter who was still standing behind him. "How long has he been like this?"

"Most all week."

"Have you had a doctor to see him?"

"Didn't think it was that bad." She dropped her eyes. "We, we can't afford to have a doctor out," she confessed.

"Well, I aim to call Doc Hudson anyway."

"But, but…."

"No buts! If he's got somethin' catchin', I want to know about it. Don't worry about payin' the doc. We can work somethin' out. Half the folks in this end of the county owe him already. I don't reckon one more will make that much difference.

"I, I...." She broke off and went back to wringing her apron. "Is there anything else? I'm awful busy."

"Yes, maam, there is one more thing. I understand Billy Larkin was here on Tuesday."

It was as though she had been struck by a hot poker. "Not long! Not long! He just stopped by for a drink of water!"

"What time was he here, Mrs. Carter?"

"I, I'm not sure. A little after one, I guess."

"How long did he stay?"

A, about five minutes."

"That's all?"

She nodded emphatically.

"Odd. Someone you ain't seen in a couple of years comes by and you only talk for five minutes."

"We don't have much in common with his kind."

"I sure won't argue that. Did he say where he was goin' after he left here?"

She shook her head.

"Did he mention any names, any names at all?"

Again she shook her head.

"Well, I thank you for your help, maam." He started to turn away but then caught himself. "Oh yes, there is one last thing. It's about your daughter, Sally."

She looked startled. "Sally? What about her?"

"Why won't she write Jimmy? He ain't had a single letter from her."

"I, I guess she's pretty busy takin' care of her aunt."

"Too busy to write a few lines?" He paused a moment. "Look, Mrs. Carter, if Sally's found somebody she likes better, I can understand that. It happens. But Jimmy has a right to know. She shouldn't just leave him hangin'. Let him have his hurt and get it over with. It'll be better for ever'body."

"I, I'll speak to her about it in my next letter."

"I'd appreciate that, maam." He fingered his straw hat a moment. "Well, I'll be goin' now. And you be lookin' for Doc Hudson."

"I will. Good-bye."

Joe climbed back up on Suzy and turned her toward the highway. Odd, very odd behavior on the part of Mrs. Carter. But, of course, she was terribly worried about John. There was no good time for a farmer to get sick, but the growing season was the worst of all possible times. As Joe surveyed the farm, he noted several little things that needed doing. It was astonishing what could happen to a place after only a few days of neglect. If John did not get back on his feet very soon, the Carter family was going to have a hard time of it. Joe decided to stop by the Larkin place and call Doctor Hudson from there.

*****

The fire in the stove had gone out hours ago, leaving the coffee in the pot as near ice cold as the July heat would allow. He didn't bother to rebuild the fire, but contented himself with a cup of the thick, tepid brew. It tasted predictably awful. Plopping onto the sofa, he stared grimly at Friday night's wreckage still waiting to be picked up. Well, it would just have to wait a little longer.

Force of habit caused thoughts of food to drift into his mind. He quickly suppressed such ideas. His stomach was still doing flip-flops, making supper a risky proposition. He decided to lie down and rest his eyes for a few minutes.

Somebody was pounding on his head with a baseball bat, causing a hollow, thumping sound. At last it became more than he could stand but not because of the pain for, oddly, there was no pain. The sheer monotony of it finally overwhelmed him. He blinked himself awake in a room even darker than the nearly lightless sky outside. The pounding continued, but it was no longer on his head. He groped for his cane, found it and struggled to his feet.

"Just a minute!" he called while searching his pockets for a match to light the lantern. Finally he had the room filled with a musky, oily smelling light. "Come in!" He checked his Illinois pocket watch against his mental clock. Seven forty five. He had not been far off.

"I dropped by like you asked me," announced his visitor.

"I appreciate it, Doc." Joe motioned toward the sofa and the old man eased himself onto it. "What's wrong with him?"

Hudson pulled at his chin and surveyed the room, habits he had acquired over the years when he wanted to stall for time while formulating an answer. "What in the world happened here?" he asked.

"Somethin' foolish," admitted Joe.

"So I see." His eyes fell on the whiskey jug.

"C'mon, Doc, what's he got?"

Hudson dropped his eyes and shook his head. "I'm not sure, Joe. He's feverish, almost delirious. It's a little like pneumonia, but he's missing some important symptoms. It could be any number of things. I just can't say yet."

"What about quarantine?"

"I've already done that. It's just a precaution until I know what it is." He gave Joe a sour look. "I guess you know you've ruined my whole weekend. I'll have to spend every waking minute going through my books until I figure this thing out. It seems the least you could do is offer me a drink."

"Sorry, Doc." Joe searched the cabinet until he found a reasonably clean glass and then poured a stiff shot for Hudson. "How much for the house call, Doc?"

Hudson shrugged aimlessly and mumbled something incoherent.

"I know the Carters can't pay you nothin', so I aim to take care of it."

"I suppose you're rolling in money now," drawled Hudson sarcastically.

"I got somethin' even better." Joe went back to the cabinet and took out a virgin jug of ARKANSAS PYZZON. "Call it even?"

Hudson gazed covetously at the gallon container. "There won't be anymore of that, you know" he reminded. "Have you got enough to be swapping it off?"

"Enough to make do for a while."

Hudson was not disposed to argue the point. He accepted the jug. "Even," he confirmed. He struggled tiredly to his feet. "I have work to do tonight. If I need to talk to you again, I'll leave a message with Mrs. Larkin. You might check there from time to time."

"Will do, Doc. And thanks for comin' out."

Hudson waved off the thanks and tottered to the door.

Joe flopped back onto the sofa. Well, here was another tidbit of strangeness to add to an already bizarre situation. After years of tedium, Burnham had suddenly become an exciting place. What next? he wondered.

As if on cue, he heard rapid hoof beats pounding up his driveway. "What the hell?" he muttered.

Laura Andrews suddenly appeared in his doorway. Ignoring Joe, she gazed about the room uncertainly. "Where's that deputy sheriff?" she asked at last, her face still red and sweaty from a fast ride.

"Took the day off." Joe paused and then asked, "But really, Laura, ain't he a bit young for you?"

She shot him an annoyed glance. Joe took her by the arm and led her gently inside. "What's wrong, Laura?"

"I, I...," she stammered. "It, it's nothing, Joe. I was just taking some night air."

"You're the world's worst liar, Laura. Somethin's happened or is fixin' to happen and you figured it would take me and the deputy both to handle it. Since he ain't here you don't want to tell me. But you ought to know me better than that, Laura. Now I'll have to go out lookin'. It would be more convenient and a whole lot safer if I knew what I was lookin' for."

She eased herself onto the sofa. "May I have some of that, please?" She was pointing at the whiskey bottle on the table.

Joe poured her a small shot and she promptly choked on it. "That's awful!" she exclaimed with a grimace.

He took the glass away. "What's wrong, Laura?" he asked again.

"I, I think there's gonna be bad trouble tonight. I was out in my garden when some men rode by. They was wearin' white sheets and hoods and laughing about how they scared those Lucas boys."

"Bastards!" muttered Joe angrily. Laura pretended not to hear the profanity. "How many?"

"Six or seven. I'm not sure. Anyway, I heard one say they should get together again after supper and go after the darkies. I'm sure they meant the Claytons."

Joe took a deep breath and stared for a moment at the floor. He did not relish the idea of confronting neighbors.

"They, they had guns, Joe, and they had been drinking. I saw a bottle changing hands."

Joe quietly arose and hobbled into the bedroom. He soon returned. About his hips was a gunbelt holding the old army .38. Under his left arm was a booted rifle. Easing back onto the sofa, he drew out the long gun to check its load. It was a Winchester

.30-30. Laura's face went pale at the sight of it. Satisfied with the condition of the rifle, Joe slid it back into its boot. Then the revolver received a minute examination.

"You rode Jimmy's gelding?" he asked. She nodded. "Why didn't you send Jimmy?"

"I was afraid he might try to follow you."

Joe nodded. "Good thinkin". He arose.

"Laura, I want you to stay here 'til I get back. I don't want to take the chance of you meetin' some of those fellows on the road. Anyway, I'm gonna borrow the gelding. He's faster than Suzy." He groped through his pockets until he found the tin constable badge, then pinned it onto the bib of his overalls.

"Joe, be careful."

"I will, Laura."

*****

The Clayton house lay in total darkness and for a moment Joe allowed himself the faint hope that they had taken his advice and gone away for the weekend. That was highly unlikely, though. This farm was the dearest thing to Samuel's heart and he would never abandon it even for a moment. However, the total absence of activity was good evidence that the women and children were away. That was something at least.

He wondered if Samuel was in the house. Probably not. He would have enough sense to sleep out in the bushes. That would give him room for maneuver, and that was the only way a single man could fight a mob. Howard might be along for moral support, but the fight, if it came to that, would be Samuel's

"Hello, the house!" he called at last. When there was no answer he called again. "Hello, Samuel! This is Joe Potts! I need to talk to you!"

A large, dark form suddenly rose up to Joe's left. Had Samuel had killing on his mind, Joe would no longer be of this world. "What you want, Potts?"

"Some men are comin' here, Samuel. Ku Kluxers. About a half dozen. I'm gonna try and stop 'em, but in case I can't I want you to know what you're up against."

"I ain't askin' you to fight 'em fer me!" The tone was very bitter.

"I know you ain't, Samuel. I'm a lawman. It's my job."

"You ain't no lawman in Mount Moriah."

"But these men are from Burnham, so I feel responsible." He hesitated and then asked, "Is Howard here, too?" another silhouette appeared and even in the darkness Joe could sense the stark terror. He touched the brim of his hat. "Samuel, Howard, you boys take care of yourselves now."

He started to turn the gelding, but Samuel came forward a few steps. "Potts, I 'preciate the warnin'."

Joe stared down at him a moment. "Just keep your powder dry, Samuel. You may need it before the night is out." Then he was gone.

Joe picked his spot near the end of the Burnham-Mount Moriah Road. This was a lonely stretch crawling along the north base of no-name hill and heavily wooded on both sides. There were no houses nearby, so if shots were fired hopefully no innocent citizens would be hit. He eased off the road on the down slope side. If he had to hoof it away from there it would be easier going downhill. After picketing the gelding far back in the timber, he chose a large hickory next to the road for cover and sat down to wait.

Night sounds closed in around him. Crickets resumed their infernal grating. Something stirred in the tree overhead. A coon or maybe a 'possum. An owl hooted not far away. Joe's Indian striker back in the war always maintained that owls signified death. But there were owls everywhere, Joe had argued. Yes, and there was death everywhere had come the reply. It made as much sense as most beliefs, he reasoned.

He shifted his position and gripped the Winchester more tightly. Would they even come at all? he wondered. After getting their bellies full, maybe they would call it a day. This thought reminded him he had not eaten all day. Well, maybe it was better this way. If he got a belly wound, chances of recovery would be better if he hadn't eaten. A mosquito nailed him on the right side of the neck. At least someone was getting a good supper tonight, he thought grimly.

He had never dwelt much on his own mortality. He supposed he was like most other people in that regard. It was just a quietly ticking time bomb in the back of your mind that you spent your whole life trying to ignore. Either that or cushion the inevitable blast with hymns and hallelujahs. If you were lucky the explosion came at an unexpected moment and it was all over with before you had to stare the Grim Reaper in the face.

A light breeze rustled its way through the treetops. A three-quarters moon forced sporadic beams of powdery light into the inky blackness of the woods. For a wild, disorienting moment, he thought himself back in the freakish jungles of Cuba. Yellow fever had been the greatest killer, but men still feared bullets the most. They understood bullets better.

Once, a single sniper had forced an entire encampment into a night of still, motionless terror. The slightest movement would result in a flash and a roar. Several of the best shots in the regiment had laid for the sniper, and someone had finally ended his career. It could have been Joe; it could have been anyone. Odd, how a memory like that could stay with a man so many years and then suddenly pop up unbidden like an unwanted relative. Was he actually scared? he asked himself.

"No Goddamned doubt about it!" he muttered.

What if he died tonight? How would he be remembered? What kind of eulogy would Reverend Watson preach over him? Here he was, a forty-five year old oddball who had never done anything noteworthy, hiding behind a hickory with a Winchester rifle while lying in wait for a pack of ignoramuses filled with more liquor than sense.

So where was it chiseled in stone that a person had to do something noteworthy? Most people lived, died, were buried and that was that. Maybe life was supposed to be like a work of art, simply something to be experienced. But there was a world of difference between a masterpiece and a child's aimless daubings on a wall. Most people merely daubed on walls and not a few scribbled obscenities. There were few masterpieces.

Something was crawling across his shoulder. He picked it off with a thumb and forefinger and discovered it was a tick. Rolling it around, he finally trapped it between two thick, blunt fingernails and popped its life out. And that was that. Whether a tick or a person, it was just that easy. He wished to hell they would come so he could get this over with, one way or another.

He dozed. Wednesday's rain had come and gone, and now the road had regained its normal summer mantle of thick dust that could muffle the slow hoof beats of walking horses. They were almost even with him when he suddenly jerked awake. Six, no, seven he quickly counted. He levered a round into the chamber, a distinctive metallic sound that could be mistaken for nothing else. This brought them up short.

"That's far enough, boys!" he called. "There ain't gonna be no necktie party tonight!"

"Who is that?" called one of the men. "Who's there?"

"It's Joe Potts, Harley!"

Even in the darkness and with a hood over his head, Joe could sense Harley's annoyance. "Dammit, Joe, you ain't supposed to know who I am!"

"Hell, I know all of you! Ed, that piebald you're ridin' gives you away. Ralph, you always slump in the saddle the same way, sheet or no sheet. Horace, you're the only man I know who owns an Enfield musket."

"Well, it don't make no never mind if you know us or not!" pronounced Harley. "We're fixin' to settle with them darkies once and for all! Shoulda done it years ago!"

"Boys, you're gonna have to get by me first," answered Joe solemnly.

"Joe, don't make us hurt you!" Harley fumbled under his sheet for the old Smith and Wesson Schofield inherited from his grandfather.

A single shot shattered the stillness of the night. Harley screamed and slumped forward in the saddle. The other men backed their horses away a few steps and watched in horror as Harley slowly slipped sideways, reached the point of no return, then suddenly dropped onto the road with a dusty thump. He sat up and gripped his right shoulder where his white sheet was rapidly being stained red.

"Boys, this is startin' to get serious!" called Joe. He levered in a fresh round to emphasize the point. "Throw down your guns! Now!"

"Somebody help me!" moaned Harley.

"Joe, let me help him!" pleaded Ed.

"Sure. Just as soon as you all throw down your guns."

"Do it; do it!" howled Harley. "I'm bleedin' to death here!"

There was a series of thumps as an assortment of mostly antique weapons dropped onto the dusty roadway. Ed started to dismount. "Not yet!" ordered Joe. "Take off them sheets so I know nobody's hidin' nothin'."

Sheepishly, they began to pull off their hoods and robes and drop them onto the road. "All right, Ed," pronounced Joe at last, "you can stay. The rest of you get on back home. And if I hear anything short of a gallop, I'm gonna start shootin' blind." There followed a stampede of hooves beating their way back eastward.

The original seven were now reduced to two, one with no fight left in him and the other too embarrassed to do anything. Joe hobbled out of the woods and stood over Ed who was kneeling while trying to treat Harley's wound. He watched for a moment and then walked over to Harley's horse and fumbled around until he found the inevitable jug hanging from the saddle horn by a cord. He uncorked it, took a sip and immediately spit it out. He then smashed the jug by the side of the road.

"There's only one man who can make whiskey that bad," he said.

"Joe, he's bleedin pretty bad," complained Ed. "You know how to get it stopped?"

Joe came over and dropped gingerly to his knees. "Damn, Harley, you're bleedin' like a stuck pig! I doubt a man could last more'n five, six minutes at the rate you're goin'."

"Joe, you gotta do somethin'!" he wailed.

"Sure, Harley, sure; I'll try. No harm in tryin'. But you gotta do somethin' for me first. You gotta tell me where Floyd Neely is."

"Pine Holler! He's in Pine Holler! He's got his still set up there!"

"Well, sure, Harley, I figured he was in the holler somewhere. But it's a pretty big place, Harley, and hard as hell to get around in. I wouldn't want to stumble around for a half a day and then find out I'm lookin' in the wrong end." He began probing Harley's shoulder, looking for the pressure point.

"West end!" cried Harley. "Over near Satan's Hoof-print!"

"I know the place." Joe guided Ed's hand onto Harley's shoulder. "Just keep your finger right there and push down hard as you can."

"How long?" asked Ed in a shaky voice. The warm, sticky fluid beginning to cover his hand had him badly rattled.

Joe didn't answer, but just kept wrapping strips of sheet around Harley's chest and over his shoulder. He concluded by rigging a sling for the right arm. "There, that ought to do it."

He reached into his bib pocket for his corncob pipe and soon had a tiny glow going. "You boys sure are thoughtful to bring your own bandages," he quipped.

"What now?" asked Ed.

"Get him on his horse and take him to Doc Hudson. "I know he'll just be tickled pink to see you." Ed pulled the weak-kneed Harley to his feet. With Joe's help, he finally managed to get him mounted.

"Ed." He reined in and looked down at Joe. "If you boys want to do somethin' useful instead of scarin' kids and darkies, John Carter's fields could use some work. But don't go near the house. It's under quarantine."

Ed digested this, nodded and rode away, leading the moaning Harley's horse. Joe watched them recede, then began gathering captured weapons in one of the sheets.

"It could have been worse," he muttered while hobbling into the woods to retrieve the gelding. "It could have been a damn sight worse!"

He rode back to the Clayton house. For the last hundred yards he constantly announced himself in a loud voice and assured them that the Ku Kluxers were gone. He was not worried about a panicky shot from Samuel, but Howard was a different story. He reined up in the middle of the yard and waited for someone to appear. Samuel finally stepped out of the bushes, an ancient black powder double barreled shotgun cradled in his arms.

"Didn't expect to see you again, Potts."

"Thanks for the vote of confidence," he replied dryly.

"I heard a shot."

"I had to put a bullet in Harley Simpson's right shoulder." Joe glanced quickly around the yard. "Where's Howard?"

"Ran off!" spat Samuel with disgust. "When he heard that one shot, he jest up and hoofed it fer that hill yonder. I felt like shootin' him my ownself!"

"Don't be too hard on him, Samuel."

"He's jest a yella belly! That's all he is!"

"Not all men have your courage, Samuel. Your brother's a hard worker and a good provider for his family. I know a lot of brave men who won't do as much. Accept him for what he is and count yourself lucky."

Samuel considered this for a moment. "Guess it was partly my fault anyway. I's the one made him stay." He looked up at Joe. "You won't say nothin'? About him runnin' off, I mean."

"No need anyone else ever knowin', Samuel."

He nodded his thanks. "You sure they won't be back?"

"As sure as I am of anything."

"Then I'll sleep in the house tonight after all."

"What about Howard?"

For one of the few times in his life, Samuel Clayton actually smiled. "Let the skeeters eat him up!"

"Good night, Samuel."

When he arrived back at the cabin the first thing he saw was the Model T parked in front. Martin and Laura came out to meet him, both with a thousand questions that he grunted away. They followed him to the back of the house and watched while he stripped the saddle and blanket from the gelding. After wiping the animal down, he put him in a stall next to Suzy who flicked an ear and switched her tail at this unwarranted intrusion. At last he turned to the deputy.

"I thought you had a social life."

"She had to be home early. The church is having a picnic tomorrow and she is one of the organizers."

"Hope you ain't countin' too heavy on goin'."

Martin looked surprised. "As a matter of fact, I am. Any reason why I shouldn't go?"

"I'm ridin' into the holler tomorrow mornin' to arrest Floyd Neely."

"You're really going to do it, then?"

Joe nodded. "Laura, I'll want to borrow this gelding. Charlie will need somethin' to ride."

"I didn't say I'd go!" Joe and Laura both stared at Martin blankly. With a sigh, he added, "But I will."

Grinning, Joe shouldered the Winchester and handed Charlie the white sheet now heavy and bulky with captured weapons. He then led the way through the back door into his cabin. But then he stopped so suddenly the others bumped into him.

"What the dickens happened in here?"

"I straightened a few things while I was waiting," confessed Laura.

"Well, you're a regular little homemaker, ain't you?" he drawled. "Where's that jug? I could use a little sip."

"I'll get it," volunteered Laura. "You sit down."

Charlie dropped the heavy sheet onto the floor with a noisy clatter, but then curiosity forced him to unfold it and look inside. "My God! You disarmed them all?"

"It seemed the thing to do at the time."

Martin sat down across from Joe. "I met your two Klansmen and drove them to the doctor. They wouldn't say much about what happened, though."

"They ain't my Klansmen!" grunted Joe.

"Well, they're somebody's."

"Larkin's." Laura served them their drinks and even had a small one herself. This time she didn't choke on it. Joe smacked loudly and slapped his glass down.

"Fact is," he continued, "they ain't even real Klansmen. I mean, they ain't part of no national or state organization."

"I don't understand."

"They started out just a bunch of coon huntin' buddies. Bought dogs and sometimes whiskey from Larkin. He decided to put 'em to use. He give hisself a title, preached some kind of mumbo-jumbo and sicced 'em on the few darkies we had in these parts. I reckon he managed to run 'em all off except for the Claytons."

"He hated colored people that much?"

"No more'n he hated white folks. All he wanted was to scare 'em off their land so's he could buy it up cheap."

"Did he ever attack the Claytons?"

"No. He respected Samuel."

"You mean he was afraid of him."

"No!" Joe shook his head vehemently. "Larkin didn't fear nothin' on this earth. But the one thing he respected, even admired I guess, was strength. He would never have bothered the Claytons so long as Samuel lived. All any man had to do was stand up to him. Larkin despised weakness."

"Did you ever have to stand up to him?" Martin suddenly asked.

Joe leaned back and smiled. He pushed his glass to Laura for a refill. "Once," he admitted. "Folks got to compainin' about the racket his dogs was makin' at night. I went to talk to him about it."

"And?"

"He attacked me."

"I suppose you whipped him as easily as those three men in the bar." Laura raised an eyebrow at this bit of news.

Joe shook his head. "Nope. He broke my cane in two and threw it on the ground. He had a knee in my gut and both hands around my throat so tight my tongue was stickin' out." He suddenly stopped and got a faraway look in his eyes.

"Well?" demanded Martin impatiently.

Joe reached into a pocket and pulled out a two barreled over and under Remington Derringer. "You know," he drawled, "it's truly marvelous how reasonable a man can get when you stick one of these next to the family jewels."

He suddenly remembered Laura and glanced over, expecting to see her blushing. He was somewhat vexed to find her concealing a coy smile. "Sorry," he mumbled.

Well," announced Laura arising, "if you two expect to get an early start tomorrow morning, I suggest you get some sleep."

Pointedly, she took the jug of whiskey and put it back inside the cabinet. Charlie smiled and raised an eyebrow. Joe shrugged and turned his glass upside down.

"Charlie, you mind drivin' Laura home?"

"Sure," He arose and went out to start the car.

Laura started to follow, but Joe caught her by the arm and pulled her back. "Thank you for comin' and for carin'."

She started to speak, but he bent forward and kissed her lightly on the lips. Quickly, he pulled back before it could become more serious.

There was surprise in her eyes and perhaps a little sadness as well. "Good night, Joe." She turned and hurried out the door.

He watched from the doorway until the car was out of sight. He then stepped to the cabinet to get the jug again, but paused and finally decided against it. After all, it had been good advice. Instead, he rummaged about until he found the makings for a quick, easy meal.

Fifteen minutes later Charlie was back. The deputy was already pulling off the sweaty uniform shirt before he made it through the door. Joe washed down the last of his sandwich with a glass of water.

"Charley, why did you come back here tonight?" he quietly asked.

"The sheriff has gotten an arrest warrant for Billy Larkin."

Joe looked at him with surprise. "You mean he's quit tryin' to make this a syndicate thing?"

"I'm not sure, Joe. He was acting mighty strange. He kept talking about that friend of yours, the one in the bar."

"Prentiss?"

Martin nodded. "I believe he's got something in mind he's not telling anyone. In spite of the warrant, I don't think he means to charge Billy. But he told me to do whatever was necessary to bring Billy in. Faulkner wants him very badly."

Joe smiled grimly. "Well, Billy is who we're really goin' after tomorrow. Floyd can point us in the right direction."

"Faulkner is going to frame Prentiss just like you said, isn't he, Joe?"

"Maybe it won't be a frame, Charley. We still don't have any idea who killed Larkin." He arose tiredly. "Time to get some shuteye, Charley. We got a big day ahead of us tomorrow."

CHAPTER SIX
Sunday, July 26

Despite his best efforts to stay awake, Martin kept nodding and dozing in the saddle. It had been years since he had risen long before the sun was even giving a hint of things to come. He wondered how Joe had managed to awaken at such an ungodly hour for he had no alarm clock. Some people, though, seem to have a mental clock and he decided Joe must be one of them.

Martin's father had been another and a very light sleeper as well. Having spent the greater part of his adult life tracking various bad men across the wilds of eastern Indian Territory, these had been very helpful traits. Martin wondered, was this early morning trek just a small sample of what his father had done for a living? A powerful hand was suddenly shaking him awake.

"Best keep your eyes open now, Charlie. We're fixin' to cross a hill." Joe gave him an amused glance. "There's a knack to dozin' in the saddle and I ain't sure you got it down pat yet. I wouldn't want you to tumble off and get your deputy suit dirty."

Martin stifled a yawn and gazed around. As Joe had explained earlier, the narrow lane that cut from Highway Ten to the Mount Moriah Road continued along a section line up and over the low hill to the south. The lane was fenced on both sides, and beyond were fields of corn and cotton. Why didn't these people raise a greater variety of crops? he wondered. As if on cue, they came to a field of potatoes. Martin yawned again and rubbed sleepy eyes.

Halfway up the hill they were suddenly among trees. But unlike the occasional hickory, oak or walnut down in the valley, these were scrawny, glowering blackjacks, each with an almost impenetrable tangle of branches reaching to the ground. In every case, the lower ranks of these limbs were dead, but refused to detach themselves from the living body.

Martin was suddenly struck by the idea that here were the hoi polloi of the wooded world. Unlike humans, however, the aristocracy resided in the valleys and the peasants on the hilltops. Significantly, though, most of the royalty had fallen, hewn down years ago for railroad ties and mine timbers.

The horses were now walking upon a thick mat of dead leaves, the accumulation of years from the nearly complete canopy overhead. Oddly, though, they did not rattle like dead leaves are supposed to. Curious, Martin bent and peered more closely. With every plodding step of the horses, water squished out. Down below, the domesticated valley was again burned almost dry by the July sun. This wild country, though, still hoarded the precious water from Wednesday's rain.

Still gazing at the ground, Martin did not see the blackjack tentacle that swept off his cap. He reined up and started to dismount in order to retrieve it. Joe pulled Suzy around, bent low to his left and scooped it up without leaving the saddle.

"Best watch where you're goin', Charlie," he advised. "One of those limbs hits you in the wrong place, it could cost you an eye."

Embarrassed, Martin accepted the cap and put it back on. "Thanks," he mumbled. "I'll be more careful."

Joe tapped Suzy with his heels and continued on up the hill. In the east a thin band of pink had appeared. The woods began to come to life. Nearby, a mockingbird broke into a raucous reveille. This was followed by a chorus of trills and twitters as the grumbling troops roused themselves. A fussy little warbler with a yellow stomach flitted from branch to branch, always keeping itself between the noisy interlopers and a two inch hole containing four tiny fluff balls.

The leaves overhead rattled and shook as a squirrel bounded through the treetops. A ponderous diamondback terrapin gazed at them without expression and then ostrich-like withdrew from the world. Off to the left, a small creek gurgled as the hill grudgingly relinquished its life-fluid to nourish the valley below. After topping the hill, they dropped into another valley, smaller than the one they had just left and with fewer farms.

"Is this Pine Hollow?" asked Charlie. It was not nearly as wild as he had imagined.

"Not yet. We gotta get over that first."

Martin gazed with dismay at the mountain before them, much higher and far steeper than the one they had just crossed. Also, the timber was much heavier and there was no convenient lane running across it. This would be a case of plunge in and hope for the best. Quietly, they rode across the small, half civilized valley. When they finally reached the timber at the base of the mountain, Joe reined up and took out his canteen along with two tin cups.

"Been wantin' another spot of coffee," he remarked, "but we needed to get across this valley before people started gettin' up and about."

Charlie accepted a cup, knowing the liquid would now be only lukewarm at best. "You don't want us to be seen?" he asked.

"I doubt any of these folks would take the trouble to warn Floyd even if they knew he was anywhere around. Still, I'd just as soon not take the chance."

Martin took another sip and gazed up at the mountain looming before them. "Is there any easy way to get over that?" he quizzed hopefully.

Joe shook his head. "Afraid not. We could have gone in at the end of the canyon, but it would take us even longer to get where we're goin'. And we'd likely be seen before we got very far."

"Seen? By whom?"

"There's more'n one moonshiner usin' the holler." Joe tossed the dregs from his cup. "Well, this ain't gettin' us up the mountain."

Martin returned his cup and pulled his cap down more tightly. "Lead away. I'm right behind you."

The climb, however, proved not nearly as brutal as Charlie had feared. Instead of tackling the mountain straight on, Joe began zigzagging, sometimes riding a hundred yards or more along the side of the mountain in order to gain only twenty feet. Even though there was nothing resembling a trail, they somehow managed to avoid the heaviest timber and brush. Clearly, Joe was no stranger to this mountain.

And if he were familiar with the mountain, wouldn't he also be familiar with the canyon beyond? Martin began to entertain the faint hope that they would be able to pull off this caper without getting shot at.

Something large and noisy crashed through the woods ahead of them. Alarmed, Martin drew his revolver as his mind filled with dreadful fantasies of ambush by scores of enraged moonshiners. Joe, however, had merely reined up and was gazing quietly, his hands resting on the saddle horn. He had drawn neither his Colt nor the Winchester. Martin eased the gelding alongside him.

"What was it?" he whispered.

"Whitetail buck. Likely just returnin' from a nighttime visit to somebody's cornfield. I'll come back this fall and get him. He ought to be good and fat by then." He glanced over and noticed the drawn revolver. "It ain't huntin' season yet, Charlie," he chided.

Blushing, Martin returned the weapon to its holster. "Do seasons and limits have any meaning to you?"

"Not much," admitted Joe.

"How many do you usually kill?"

"Half dozen or so."

"Do you use all the meat?"

"Sell most of it. Hides, too. When it turns cold, I'll run a few trap lines."

"I've wondered how you support yourself. I know you can't make much from this job."

"I do a little bit of ever'thing, Charlie. Some blacksmithin'. A touch of woodworkin' Even fix a few guns now and then."

"A jack-of-all-trades."

Joe nodded. "But I only do as much as need be to keep grub on the table and buy the few other things I need." He glanced over. "It don't take as much effort as most people think to stay alive."

"But is that really living? Just squeaking by, I mean."

"Life is what you make it, Charlie. Trinkets and baubles don't add much." He goaded Suzy on up the mountainside.

Undoubtedly, Joe's choice of route had made the climb much easier. Even so, by the time they reached the top both men were soaked with sweat and the animals well lathered. Charley, however, completely forgot his exertions as he stared in awe at as wild a scene as he had ever viewed. No wonder the moonshiners so adored this rugged canyon! What revenuer in his right mind would even attempt to come in here?

Beginning in the east as a narrow slash, the canyon deepened and widened as it ran to the west. Yet the walls remained just as precipitous. The slope directly before them was so steep as to release a bushel of butterflies deep in his belly. There were also a few scattered hillocks in the western end, but these only enhanced the chaos and confusion. The whole abominable pit was a solid web of scrub timber and briars. There were not so many gentle pine trees as the name implied.

"How in the world are we going to get through that?" gasped Martin. His mouth refused to close.

"There's a few trails if you know where they're at."

"Won't they be watched?"

Joe shook his head. "Not likely. Nobody's ever bothered the 'shiners in here before."

"So they won't be expecting us?"

"Nope." He glanced slyly at Martin. "Leastways, I hope not."

Charlie gave him a sour look.

Joe swung down from his mule. "It'll have to be on foot 'til we get to the bottom, Charlie."

Martin also dismounted. "Why?"

"Too rough to risk mounted. If one of these critters decides to fall, it'd be a good idea not to be on top of it."

He glanced again at Martin. "Never been in rough country much, have you?"

The deputy shook his head.

"Comes as a surprise to most folks, but almost any man is more sure-footed than any horse. A man can go places no horse or even mule can. Back when I was a youngun, I could have run any mounted man ragged in this place."

He glanced down in disgust at his crippled right foot. "Wasn't for this, I'd hike in there and have Floyd halfway out before he figured out what was goin' on."

Martin followed Joe's gaze to the twisted appendage. "Will you be able to make it?"

Joe looked at him sourly. "Let's go!" he snapped, leading Suzy over the edge.

Martin was not only embarrassed but also a little perturbed that he was panting more loudly than Joe when they finally reached the bottom twenty minutes later. Joe gave him an amused glance.

"I think I'll be able to make it, Deputy," he drawled. He brought out the canteen and again filled their cups. The coffee was now completely cold, but Martin gulped it greedily anyway.

"How far do we have to go now?" he gasped.

"About a half mile."

"Is that all?"

"You ain't traveled that half mile yet. Wait 'til we get there and ask me that again."

Joe climbed back on Suzy. Charlie wiped his mouth on a sleeve, dabbed at his sweaty forehead and boarded the borrowed gelding.

It was an exceedingly difficult half mile. Every twenty feet or so seemed to bring them face-to-face with an impenetrable blackberry thicket that had to be bypassed. At almost every other step, one or another of the animals would either stumble on loose pebbles or else sink knee deep into a deadfall. Several times they had to pick their way carefully past a fallen tree overgrown with briars and brush.

Other casualties of nature leaned at crazy angles, their dead limbs entangled with those of the living. These were a perpetual hazard for they could break free and tumble down at any moment. Perversely, Martin wondered if Joe were still picking the easiest route. But he had to travel it, too, and he was in the lead.

At last they came to a sight so fantastic that Martin just had to dismount for a closer look. Thrust up out of the ground was a flat slab of rock about ten feet across and almost perfectly smooth along the exposed surface. Near the center, however, were three splayed out slashes and at their point of origin a shallow depression. Martin squatted and peered closely to see whether these marks had been chiseled. Joe turned back to see what was keeping his companion and found the deputy on his hands and knees tracing one of the grooves with a finger.

"Satan's Hoofprint," volunteered Joe.

"What do you suppose made it?" Apparently Martin was not the kind to be awed by demons or devils.

"I don't know," sighed Joe. "One of those old timey lizards you hear tell of or maybe a bird of some kind. A very big bird. I doubt a sparrow made it." He paused for a moment and added dryly, "I think it happened a long time ago, Charleie I doubt we can pick up the trail now."

Martin was gradually learning to simply ignore such snideness. "It should be in a museum."

"And just how would you get it out of here?"

Martin raised his head and looked around. "I see your point."

"Come on. We're wastin' time."

Charley remounted but paused for one final, wistful look. At last he nudged the horse forward, not wanting to get so far behind that he lost sight of Joe. If he were left behind, it would probably take a whole day of stumbling around to get out of this dismal canyon. That was a bleak prospect indeed!

A few minutes later they came to a trail. It was not much of one, just barely adequate for a man on horseback. Martin breathed a sigh of relief for now they would be able to travel much faster. Or at least so he thought.

Joe, however, now seemed to be going even slower, stopping frequently for no apparent reason. Martin was growing impatient and on the verge of complaining when he suddenly detected a faint scent carried on a weak westerly breeze.

"Joe, I smell smoke!" he hissed.

Joe nodded and dismounted. We'll tie the animals here and go the rest of the way on foot."

Martin also swung down. "Why?" he asked.

"They'll have horses, too. If ours get too close, they'll start whinnying to each other."

"They?"

"Floyd's likely got his cousin Luke along to do all the heavy work."

"Will they be armed?"

"I'll be surprised if they ain't."

"Why, if nobody bothers them?"

"There's wildcats and a few bears in here."

Martin looked around nervously for this possibility had not occurred to him. "Bears?" he echoed numbly.

"Yep! And they're sometimes drawn to the smell of sour mash. You got a watch?"

He was taken aback by the sudden question. "Why, yes." He flipped open the pocket watch that had also belonged to his father. "It's a quarter past eight." He then noticed Joe looking at his own watch.

"I want you to wait here for thirty minutes," he told the deputy. "Then follow this trail on into their camp. It'll be about a hundred and fifty yards. Maybe a bit more. Be as quiet as you can and don't let them see you. When you get close to the edge of the clearin', just stop and wait. I'll make the first move. You got any spare ammo?"

"Uh, yes, a whole boxful. It's in the saddlebag."

"Get it out and fill your pockets with cartridges. If you need 'em, they won't do you any good back here."

"What are you going to do?"

Joe nodded toward a low hill that had sprouted up to their left. "Gonna cut around behind there and come up on their rear." He checked the loads in both weapons and then patted his copious overall bib that bulged with ammunition.

"Do you think there will be shooting?" asked Martin nervously.

"It's always a possibility, Charlie." He looked intently at the deputy. "You be careful now. And take off that badge and cap. You're showin' way too much metal. It can catch the sun and give you away."

Joe paused, wondering if there was anything else he should say. There was.

"Just one more thing," he added quietly. "There's a fair chance they'll have a dog. If they do, we won't get much closer without them knowin' it."

"What then?"

"Then it's ever' man for hisself, Charlie. In football, it's what they call a busted play. All bets are off." He hesitated. "If bullets go to flyin', Charlie, shoot to kill 'cause that's damn sure what they'll be doin'."

Martin nodded grimly. Joe clapped him on the shoulder and gave him a reassuring smile that did not in fact reassure him at all. He then vanished into the thick foliage.

There followed the longest thirty minutes Charlie could ever recall. The hum of forest insects closed in on him like a terrible roar. It was as though they were all pointing their feelers at him and chirruping, there he is; there he is! There came an incredible din from overhead. It seemed as though every bird in the forest had built its nest in this one tree and was now cursing the trespasser.

How could one stand in the middle of a wilderness and still feel conspicuous? He eased himself onto the ground and spent what seemed an eternity watching a procession of red ants marching back and forth across the trail. At last he checked his watch. It had been all of eight minutes since Joe departed.

So this was how his father had spent most of his adult life, hiding in the woods and waiting to pounce on the bad guys.

What a way to make a living and not much of a living at that! Was he afraid? Hell, yes! The boulder in his belly was sufficient testimony to that. To pass the time, he unloaded the .45 and wiped clean both the weapon and the cartridges. It was something he had seen his father do many times. A clean weapon, he had emphasized, could mean the difference between living and not living.

He was suddenly struck by a frantic thought. What if one of the moonshiners came walking down the trail right now for some reason? Hastily, he shoved the cartridges back into the cylinder. An empty gun could mean the difference between living and not living, too.

And why were they here taking the chance of getting killed in the first place? To arrest a pair of moonshiners? Of course not! Joe clearly had no interest in enforcing Prohibition. In fact, none of the local lawmen did. Why, then? Because Floyd Neely could tell them where to find Billy Larkin. Maybe. But Billy had not killed his father and probably had no idea who did.

Yet Sheriff Faulkner wanted Billy for some mysterious reason. And Joe wanted Floyd for devious reasons of his own. Moreover, none of this had anything to do with catching Larkin's killer. Martin felt like a spectator at a game whose rules he did not understand. Indeed, there seemed to be few rules.

Charlie glanced again at his watch. It was finally time. Drawing his revolver, he put it on half cock and started down the narrow, twisting trail. He glanced often at the ground to make certain there was nothing brittle to step on. Once he saw some species of snake slither from one wall of wilderness to the other. This helped his nerves not at all.

At every turn in the trail he stopped and peeped around cautiously before proceeding. It was slower this way but avoided potentially nasty surprises. Why hadn't he paid more attention to his father's tips on woodcraft? Perhaps it was because his father had seldom been home and then died shortly after retiring.

He had proceeded about fifty yards when he was suddenly brought up short by a deep guttural growling. It soon erupted into a spate of angry barking. So they did have a dog, he realized with a sinking feeling! The game was up. And perhaps more than that. The barking was becoming louder and there was a noisy crashing coming up the trail toward him. The dog! And certainly behind the dog was a man, probably armed!

What to do; what to do? Step off the trail? But the dog had his scent and could certainly get through the brush much easier than he. Glancing over his shoulder, he backed up the trail to the last turn. The dog would certainly appear first. Now he would have over ten yards for a clear shot before it could reach him. After that he could decide what to do about the man. First things first.

The dog popped into view, at least eighty pounds of growling, bristling fury. It seemed to be a mixture of German shepherd and God only knew what. Upon sighting Martin, it did not stop or hesitate, but charged even faster. This was an animal that harbored no doubts or discretion. And no pity. Suppressing his fear by sheer force of will, Martin put the revolver on full cock and brought it to eye level. Steady, steady! Make sure of the shot. Don't rush it.

But don't take too long either. The vicious mongrel had already covered half of the thirty feet. It was a matter of seconds now. He fired.

The explosion sounded unnaturally loud. The noisy insects instantly ceased jabbering as though dismayed by this unexpected turn of events. The complaining birds fell back to reconsider. He cocked the single action weapon again, but then eased the hammer back down.

The dog was lying on its side, bleeding heavily from the chest while its paws clawed with dying agony at the brush and rocks. Red foam and a pitiful whimpering came from its quivering mouth. A killing headshot would be merciful, but he could not risk it. The crashing down the trail had stopped as the moonshiner stood poised, looking for the source of the shot. A second shot would pinpoint Martin's position. The muzzle flash would give him away.

Martin advanced cautiously toward the dying animal and when nearly upon it, sidestepped into the woods. Gone for the moment were any fears or even thoughts of snakes. Slowly and quietly, he advanced a short way past the dog and crouched down to wait. He left the revolver on half cock. Why were his lips so dry and his palms so wet? He could barely hold onto the polished walnut grips.

It seemed he waited an eternity, but in fact it could only have been a few minutes. A head wearing a straw hat finally peeked around a turn in the trail. Soon, the whole man appeared. He was large, well over six feet tall and husky. Floyd Neely was supposed to be skinny, so this had to be his cousin Luke.

At least Martin hoped it was Luke. If it weren't, that would probably mean three men in the camp. Or more. Clad only in overalls, the man's sweaty, rippling muscles glistened in the morning sunlight.

Anger flashed from the man's dark eyes as he spotted the now dead animal. He strode quickly up the trail, stopped and stared down at the unmoving form. Suspicious eyes darted to both left and right, the twin bores of a scattergun following his gaze. Then he spotted footprints leading almost to the dog. Martin decided he could wait no longer. In one fluid motion, he arose, stepped from the brush and thrust the muzzle of his revolver into the small of the man's back.

"Drop it!" he ordered with as much sternness as he could muster. The revolver went to full cock with a noisy, distinctive click.

"Who are you?" demanded the moonshiner belligerently. He did not throw down the shotgun.

"Deputy Sheriff Charles Martin! I'm placing you under arrest! Throw down your weapon!"

"You killed my dog!" the man accused in an almost whining voice. He still did not throw down the shotgun.

Martin was becoming exasperated. He had no idea whether someone else might be coming up the trail that very instant. And here he would be with his back to him while trying to talk this ignorant hulk into throwing down his weapon! He did not have time for this jabbering. He suddenly made a decision and hoped he would be able to abide by it if necessary.

"Look, you son of a bitch!" he hissed. "Drop that goddamned shotgun right now or I'll blow your guts all over that mangy mutt!"

The shotgun struck the ground with a suddenness that astonished him. Perhaps you had to talk to people like this in just the right way. He hesitated, uncertain how to proceed. He couldn't take the chance of marching this character back to the clearing. He could not be distracted by a prisoner. This fellow, hopefully Luke, had to be put out of commission some way. A slender persimmon by the side of the trail seemed about the right size. Martin stepped back from the prisoner.

"Sit down with your back to that tree and put your hands behind it!" he ordered. The man obeyed and in an instant Martin had him handcuffed. "What's your name?"

"Luke Neely," answered the man sullenly.

Martin breathed a silent sigh of relief. "How many men are in your camp?"

Luke only glared at him.

175

Martin felt himself becoming impatient again. He gently placed the tip of his revolver across the man's left cheek so that the bore rested against the side of his nose.

"Would you like to keep that nose?" he asked matter-of-factly.

Wild, dark eyes almost crossed while attempting to focus on the big .45 barrel. "Just me and Floyd!" cried Luke. He was now almost drooling from fright.

"Good, good." At least it was good if Luke wasn't lying. "Don't go away now," he commanded airily. "I'll be right back."

Good Lord! Was Joe's snideness contagious?

The butterflies returned to his stomach as he continued down the trail toward the camp. Where was Joe? he wondered. Hiding in the bushes outside the camp? Or maybe still thrashing around behind that hill and wondering what all the commotion had been about? At least there had been no more shooting. Ahead of him all was silent as a tomb. He immediately cursed himself for an unfortunate wording of his thoughts. Still, the only sounds now were his own heavy breathing and clumsy attempts to tread softly.

Sunlight glinted on metal just ahead. He dropped to his belly and lay still. There were no sounds, no movement, no anything; just burning, salty sweat stinging his eyes. He began to inch forward slowly, stopped, reconsidered and then rolled off the trail into the brush.

The going was much slower now. Thorns tore at his clothing and flesh. He wondered where the snake was he had seen earlier. Something poked at his eyes and he thought profane thoughts. But at last he was at the edge of the clearing. Tenderly, he pushed a weed aside and peered through.

It was the first operating still he had ever seen. At the center of the camp a large fire was burning. Nearby was the vat of sour mash being heated by coals carried from the fire. Coils and tubes seemed to run everywhere in some crazy pattern, into a barrel and back out of it and then into another. The cauldron bubbled and simmered and stank.

At one edge of the camp was a large pile of dead limbs to feed the fire when necessary. There was little smoke, certainly not enough to give away the location for any meaningful distance. Along another side of the camp were several ten gallon milk cans, almost certainly the source of the metallic glint that had spooked him earlier.

Where was Joe? Where was Floyd? He couldn't see anyone anywhere. This impasse could go on indefinitely, and he did not propose to spend the whole day lying on his belly in the woods while being eaten by ticks, chiggers and snakes.

"Floyd!" he shouted. "Show yourself and keep your hands up!"

"Afraid he can't do that, Charlie!" called back a familiar voice.

"Joe?"

Martin looked all around and then saw him hobbling out of the woods, the Winchester under his left arm and the cane in his right hand. Charlie struggled to his feet and heard the discouraging sound of cloth shredding as something clung to his back. Cursing under his breath, he ripped himself free and staggered into the clearing. Joe halted and gave him an amused glance.

"Charlie, you look a sight!"

Martin shot him an angry glance. "Where's Floyd?"

"Tied and gagged behind those milk cans."

"Did he give you any trouble?"

"Not a bit. Took him total by surprise. Just walked up behind him while he was lookin' off that way at all the racket you was makin'."

This evoked yet another angry glance. "Why didn't you say anything so I would know you had everything under control here?" He twisted to look back over his shoulder. "I've ruined another shirt! This is the third one in less than a week!"

"I didn't want to spook Luke in case he came back. Where is he, by the way?"

"Handcuffed to a tree." He turned again on Joe. "Didn't you hear the shot? Why didn't you come? I might have needed help!"

"There was just the one shot and I knew you fired it to kill the dog. Heard it yelp. You did kill it, didn't you?"

Charlie nodded.

"Thought so. That was a death yelp if I ever heard one. Anyway, when I didn't hear no more shootin', I figured you either captured Luke or he turned back or run off. I didn't come 'cause I figured there was too much chance of us shootin' each other."

He looked deeply into Martin's eyes. "If I'd thought you was in trouble, Charlie, I would of come."

Martin sighed, glanced down at the revolver still in his hand and holstered it. "I know you would have, Joe. But that waiting was starting to get to me."

"Gettin' to me a mite, too, Charlie," admitted Joe.

"Should I go get Luke now?"

"He'll keep."

Joe hobbled over to the milk cans where Floyd was lying. A scrawny man with a sallow face and dark, matted hair stared up at them with jaundiced eyes that contained more hurt and fear than anger.

"Charlie, take off his gag."

Martin removed the gag and helped Floyd to sit up. Most of the terror suddenly vanished from the man's eyes. Now they appeared on the verge of tears.

"What's this all about, Joe?" he pleaded. "Why you got me all tied up?"

"Why, I thought you knew, Floyd," drawled Joe. "Makin' whiskey's against the law. Has been for quite a spell now."

Floyd, his mouth open and eyes vacant, tried to assimilate this explanation. However, the effort simply overwhelmed him. "But, Joe, you ain't ever arrested nobody for makin' whiskey before!"

"I know, Floyd. But you see, I'm tryin' to mend my ways." He sat down atop one milk can and began prying the lid off another. "Anyway, Floyd," he continued, "your whiskey is so God-awful bad it would still be a crime to make it even without all those silly laws."

Joe finally got the lid off and leaned over to smell the contents. He immediately jerked back in disgust. Martin peered inside, expecting the can to contain whiskey. It didn't. It only contained water, but still smelled like seven kinds of mortal sin.

"Dammit, Floyd!" growled Joe. "I told you years ago you shouldn't have your privy right next to your well. But you always were a lazy cuss, too lazy to move it or build a new one. I always figured the reason your whiskey was so bad was because of this slop you call water. A man ought to have more pride than to let his younguns drink somethin' like this."

"I'll build a new one, Joe! I promise! I'll start on it first thing tomorrow!"

"Floyd, your good intentions don't last no longer than the scare. Anyway, I figure you'll be in jail tomorrow."

The fear returned to Floyd's eyes. "You're not really gonna arrest me, are you, Joe?" he whined pitiably.

Joe took out his pipe and began to load it. "It depends, Floyd." He popped a match to life with a thumbnail.

"Depends on what, Joe?"

"On whether you'll help me."

Floyd ventured a twisted smile that was supposed to signify cooperation. Instead, it made him look like someone who had just passed gas that turned out to be a bit more than gas.

"Sure, I'll help you, Joe! Just name it!"

"Where's Billy Larkin these days?"

The cringing smile evaporated and the eyes again clouded with fear. "I, I don't know," he stammered. "I ain't seen hide nor hair of Billy for months."

"Well, let's see," drawled Joe while puffing idly on his pipe. "We've got you for moonshinin', resistin' arrest and now perjury. How many years will that get him, Charlie?"

"About thirty," replied Martin deadpan, playing along.

"Perjury? Now hold on, Joe!"

"Sure, perjury, Floyd. You done lied to me. You seen Billy right after he killed his pa. He kept Tom's dogs at your place that night. I can prove that."

Joe suddenly stiffened as though something just occurred to him. "Hey, wait a minute. That makes you an accomplice to murder, don't it? I didn't think of that before. How many more years, Charlie?"

He shrugged, not waiting for an answer. "Well, it don't matter much. You're goin' away for the rest of your miserable life, Floyd. Prob'ly won't be long either, the way they work you down on that pea farm."

"Joe, please!"

"Wait!"

The command was so sharp that even Charlie jumped. Joe narrowed his eyes and stared intently at something no one else could see. He clamped his forehead with his left hand and tapped the cane nervously with the right. A trembling Floyd mindlessly followed the intent stare with no idea what he was supposed to be seeing. Joe finally dropped his left hand, stilled the cane and fixed Floyd with a look so harsh it made him cringe.

"I just thought of somethin'," intoned Joe in a low, ominous voice. "Maybe Billy didn't kill his pa after all. Maybe you killed him, Floyd."

"Me!" he squealed. "My God! Are you crazy? Me kill Tom Larkin?

Even Joe silently admitted the idea was ludicrous. But that did not stop him from using it to hammer Floyd whose thought processes were not terribly sound even on his best days.

"Greed can give a man false courage, Floyd."

"Greed? What are you talkin' about, Joe?"

"Why, your oldest girl is carryin' Billy's child, ain't she?" Floyd's mouth dropped open. How did Joe know that? "Wanda, ain't that her name?" Joe puffed at his pipe and winked knowingly.

"That'll make the baby a Larkin heir," he continued. "All you gotta do is get rid of the old man and twist Billy's arm some. Then the Neely clan is sittin' prettier than it ever has before."

"I didn't kill him, Joe!" pleaded Floyd. "I swear to God I didn't ! You gotta believe me!"

"Don't matter if I believe you, Floyd. It's a jury of your peers you gotta convince."

Unbidden, Joe visualized a jury of Floyd Neelys. He had to shake the idea off before it caused serious mental damage. He removed the pipe from his mouth and examined the bowl.

"Havin' those dogs at your place is gonna look real bad," he continued. "I guess Billy's the only one who can clear you on that point. Trouble is, no one knows where to find him."

He turned his eyes back on the prisoner, shook his head and sighed loudly. "So I guess you're just stuck, Floyd. Looks like you're goin' down for the murder of Tom Larkin."

"Moffett!" squealed Floyd. "He's runnin' a still in the Moffett bottoms!" This was a small town populated mostly by Blacks just across the border in Oklahoma. It lay along the west bank of the Arkansas River where it looped to the north.

"That's a right sizable strip of territory, Floyd. Whereabouts exactly?"

"A mile west of town! He pays the darkies to warn him if anybody's lookin' for him!"

Joe tapped out the bowl of his pipe. "You've been right helpful, Floyd. Maybe I was wrong about you killin' Tom. I reckon you won't fry in that new-fangled electrical chair after all."

"Then, then you ain't gonna arrest me?"

"Yes, Floyd, you're still under arrest. Makin' whiskey is against the law."

"But, but you promised, Joe! You promised you wouldn't arrest me if I helped you! Well, I helped you! I told you where to find Billy!"

Joe was nodding enthusiastic agreement on every point. "I know you did, Floyd, and I appreciate it. I truly do. And I know I made you a promise. But you see, Floyd, it's like this. I lied."

Floyd was suddenly struck dumb, his eyes blank and mouth hanging open. He was utterly incapable of taking in the situation.

"That's right, Floyd," continued Joe. "I just told you a downright lie, no doubt about it. It was a sure enough awful thing to do, and I'm gonna feel real bad about it tomorrow. I just know I am."

Joe crawled off his milk can perch. "Charlie, I reckon it's about time for you to bust this place up."

"Me!" The deputy looked around uncertainly. "How do you go about it?"

"You mean you don't know? I figured you'd at least read about it in one of your lawman books." Joe shrugged. "Damned if I know either. I ain't never busted up one of these places."

He turned to the prisoner. "Floyd, can you help us out?"

But Floyd was no longer being cooperative. Joe shrugged again. "Reckon the first thing to do is put that fire out. Cut Floyd loose and have him tote these cans of so-called water over there and douse it. If he tries to run away, shoot him in the butt."

Joe hobbled over to the tubes and coils and merrily wielded his cane to shatter the glass. Martin, meanwhile, cut Floyd free and inflicted upon him the indignity of helping bust up his own still.

An hour later Floyd was tied up again, shoved onto his horse and led away from the clearing. They stopped on the way to pick up Luke who was still handcuffed to the persimmon and still sulking over his dead dog. He was quickly hoisted aboard his own horse. He looked at Joe with an expression both hurt and dumbfounded.

"That deputy threatened to shoot my nose off!" he complained.

"Now why in the world would he do somethin' like that, Luke?" quizzed Joe, genuinely mystified.

"He wanted to know how many men were in the camp."

"And did you tell him?"

Luke looked astonished. "Well, sure. If a man says he's gonna shoot off your nose, you oughta do what he says."

"You made a wise decision, Luke," replied Joe solemnly. He glanced at Martin. "Unusual technique. Is that what they're teachin' young lawmen these days?"

"My father used the threat once to make a man talk." He paused. "He said he had to use it a second time to make him shut up."

Joe did not say anything for a good twenty yards. "Shoot off the nose," he muttered at last. "Have to remember that one."

*****

By three o'clock that afternoon, Floyd and Luke were settling into their new accommodations provided without charge by Sebastian County. Joe and Charlie, meanwhile, were deep in a conference being held in Sheriff Faulkner's office. On a Sunday afternoon, the courthouse was abandoned and silent as a tomb. Justice had taken the weekend off.

A fourth man was also present, Prosecuting Attorney Wayne Saunders, one of the most promising talents coughed up by the party machinery in many a moon. Of medium height and build, Saunders was forty, blond and looked disgustingly handsome in a business suit. He smiled so easily and effused so much charm that a Vermont Republican would have voted for him and been happy for the chance. But if one looked very closely, there was something hard and even dangerous in those steely blue eyes.

No one seemed to know very much about him. He had simply shown up ten years ago, presented a law degree from an out of state university, paid his dues and joined the ranks. The party bosses congratulated themselves on this stroke of luck while all the local hacks stepped discreetly aside to make way for this natural superior. The pecking order quickly rearranged itself. When the war came a few years later, Saunders took a leave of absence from party duties. Naturally, he returned as a major and with the left breast of his uniform filled with ribbons. The pecking order rearranged itself again.

In 1920, he became the county prosecutor. A six year apprenticeship, however, was sufficient. Next spring, he would enter the primary for state attorney general. There would be no meaningful opposition. The party would see to that. The deals had already been cut. And in a one party state, the primary was the whole shooting match. The local bosses would lose a superlative operative, but it would be worth it. At long last, Fort Smith would have a voice in the halls of the mighty in Little Rock.

With someone as prominent as Wayne Saunders present, Faulkner was compelled to yield up one of his treasured bottles of Scotch and serve a round. He took out his bitterness by staring with disapproval at his deputy's shredded uniform.

Joe smacked his lips loudly. "Mighty fine sippin' whiskey, Sheriff," he complimented. "Yes sir! Mighty fine!" He set the glass back down on Faulkner's desk.

"What's this about a big break in the Larkin case?" demanded the sheriff as he gazed with dismay at the inroad on his last bottle of Cutty Sark. How had Potts gotten his hands on the bottle to pour the drinks anyway?

"We've found where Billy Larkin is keepin' hisself."

Faulkner sat up quickly, his eyes beaming. "Where?" he demanded almost greedily.

Joe smiled faintly and held up a hand. "Now first, you oughta know one thing. Floyd and Luke, them's the two 'shiners we just brought in, they've suddenly got stubborn for some reason and ain't gonna say no more 'til they see a lawyer. 'Course, any lawyer worth his salt is gonna tell 'em to keep their mouths shut and try for a deal of some kind."

"What are you gettin' at, Potts?" growled Faulkner.

"What he's getting at, Sheriff," interrupted Saunders, "is that you will get nothing out of the prisoners. To learn of young Larkin's whereabouts, you will have to deal with Constable Potts." He leveled those powerful eyes on Joe. "Is that not correct?"

"Right as rain, Mister Saunders," replied Joe lightly.

"Can he do that?" demanded Faulkner. "Withhold evidence, I mean."

Saunders chose to ignore such an asinine question. "What is it you want, Mister Potts?"

"Three things. First, about the two men we brought in today. I don't want any deals made with 'em. They're both to do hard time."

"I see no problem with that," replied Saunders.

"Second, I want an arrest warrant for Neely's wife."

Saunders furrowed his brows doubtfully. "That is very shaky ground. Arresting a woman can blow up in all our faces. The public frowns on it unless the charges are very serious indeed."

"I don't aim to arrest her, Mister Saunders. I just want an official paper so's I can scare the bejesus out of her. And that leads to the third thing I want. I want a court order to take the Neely children. With Floyd goin' away for a long time and an arrest warrant over her head, she'll give 'em up without a squawk."

Saunders rubbed his chin reflectively. "How bad is this domestic situation?" he asked.

Joe explained a few salient points.

Saunders considered for a very long time. "All right, Potts," he agreed at last. "I'll arrange all the documents you need this evening. You can pick them up first thing in the morning. They will be expecting the children at the county youth home tomorrow. I'll leave it to you to get them there."

Joe grimaced. "Well, sir, I reckon there's a fourth thing I need. You see, I've already found a foster home for 'em in Burnham. I guess I'll need somethin' to make it official."

Saunders stiffened. "Who are these foster parents?"

"Parent," corrected Joe. "Just one. Mrs. Larkin."

Saunders shook his head doubtfully. "The court prefers that a foster home include both a father and a mother. Especially in a case where the previous home has been so, ah, unsatisfactory."

"Well, there ain't no father. Fact is, I wouldn't recommend such a thing if Tom Larkin was still alive. But there will be a man present, the hired hand, Mase."

"That dummy?" exploded Faulkner.

"He ain't no dummy, Sheriff!" snapped Joe. "He can't hear or talk, but he's smart enough to run a farm and a truer man than most I know."

Joe turned back to the prosecutor. "Look, Mister Saunders, the younguns will be eatin' three proper squares a day, sittin' in church on Sunday and goin' to school once it starts up again. That's a whole sight more'n can be said about 'em now. And it won't cost the county one red cent."

"You certainly want a lot for your information, Mister Potts," remarked Saunders coolly.

"Just tryin' to give some younguns a real chance in this world." Their eyes locked in a long, silent exchange.

"Very well," relented Saunders at last. "I will arrange everything." He pointed a finger sharply at Joe. "But you damn well better know what you're doing."

"Thank you, Mister Saunders."

"Is that all settled?" demanded Faulkner impatiently.

"Seems to be, Sheriff," replied Joe airily.

"Then where the hell is the Larkin kid?"

"Runnin a still a mile west of Moffett." He glanced with sympathy at Saunders. "That'll mean extradition."

Saunders shook his head with disgust. "You've certainly ruined my Sunday evening, Potts."

Joe turned back to Faulkner. "It'll mean somethin' else, too, Sheriff."

Faulkner narrowed his eyes suspiciously. "What?"

"Billy's payin' some locals to keep a lookout. But he'll also be payin' protection money to Marshal Sims unless I miss my guess. So the marshal will also need a reason to cooperate.

Otherwise, whoever goes in after Billy ain't gonna find nothin' but where he used to be."

This frank acknowledgment of police corruption surprised no one, not even Charlie at this point. "Any suggestions, Potts?" asked Saunders.

Joe nodded. "Billy's father, Tom, was a Grand Dragon in the Klan."

"He was not!" exploded Faulkner hotly.

Everyone looked at him. "How would you know, Sheriff?" asked Saunders quietly.

His face bright red, Faulkner merely mumbled. "I just know, that's all."

Joe shrugged. "Anyway, he called hisself one which amounts to the same thing, I reckon. That won't set at all well with the colored folk around Moffett. And what don't set well with them won't set well with Marshal Sims. When they learn about Tom, Billy will be finished in Moffett. He'll be a sittin' duck for whoever goes in after him."

Saunders put aside his glass and arose. "Well, gentlemen, it seems we have now covered everything, so if you will excuse me I have a great deal to do."

Saunders started for the door, but then paused and glanced down at Martin who had said nothing during the entire meeting. "Young man," intoned the prosecutor severely, "you should take better care of your uniform." He departed, leaving a crushed and blushing deputy in his wake.

Joe drained his glass and slammed it down. "Charlie, I think that's all the damage we can do. You ready to go?"

"Potts!" growled Faulkner. Joe turned to him. "I ain't gonna forget how you held me up today!"

Joe smiled at him and winked. "I don't expect you to, Willie Don." He hobbled out of the office. Charlie arose to follow him.

"Martin!" It was Charlie's turn to stop and look back. "You have no more business in Burnham. You will report here tomorrow morning."

"Yes, sir."

Joe and Charlie paused for a moment on the sidewalk outside the courthouse. Fort Smith was a dormant city today, the streets nearly deserted as people sought shelter from the fierce July sun. Directly across Sixth Street stood the Post Office, another government establishment in the sterile classical style. Not far away was the old courthouse of Judge Isaac Parker who had dispensed hemp justice on a volume basis. Those were the good old days of extreme, straightforward and highly effective solutions to social problems.

"I don't understand what you're doing, Joe," complained Martin. "We know Billy is innocent, yet you've turned him over to Faulkner on a silver platter."

Joe stared off into space for some time. "He was gonna get him, Charlie. It would of took longer, but Faulkner was gonna get him sooner or later 'cause Billy ain't got sense enough to keep his head down. This way, I got somethin' out of it I wanted."

"The Neely children."

Joe nodded.

"Are they really going to stick Billy with this?"

Joe thought for a moment and then shook his head. "I ain't really sure who's plottin' what, Charlie, but no, I don't think Billy is the one they're really after. He's just a tool to get somebody else."

"Prentiss?"

Joe nodded. "Likely."

"And he's innocent, too?"

"I think so."

"Where is there any justice in all this?" cried Martin with exasperation.

"Justice ain't nothin' but an accident lurkin' around and hopin' to happen."

It isn't right! None of this is right!"

"No, it ain't right, Charlie," agreed Joe quietly. "But it's the way things are done."

"I may just quit!"

"No, you ain't gonna quit, Charlie. This is what you want to do. Quit and your life is over." He paused. "Folks need men like you, Charlie. More'n they'll ever realize. If all your kind quit, there wouldn't be nobody left to even slow up the Faulkners of this world."

Martin gazed at his shoes self-consciously. "Can I drop you anywhere?"

Joe shook his head. "Ain't far to Bonnie's. I'll walk."

"You're going to spend the night in a, a brothel?" asked the deputy with astonishment.

"Charlie, I can't think of a finer place," he drawled.

Martin shook his head with dismay. "To think there is a brothel within walking distance of the courthouse!"

"Look, Charlie, go home. Change clothes. You can still make the tail end of your church picnic. You'll feel better."

"I don't suppose you'd come with me?"

Joe looked shocked. "You gotta be kiddin'!" He stuck out his hand. "Charlie, I'll be seein' you around."

Martin watched him hobble down the street. At last, he cranked up the Ford and drove away.

CHAPTER SEVEN
Thursday, July 30

It was nearly nine o'clock on another sweltering July morning when the Model T chugged to a stop in front of Joe's shabby cabin. He glanced over at Martin and smiled sympathetically at the deputy's hopelessly ripped shirt. It was the fourth one he had ruined since the Larkin case began. During the long ride home the ugly scratch on the deputy's side had reopened, allowing a trickle of blood to stain not only his trousers but the car seat as well.

"It's been a long trip, Charlie. Want to get out and stretch your legs. I'll put on some coffee."

Martin shrugged and killed the engine.

It had been somewhat of a surprise to Joe when Martin drove up to his cabin on Tuesday night. Hadn't Faulkner taken him off the case? Yet there was a new wrinkle, or so Faulkner claimed. He had received secret information that Larkin was the victim of a conspiracy between certain moonshiners to eliminate a competitor. It sounded lame, but still had to be investigated.

As luck would have it, Federal and Scott County officials were planning a raid the very next day on one of the moonshiners in question. As a polite gesture, a couple of Sebastian County officers would be allowed to accompany the operation as observers. Joe was unclear why both he and Martin had to go, but Faulkner was the chief law enforcement officer of the county and those had been his orders.

Arising long before the sun on Wednesday morning, they had driven south to the Scott County seat of Waldron and arrived just in time for the eight o'clock briefing. Then came the twenty mile mounted march across heavily timbered mountains, a journey that had taken only six hours in spite of two federal

191

agents who kept falling off their horses. At three o'clock in the afternoon they had fallen on a totally surprised encampment and taken three prisoners without a shot being fired.

While the federal men demonstrated their expertise at destroying a still, Joe and Charlie interrogated the prisoners. But no matter how many noses they threatened to shoot off, they came up empty. These characters had clearly never even heard of Tom Larkin. Joe quickly began to suspect they had just chased someone else's wild goose. After spending Wednesday night in Waldron, they then bid good-bye to Scott County and its loudly smirking lawmen.

The first thing Joe saw when he stepped into the cabin was a page from a Big Chief writing tablet tacked securely to a cabinet door where he could not possibly miss it. He immediately recognized Laura's small, neat handwriting. Martin noted the concern on Joe's face as he read the message and began to suspect he would not be getting the promised coffee after all.

"What is it?" he asked.

"Not sure," muttered Joe, "but Laura wants me to come over to the Larkin place the minute I get back." He glanced up from the page. "Charlie, you mind takin' me over there? I left Suzy with Art Jackson to look after while I was gone."

"Of course."

By this hour of the morning the big Larkin farm was a beehive of activity. One Neely boy was in a field plowing. Another was in the shop with Mase who was doing something at the forge. The smaller children were in the garden hoeing down the few weeds that had encroached there. Unaccustomed to such activities, this was all a novelty for the moment. There was considerably more laughing than groaning. Martin had barely killed the engine when Laura appeared on the porch to greet them.

But this was no friendly greeting; in fact, there was no greeting at all. She plunged straight to the heart of the matter. "Joe, something awful has happened. Sheriff Faulkner was here yesterday."

Joe's face suddenly turned cold. "What did he want?"

"He made Mrs. Larkin sign a statement."

"What did it say?"

"It said that both she and Billy saw Tom murdered, that the killer was somebody named Prentiss."

"That son of a bitch!" hissed Joe.

So that was the reason for the Scott County escapade. Faulkner wanted Joe out of the way while he extorted Mrs. Larkin's signature to a false statement.

"How did he get her to sign it?" But again, he thought he already knew.

"He said that if she didn't sign, both she and Billy would be charged with the murder, that they did it to get Tom's property."

"Were you here when all this happened?"

"I was here when he arrived. He thought I was Mrs. Larkin at first. When he found out I wasn't, he ordered me to leave. When I protested, he, he…."

"He what?" demanded Joe.

She dropped her eyes. "He threatened to arrest me for obstructing justice. I, I left like he ordered."

Martin noticed Joe's knuckles turning white as he gripped his cane with both hands.

"Where is Mrs. Larkin now?" asked Joe tightly.

"She's taken to her bed. She wouldn't even get up for breakfast." Laura looked at him with tears in her eyes. "Joe, you should have seen her Tuesday. Smiling and laughing all the time. I've never seen her so happy. These kids gave her a reason to live again. Now I think she just wants to die."

"I'll have to talk to her, Laura."

"I know."

He turned to Martin. "Charlie, you're gonna have to decide where you stand in all this. I'm goin' after your boss now. But there's no guarantee I'll get him. You could get smelly stuff all over you. It could mean your job, maybe even your whole career in this business. If you want to pull out, I'll understand."

Martin looked almost angry at the suggestion. "I want justice done! If I can't have that, I don't want this job at all! I am damned tired of these silly games!"

Joe nodded, feeling more gratitude than he expressed. His opinion of Martin went up a few more notches. "All right, Charlie, no more games. Let's go talk to Mrs. Larkin."

"Joe, there's one more thing," spoke Laura. "He made Wanda Neely sign a statement, too."

"Wanda?" His face went totally blank. What kind of statement could she make, true or otherwise? "What did it say?"

"I don't know. She won't tell me.

"We'll want to talk to her, too. Come on, Charlie."

This time Mrs. Larkin's faithful rocker had been abandoned. She now lay in bed on her back, covered to the chin with a light quilt. She looked very old and very sick. Joe wondered for a moment if Doctor Hudson should be called, but finally decided there was little point. This was a sickness of the spirit. The band-aids and little white pills of the medical wizards were of no avail in such things. He pulled the rocker over to the bed and sat down. Charlie had two good feet. He could stand.

"Mrs. Larkin, it's me, Joe Potts."

"I should have sold the place, Joe Potts," she announced weakly. "I should have sold it like I meant to do in the first place and moved away from here." She turned her eyes away from him. "This place is cursed. Nothing but evil can happen here."

"The evil didn't come from here," corrected Joe. "It came from a little fat man in Fort Smith."

She shook her head at this reasoning. "It's all the same," she argued. "This place draws evil. There's too much of Tom in it."

"Maam, did the sheriff say anything about Billy?"

A trundled and terrified Billy Larkin had been delivered to Sebastian County officers Tuesday afternoon. Saunders had wasted no time pulling extradition strings, and Faulkner had wasted no time getting Joe out of the way. Were they in this together? Joe wondered.

"He said that Billy had signed a paper that we both saw this man...." She hesitated. "I can't even recall his name! I have falsely accused him, and I don't even know his name!" She looked at Joe with beseeching eyes. "Is signin' a piece of paper the same as swearin' on the Bible, Joe Potts?"

"No, maam, signin' a paper ain't quite the same as testifyin' in court." He paused a moment. "The man's name is Prentiss, Jackie Prentiss."

She nodded. "I recall it now." She looked at Joe hopefully. "Is he the one who killed Tom?"

Joe shifted uncomfortably in the rocker. "He could have been, maam," he lied. Martin raised his eyebrows at this.

"But you're not certain?" she persisted.

Joe laced his fingers, dropped his eyes and shook his head. "No, maam, we can't be sure of much of anything."

She turned her eyes away from him and stared vacantly at the ceiling.

"Maam, what did your statement say? As best you recall."

"It said we heard the shot, looked out the window and saw this man runnin' away, that Billy told me who he was." She paused, trying to remember everything." It described him as a large man with black hair and carryin' a shotgun."

"The sheriff must figure you and Billy to have powerful eyesight. It's a good three hundred yards from the house to where Tom was killed."

She turned her eyes on him again. "I will not speak these things at a trial. I will not swear on the Bible and then speak untruly. I told the sheriff that. He laughed and said it didn't matter, that there wouldn't be a trial. With Billy's statement and mine, this Prentiss would confess and plead guilty."

"He lied to you, Mrs. Larkin. I know Prentiss. He'll never confess. Faulkner means for Billy to take the stand and just use your statement to back him up."

Her eyes widened. "Then my statement will be like swearin' on the Bible after all!"

Joe sighed and nodded. "I never thought of it that way, maam, but I guess you're right. Billy will lie under oath and your statement will support him." Her face turned pasty as she contemplated the certain fate for such a mortal sin.

"What else did the sheriff say?" pressed Joe. "What did he say he would do if you didn't sign?"

"He said he would charge both me and Billy with the murder; that even if he couldn't prove it that, that the shame…." She couldn't finish.

Joe turned to face Martin. "Charlie, what is it they call that? Forcing testimony under, what is it?"

"Duress."

"That's it; that's the word!" He turned back to Mrs. Larkin. "Maam, your statement don't mean nothin' 'cause he forced it from you. But we're gonna have to be able to prove it and that means makin' another statement to me and Charlie here."

"Another piece of paper? I am very tired of these pieces of paper, Joe Potts."

"I know, maam. But this one won't have nothin' but the truth on it, nothin' more and nothin' less. Things just have to be set right, maam, and this is the only way to go about it."

She turned tired eyes on him again. "Very well, Joe Potts, I will sign your piece of paper, shame or no shame."

He smiled down at her. "Charlie here will write it all down for you. He can do these things a whole lot better than I can. I just have one more question, Mrs. Larkin. Was anyone else with you and Faulkner when he made you sign that statement?"

She shook her head. "Some other men came with him. They was wearin' uniforms like his." She pointed to Martin. "Except theirs was clean and not tore up so." Joe suppressed a smile. "But they stayed outside while I was makin' the statement. It was just him and me. He even made the children go outside."

"Thank you, Mrs. Larkin," said Joe arising. "Charlie, be sure to get it in there that Faulkner didn't allow no witnesses. When you get it done, we'll leave it with Laura for safekeepin'."

"But...."

"No buts, Charley. We'll use this statement when it will do the most good and not one minute before." He paused. "I ain't tryin to play a game, Charlie, but it don't make no sense to tip our hand before the bettin' is over."

Martin smiled thinly at the analogy. "I've never played much poker, Joe. Is that the game now?"

Joe sighed loudly. "Ever'thing's a poker game, Charlie. I'll send Laura up with paper and pen." He turned and hobbled out of the room, closing the door behind him.

With brown hair and eyes, Wanda Neely was sixteen years old and carried a six month hump in her belly that the blue flour sack dress did little to conceal. A typical Neely female, barefoot and pregnant, she now sat on the living room sofa and twisted nervously at a pot holder. Her face and manner indicated a vague embarrassment. It was clear she would have preferred to be elsewhere.

Joe seated himself on a brand new easy chair directly across from the matching sofa. He had spent much of Tuesday afternoon helping haul the new furniture from Greenwood. A dainty, highly polished coffee table straddled the neutral zone between them.

"Wanda, I reckon you remember me?" he began gently.

She nodded shyly. "You're the man who arrested my pa."

"I need to talk to you about Sheriff Faulkner's visit yesterday."

"He's got Billy in jail!" she complained in a whiney voice.

"I know. He's bein' held as a material witness." He paused. "Did you sign a statement for Sheriff Faulkner?"

"Yes, sir."

"Would you tell me what it said?"

She looked up quickly with terrified eyes and then lowered her head again. "He said I shouldn't say nothin' to nobody."

"I know he would say that, but do you see this?" She glanced up at a stubby finger tapping the battered star on his chest. "I'm a lawman, too, so it's all right to tell me."

"I, I don't know," she mumbled.

"You want to help Billy, don't you?"

She nodded without looking up.

"Billy made a false statement, Wanda. Sheriff Faulkner tricked him into makin' it. Now he's gonna repeat it in court. That's called perjury. Did you know he can go to prison for that?"

She looked up quickly, abject terror in her face.

"Your statement was false, too, wasn't it?"

Again the face dropped. She nodded weakly.

"What did it say?"

"It said this man named, uh…."

"Prentiss."

She nodded. "That's the one. That this man Prentiss came to our house the night Mister Larkin was killed and threatened to kill Billy if he told what he saw."

"What was it Billy was supposed to have seen?"

"Prentiss kill Mister Larkin," she squeaked.

"Did Billy tell you he saw that?"

She shook her head. "No, sir. Billy told us he didn't know who did it, just that he was glad it happened. But, but the sheriff said that if Billy didn't help convict Prentiss, then Billy would be charged hisself. He, he said my statement would help make Billy co, co...."

"Cooperate?"

She nodded. "I didn't want Billy to go to prison. Not my pa neither, though I don't care so much about him."

"What did the sheriff say about your father?"

"He said if I signed he would let my pa go."

Joe suppressed the anger. "Did he say anything else?"

"He, he...."

"He what?"

"He said if I signed, he'd make Billy marry me."

Joe grunted loudly. "That's a hell of a reward!"

"But I love him!" she blurted defensively.

"Wanda, if Billy was worth havin', he'd have married you when he first learned you were carryin' his child."

She started to come to Billy's defense, but Joe raised a hand to cut her off. "It's neither here nor there, Wanda. If you want to marry Billy, that's your business. All I want from you is a statement about what all happened yesterday. And be sure to put in that part about Billy not knowin' who killed his pa."

"I, I don't think I should," she stammered.

"You have to, Wanda. Billy's made a false statement, but if we can prove he did it under duress, it'll get him off the hook.

But if he gets on the witness stand and perjures hisself, then nothin' can save him. He'll get sent to prison for a very long time. He won't do you much good there, Wanda."

"I, I...."

Martin chose that very moment to come down the stairs and place on the coffee table a creamy white sheet of paper almost completely filled with his cramped, neat handwriting. Joe quickly scanned it and then signed his name in the appropriate place.

"You did a real good job on this, Charlie," he complimented. "Laura, come in here a minute, please. I want you to sign somethin' as a witness."

"Wha, what is that?" squeaked Wanda who had now come to distrust all official-looking papers.

"It's Mrs. Larkin's statement about what all went on here yesterday," explained Joe. "You're mentioned in here, by the way."

"M-me?"

"That's right. She tells how you were forced to sign a false statement, too." Laura arrived and signed her name.

"You're kinda on the spot here, Wanda," continued Joe. "If you let the truth dash on by and leave you behind, it could be a wee bit embarrassin'."

"They, they wouldn't send me to jail, would they?"

"I don't know," replied Joe deadpan. "We got us a prosecutor who's a holy terror. Ain't much tellin' what he might do."

"All right, I, I'll make a statement."

Joe turned to Martin. "Charlie, you got more scribblin' work ahead of you. Oh, Billy told the Neelys that he didn't know who killed Tom. Be sure and get that in. Come on, Laura, let's give them some privacy."

He led her onto the porch. She seated herself on the swing and immediately began wringing her hands. Joe pulled up a wooden chair and sat down, stretching out his mangled right foot that was still aching terribly from yesterday's exertions. Old Marty, Tom's sole surviving coonhound, waddled up onto the porch, plopped his ancient bones beside Joe's chair and nestled his incredibly sad face between his front paws. What could Larkin have possibly done in this world to merit such a faithful friend? Joe reached down to scratch the dog's ears, faint comfort in these trying times.

"Somethin' else is troublin' you, Laura," he ventured. "Besides all this Larkin business, I mean."

She did not try to deny it. "Jimmy got a letter from Sally yesterday. It seems when it rains, it pours."

"What did it say?"

"He wouldn't tell me," she replied evasively. "Just threw it in the trash and stomped out."

"But you got it out of the trash and read it."

She nodded guiltily. "It was short. Very short and very cold. She said she didn't want to see him anymore."

"Did she give a reason?"

Laura shook her head. "She just said they weren't right for each other and that she was going to stay in Oklahoma. I suppose she found someone she likes better."

"That's kinda what I suspected, too."

"Jimmy's not taking it well. He came home drunk last night. He was cursing, said he hated this whole place and was going to leave just as soon as he could; that he would join the army the day after he graduated."

"He's hurt and mad, Laura. He'll get over it."

"He'll get over the hurt," she agreed, "but he still means to leave here. I could see it in his eyes beyond the mad. Come next summer, he's going to enlist in the army. I just know it."

Joe sighed loudly. "Maybe that's for the best."

She looked at him sharply. "How can you say that?"

"I just mean that maybe he needs to find hisself."

"And he can't do it here? What are you saying, Joe?" Her eyes became almost angry. "Do you think I have him tied up with apron strings?"

"I didn't say that."

"But you think it."

He became very intent on scratching Marty's ears. "You can't keep him forever, Laura," he spoke quietly.

Something seemed to go out of her at this blunt pronouncement of the obvious. "And what of me?" she demanded grimly. "Am I to sit alone in an empty shack on twenty acres of gravel?"

"Why don't you move in with Mrs. Larkin? There's plenty of room, and I'm sure she'd appreciate your help with the children."

"I'm to help raise someone else's children?" she demanded petulantly.

"You've spent almost ever' minute over here the past two days, haven't you?"

"I, I…" She dabbed at moist eyes. "I just don't want to die a lonely old woman, bitter and forgotten."

"Jimmy's not gonna forget you, Laura. I can promise you that. No man worth his salt ever forgets his mama. But he needs to get away from here; he needs to find somethin' better for hisself than twenty acres of gravel as you call it. But it will be a whole lot better for both of you if he can leave here with your blessin'. Don't make him leave on a sour note, Laura. You'll both regret it."

She smiled sadly. "I remember a lot of years ago another young man who left on a sour note. Nothing's really been in tune since."

He began tapping the cane nervously. "There ain't no reason folks have to go on makin' the same mistakes over and over."

"No, Joe, there isn't." She met his eyes, but he looked quickly away. She sighed. "But I suppose there are some mistakes that can't ever be corrected."

Again with perfect timing, Martin came out onto the porch with another official-looking document. After signing it, Joe handed it to Laura. "Where's the other one?"

"Right here," replied Martin.

"Give it to Laura. Laura, I want you to find a safe place to keep these. Not in this house. Faulkner might take a fool fit to come back here for some reason. I wouldn't want him to find them."

"You're not going to show them to him?" she asked with surprise.

"Not for the time bein'. I want this to be a clean, quick kill; not messy and drawn out."

"Joe, can you really stop him?"

"I don't know," he confessed. "All I can do is try." He paused. "Are you gonna talk to Jimmy?"

She smiled sadly and nodded.

When they were in the car, Martin suggested, "We could show those statements to Mister Saunders. Or do you think he's in on the frame, too?"

Joe considered. "I just ain't sure, Charlie. He's a tough man to read. But even if he ain't, it's still just our statements against Faulkner's. He could say ours were extorted and come back on Mrs. Larkin and Wanda. It could get very nasty, and I want to protect them as much as I can."

He turned to face Martin. "When we bring him down, Charlie, it has to be all the way."

"There's only one way to do that. We have to find the real killer."

Joe nodded. Martin backed onto the highway.

*****

At half past one o'clock, they pulled up outside the county courthouse after finally finding a parking space amid a couple score of horse drawn carriages and a scattering of automobiles. Nearly all of the latter belonged to lawyers. The pursuit of justice could be very rewarding indeed. Martin started to kill the engine, but Joe grabbed his arm. The deputy looked at him curiously.

"Go home, Charlie."

"I have a few things to say to Faulkner!"

"I'd rather you didn't Charlie. There's no point in you gettin' yourself fired. You can be a lot more help if you keep wearin' that badge. Lose it and you're just an outsider lookin' in."

Martin gripped the steering wheel tightly. The games hadn't stopped after all and he still felt like someone else's pawn.

"Please, Charlie. Go on home and get cleaned up, then come back to work just like nothin' happened. If anybody asks, you dropped me off at my house this mornin' and ain't seen me since."

He slapped the steering wheel several times with both hands. "All right!" he finally grumbled. "But I'm damned tired of attacking things sideways!"

"Faulkner plays by alley rules, Charlie, and that means there ain't no rules at all. We'll Queensbury ourselves to death if we ain't careful." He clapped Martin on the shoulder. "Cheer up! Maybe we'll get to go after some more moonshiners before long."

Martin gave him a sour smile. "Go to hell!"

"That's the spirit!"

Joe got out of the car and hobbled away without a backward glance.

Once inside, he had to proceed with considerable caution for the human traffic was so heavy that one could hardly see the highly polished tile floor. Unlike last Sunday, the halls of justice were teeming on this day. Several times he was almost knocked down, the battered badge on his overalls availing him nothing. In this asphalt blighted nightmare of a human existence, hick constables rated somewhere between dogs and darkies. Thieves, pimps, whores and lawyers bustled back and forth on their various errands of so-called justice.

He halted outside Faulkner's private office and gazed at the frosted glass window with his name and title in large black letters. For a moment he considered making many pieces of one but dismissed the idea. It would be a childish and pointless display of rancor. Besides, the taxpayers would have to buy Faulkner a new and better window. He opened the door and entered, omitting the troublesome nicety of knocking.

The office was fairly crowded, but little official business was being conducted. Four fat, half drunk, cigar-chomping men were gathered about Faulkner's desk that had been temporarily cleared of its few businesslike accouterments in order to make room for a jumbo jug of white lightning and a blue-backed deck of Bicycle playing cards. Multi-colored poker chips were scattered in gay profusion.

Joe recognized one of the men as a building contractor who always seemed to get a disproportionate share of the county's building business. Another was a banker who charged a reasonable rental rate for storing what little money the county managed to keep on hand. The third was a prominent minister widely noted for his public disdain of such sins as drinking and gambling. Faulkner looked up from behind his desk, eyes angry at this unannounced intrusion and his mouth furiously boiling smoke.

"Very cute, Willie Don," intoned Joe with false sweetness.

"What the hell you want, Potts? Make it fast! I'm busy!"

"So I see." He pulled up an extra chair and straddled it, crossing his arms atop the back. "Very cute, that wild goose chase. You didn't have the guts to browbeat two women with me around. You knew I'd kick your fat ass all the way back to Fort Smith."

Faulkner slammed the desk with his fist so hard that the jug bounced and sloshed white lightning onto the banker's lap. He yelped and jerked backwards, causing a couple of supplementary aces to tumble from his sleeves. His comrades tactfully ignored this development. After all, the worthy gentleman had ascended to the bank presidency when his predecessor accidentally shot himself in the back of the head with a twelve gauge shotgun. Faulkner cut his eyes from player to player.

"Get out!" he snapped to his companions. "Let me take care of this pissant in private!"

Within seconds, the two of them had the office to themselves. "All right, Willie Don, take care of me," invited Joe quietly.

"Don't you ever say anything like that to me again!"

"Or what, Willie Don?"

The sheriff was taken aback by the cold confidence in the voice and eyes. "What do you want, Potts? I ain't got all day!"

"I want you to tear up those statements you took yesterday."

"You're crazy! With them I can nail Prentiss to the wall!"

"He didn't kill Larkin."

"So?"

Joe sighed and dropped that line of argument. "I just wanted to give you this one chance to back out of it Willie Don. You're a fool if you don't 'cause I ain't gonna let you get away with it. When I get done with you, Willie Don, you won't have a pot to piss in or a window to toss it out of."

Faulkner came halfway out of his chair, intending for one split second to wreak some physical violence. After all, Potts was a cripple. He suddenly froze. There was a hint of a smile on the constable's face and a homicidal gleam in those cool brown eyes.

Perhaps violence was not called for after all. Faulkner quickly fell back to his dependable standbys of threat and bluster. Gripping the edges of the desk tightly with both hands, he leaned forward, accidentally dropping a pile of gray cigar ashes into the poker pot.

"Don't cross me, Potts!" he growled. "Don't get in my way or I'll stomp on you like a bug!"

Joe arose slowly and easily. "Best be careful what you go stompin' on, Willie Don," he cautioned. "It may turn out to be a stinkbug and get all over you."

"Get out!"

Joe paused at the door. "Willie Don, you've dealt yourself a bad hand. This is your last chance to fold."

Joe closed the door as he left the office. However, he had only taken a couple of steps when he suddenly stopped, turned and smashed the window with his cane. So let the taxpayers buy Willie Don a new door glass. They shouldn't elect such worthless meadow muffins into responsible positions in the first place. He then proceeded directly to the prosecutor's office.

Wayne Saunders's secretary looked up and smiled with proper, mandatory civility in spite of Joe's ragged overalls and molting straw hat. "May I help you?"

"I'd like to see Mr. Saunders. Name's Joe Potts."

"Do you have an appointment?"

"No, maam, I just want to warn him about the riot."

The regulation smile vanished. "A, a riot?" she stammered. "What riot?"

"The riot that's gonna happen if I don't get to see him right now."

Eyes bulging, she hurried to the inner door, tapped gently and stuck her head inside. "Sir, there's a gentleman here to see you," Joe heard her say. "He seems to be a police officer of some kind. He's, uh, very insistent."

"What's his name?" spoke a voice from the inner sanctum.

"Uh...."

"It's Constable Potts, sir," called Joe.

"Send him in," replied the muffled voice.

Saunders glanced up from behind a mound of papers. There were no poker cronies or cigars here. "What is it, Potts?" he demanded. "More information to sell?"

"No, sir, this time the information's free."

The yellow eyebrows lifted slightly. "Now that seems very out of character. What is this free information?"

"Faulkner's runnin' a frame."

This time the eyebrows shot up noticeably. "You refer, of course, to the esteemed Mister Prentiss."

Joe nodded. "He didn't do it."

Saunders leaned back and folded curiously calloused hands over a small stomach that had a hard look even beneath the summer suit. "You can prove this assertion?"

"He had about a hundred witnesses at the time of the murder."

Saunders closed his eyes and tapped a temple. "Let's see if I can recall your exact words. 'They'd also swear you was juggling ten bobcats at the same time'." He opened his eyes again. "Or was it eight?"

It was Joe's turn to hoist eyebrows. Saunders smiled thinly. "I have my sources of information, too."

"And very good ones they are, sir. Joe sat down without awaiting an invitation. "Prentiss didn't do it," he announced flatly.

"Do you know who did?"

Joe shifted uneasily and shook his head.

"Do you suspect who did it?"

He shifted with even more discomfort. Saunders was fixing him with his best courtroom stare. It would be bad enough to face this man on the witness stand if one were telling the truth. To get a lie past him would be a tall order indeed. Joe hoped very much that Saunders was not in on the frame. If he were, Prentiss was probably done for. He could fry before the year was out.

"No, sir," Joe reluctantly admitted. "I don't even have any suspects either."

"Yet you can say with absolute certainty that Prentiss is innocent of the crime?"

"I know the man, sir."

Saunders drummed his fingers impatiently, silently considering only God knew what. "Sir, are you in on the frame, too?" Joe suddenly asked.

The finger drumming stopped and the mouth dropped open. Then the prosecutor's face flushed with anger. But this was only for a split second and then the rosiness was gone as though it had never been. This was very revealing. Here was a man who would not allow anger to rule him, not even for an instant.

But of even greater significance, that brief flush of anger was of the innocent man falsely accused rather than a guilty one identified. Joe was now fully convinced that Saunders was not part of Faulkner's conspiracy. Again fully under control, the prosecutor studied Joe with renewed interest.

"I have here the statements Faulkner took yesterday," announced Saunders. "They are very damning."

"Too damning, sir. They were extorted. Not a word is true."

"That could be very difficult to prove."

"I understand that, sir."

Again the fingers began drumming. "Why did you come to me with this, Potts?"

"First, to find out if you were part of it."

"And your conclusion on that point?"

"This is strictly Faulkner's play."

"Well, I am very touched by your confidence," he replied sarcastically. Yet something in those distant blue eyes indicated he really was. "Any other reasons?"

"Yes, sir. In case you wasn't part of it, I didn't want you took total by surprise when it blows up in Willie Don's face."

"And is it going to blow up in his face?"

"I think so, sir. It may not be before the trial. It may not be this year or even the next. The way thing are goin', it may not even be in Prentiss' lifetime. But I'll never let this thing go. One day I'll find who did it. If Prentiss has already fried for somethin' he didn't do, it could get mighty embarrassin' for a lot of folks."

"Point taken. Are you anywhere close to getting a handle on this?"

"No, sir. All trails have run cold. I'm startin' from scratch."

"I don't suppose I have to tell you that the only way to stop Faulkner, assuming he really is running a frame, is to produce the real killer."

"I understand that." Then the full import of the words struck him. "You're not convinced this is a frame, sir?"

"No, I'm not. I don't doubt your word that the statements were extorted. However, that does not necessarily mean they are false."

Joe sighed and arose. "Sir, I understand that you have to go to court with whatever evidence you are given. But I advise you to cover your tracks and watch your back-trail mighty close on this one."

Saunders smiled thinly. "I assure you, Mister Potts, I do not venture into dead end canyons." He also arose. "Tell me, where is your young friend of the torn shirt?"

Joe chuckled. "Home changin' clothes. You know, he ruined another one on that wild goose chase Faulkner sent us on yesterday. We got the moonshiners, but they didn't have nothin' to do with the killin'."

Then came the charming, endearing laugh. "We'll have to give that young man a raise just to keep him in uniform."

"Good-bye, sir."

Saunders followed him to the door. "Potts, I appreciate you coming by. I'll keep this case at arms length and delay the trial as much as I can. That will buy you a little time, but not much."

"Thank you, sir." He paused. "By the way, I suppose Prentiss has already been picked up."

"Oh, yes. Faulkner wasted no time on that score. He was pulled out of bed at three o'clock this morning while he was still half asleep. Faulkner took the entire department with him except for Deputy Martin."

"A wise precaution," conceded Joe. "Think I'll drop by and pay him a visit."

"Just be advised, he is not a happy man right at the moment."

"No, sir. Ain't too many of us very happy about any of this. One more thing, sir. Faulkner promised Floyd Neely's daughter that he'd cut her daddy loose."

Saunders stiffened. "He won't! His promises do not take precedence over mine."

Joe nodded and hobbled away.

Fifteen minutes later he had made his way to the top floor of the courthouse where were lodged those currently in disfavor with the local authorities. He paused in front of an ancient oak desk where sat a fifty year old fat man with white hair clipped brushy short. Between his teeth was clutched the mandatory cigar.

He did not deign to look up from the enthralling game of solitaire spread out across his desk. As Joe watched, Chief Jailor Walter Hanley stole an ace from one of the buried piles. The game was not blocked. Joe noticed several plays. It was just that cheating was first nature to this man.

"I'm Constable Potts," announced Joe. "I want to see Prentiss."

"Visitin' hours is over!" growled Hanley while stealing a red jack. He proceeded to play it on a red queen.

"They just opened again."

At last Hanley looked up and fixed Joe with a brutal stare. "Now you see here! This is my jail and I make the rules! You don't come in here and order me around! Now get out of here before I throw you out!"

Joe sat down on the edge of the desk, taking care to scatter most of the cards. Hanley almost lost his cigar, his mouth dropping open so wide at this unheard of affront. But before he could do or say anything, Joe was speaking again, and what he had to say was not pleasant to hear.

"Hanley, most of the department knows you cheat the prisoners on rations by buyin' garbage and pocketin' what you save, which is about half of what you're allotted for meals. What's surprisin', though, is that you ain't bothered to cover your tracks. A blind girl scout could sniff you out and not be half tryin' either. Maybe it's time the local newspaper knew about your little racket. They got a coupla muckraker wannabes on their staff."

Hanley's face skipped the angry flush altogether and went directly to pasty white.

Joe smiled maliciously. "I reckon you know we got us an ambitious prosecutor. He's tacked up a pretty impressive number of hides, but there's always room for one more on his wall. 'Specially if it's a corrupt local official. That always looks good to the voters. And it would be so easy! Why, Hanley, he could skin you right out and not even work up a sweat. Half a mornin's work. And there you'd be, an ex-jailor hoein' peas alongside killers, kidnappers and all sorts of very mean people."

Joe remained sitting on the desk while smirking at the now badly shaken chief jailor. Without a word, Hanley arose and gathered his keys with trembling fingers. Joe stood up and clapped him on the back.

"Now that's a good fellow!"

The first few cells on either side of the central aisle contained assorted riff-raff and those with vaguely mistaken ideas concerning the socially acceptable means of acquiring wealth in this world. At the very rear resided the elite of the criminal kingdom. In two adjoining cells on the left were Floyd Neely and Billy Larkin, two scarecrow-like men looking equally unhappy about the current state of affairs.

The primary reason for this generally glum mood was lodged directly across from them in the last cell on the right. Prentiss was lying on his back, hands behind his head and with his knees drawn up. This was the only way he could make the tiny bunk accommodate his huge frame. Seething rage emanated almost as a dark cloud from the cramped confines of his chamber.

"Jackie, it's real fine company you're keepin' these days," drawled Joe.

He grunted and sat up. "Got any tobacco?"

Joe pulled a small pouch from his bib pocket and tossed it into the cell. Prentiss sniffed the contents suspiciously. "Is this that homegrown hogweed of yours or whatever it is you call tobacco?"

"Secret's in the curin', Jackie."

Prentiss grunted again and shoved the pouch into a trouser pocket.

"Just don't let the mean little boys take it away from you," chided Joe.

"Very funny!" he arose and came over to the bars. "Well, I can't say you didn't warn me. So what they got on me?"

"An eyewitness."

"Who?"

"Billy Larkin." There was a noisy yelp from across the aisle. "Did you hear somethin', Jackie?" asked Joe. "Sounded a little like a pig in a slaughterhouse."

"No, it was more like a weasel gettin' its nuts cut off." The yelp trailed off into a tremulous, high pitched whimpering.

"Yep, Jackie," continued Joe, "ole Billy has pointed his finger right at you. 'Course, I don't think he really wanted to do it. He had to be encouraged a little, if you know what I mean. They way I got it figured, that's where Floyd over there comes in."

There was a yelp from the cell adjoining Billy's. Prentiss shifted his gaze to the other moonshiner. "You mean he's in on the frame, too?"

"In a way, Jackie; in a way. I expect Faulkner's done got a statement from Floyd that could hang the killin' on Billy. So you see, Jackie, Billy had to point the finger at you to protect hisself. Ain't that right, Floyd?"

"No! It's a lie! I swear it's a lie!"

"So you see, Jackie, in a way, Floyd there is the key to the whole thing." Joe smiled sweetly at the cringing moonshiner.

"My God, Joe!" wailed Floyd. "What are you tryin' to do to me?"

"Why, this is called gettin' it all out in the open, Floyd. They say it's supposed to be good for the soul. Don't you think it's good for the soul, Floyd?"

"Jesus Christ!" he hissed.

"Why, if a man goes and does somethin' foolish, Floyd, he oughta own up to it like a man, ain't that right?" He turned back to Prentiss. "Now Jackie here is a real smart fellow. He'd never do anything foolish. Would you, Jackie?"

"I've never done anything foolish in my life," he replied deadpan. "Except kill a man once."

There was a chorus of bleating from across the aisle. Joe smiled at them pleasantly. "Now don't you see? We all learn from our mistakes and Jackie ain't no different. You boys don't have a thing in the world to worry about."

The whining and jabbering indicated this latter remark was not altogether convincing. Joe turned back to Prentiss and became deadly serious.

"Jackie, I ain't gonna tell you what to do; I ain't even gonna suggest anything. Whether you stay and face the music or try to break out of this sorry excuse for a jail is entirely up to you. I'll only say this. Faulkner's put this frame together pretty tight, a lot tighter than any of us figured he could. I'm tryin' to unravel it, but I'll tell you the truth. It don't look too promisin'."

Prentiss didn't say anything for a long time. "Well, you don't candy coat it none," he replied at last.

"You wouldn't want it that way, Jackie."

"No," he agreed.

"I can promise you one thing, Jackie. No matter what happens, I won't let go of this thing. Even if it takes years, I aim to find who killed Larkin. But if you squash either of those two bugs, it won't do you a bit of good."

"I'll keep it in mind."

"Well, I'll be goin' now, Jackie. Keep your chin up."

"Right."

"And don't take no wooden nickels."

"Sure," he agreed sourly."

"Keep a stiff upper lip."

"Get the hell out of here!"

He started to turn away. "Joe?" called Prentiss. He turned back. "You got any matches on you?"

Joe tossed him a small box. "Better to light one candle than curse the darkness," he advised.

"Jesus!" exclaimed Prentiss.

Joe turned to Billy and Floyd who were cringing and moaning in their respective cells, neither of them able to take their eyes off the very big and very mean man across the aisle from them. "You boys have you a real nice day now, hear?"

He hobbled away, but there was little prospect that either Billy or Floyd would have a nice day for quite some time to come. When Joe reached the outer door he began pounding on it noisily.

"Oh, Mister Jailor, won't you let me out of here, pretty please? I'll be good! I promise!"

There was a chorus of guffaws up and down the cellblock, but when Chief Jailor Hanley opened the door he did not appear to be very amused. Indeed, Hanley looked as though he had never at any time in his life been amused.

"Should have left you in there," he grumbled.

"Oh, now you wouldn't want to do somethin' like that, Walter. 'Cause when I finally got out you'd just have to leave the state, that's all."

Hanley gave him a sour look.

"A piece of advice, Hanley. Don't let Prentiss get too close to Neely or Larkin. If you do, somebody's apt to be scrapin' blood and brains off the walls."

Hanley stiffened. "What did you say in there?"

216

"I let all the kitties out of the bag, Walter. You might tell your boss about that first chance you get."

"Jesus Christ. He's gonna have my hide for lettin' you in there!"

Joe shrugged. "Better that he has your hide than Saunders." He hobbled away toward the stairs.

When in doubt, punt, they said in football. Well, he had punted and now quite a few of Faulkner's dirty little secrets were bouncing around for all to see. There would be a mad scramble, but there was no way to foresee who might come up with what. Faulkner was going to have some unpleasant moments, particularly when Saunders confronted him with Joe's charges. But there was little pleasure in it for Joe. He was still no closer to catching the real killer. Plus, there was the added frustration of having lost control of it all.

He checked his watch. Fifty minutes until the train departed for Greenwood. It was time to get the hell out of this benighted town. Where had Jimmy gotten the whiskey to get drunk last night? he wondered. He would have to check his stock when he got home.

CHAPTER EIGHT
Monday, August 3

Joe tapped on the front door and then fidgeted with his cane while awaiting the inevitable response from inside. Behind and to his right stood Martin with a faintly worried expression as he wondered how much trouble he was going to be in for this unauthorized trip back to Burnham. Yet Joe had somehow gotten a message to him Sunday afternoon to be at his cabin bright and early Monday morning. In the note tacked to his front door, the word important had been underscored several times. Such emphasis from Joe could not be disregarded. Therefore, Martin had put his job on the line by taking the county's car and coming to Burnham this morning.

To Joe's left was Reverend Watson whose expression was of almost equal parts annoyance and curiosity. He knew just as little about this as Martin, and Watson was a man used to being in control of any situation. He had barely finished his first cup of coffee that morning when the car pulled up and Joe ordered, Ordered! him to get in. Someone badly needed help was all he had been told. He only had to time to grab his Bible and his hat. Yet these tools were all that he required to wage mortal combat against Satan, the hat being optional.

At last a tired, haggard woman with lusterless eyes came to the door. Despite an overwhelming emotional lethargy, she was struck by the realization that these three solemn men were an odd combination. Not Joe and Charlie, of course. The neighborhood was by now well accustomed to seeing them gadding about.

But Reverend Watson was definitely out of place here. Somewhere in the back of the woman's mind a tiny alarm bell began to clatter. In the front yard a small army of noisy song birds chattered raucously with early morning enthusiasm, but they seemed to have a monopoly on cheerfulness

"Good morning, Reverend Watson; gentlemen," she mumbled.

Joe nodded a greeting. "Mrs. Carter, we need to see John."

"We're still under quarantine," she reminded.

"Yes, maam. I think that's fixin' to change."

"John's sleepin' now."

"Then we'll have to wake him up."

The tiny alarm became a klaxon. Yet it was as plain as the solemn expressions on their faces that there would be no deterring these men on their sacred/legal mission. With a resigned shrug, she stepped aside to allow them entry. Joe paused to deposit his ridiculous straw hat on the coatrack just inside the door. The other headgear quickly followed. Joe turned to Reverend Watson.

"Preacher, I'd like for you to go into the parlor with Mrs. Carter. Me and Charlie need to talk to John alone. I expect he'll need to see you afterwards."

"Very well," replied Watson with barely concealed annoyance.

Joe tapped on the bedroom door, but then went on in without waiting for an invitation. John sat up and stared at them with sleepy eyes. Joe signaled for Martin to take the only chair. Then using his cane like a blind man, he tapped his way across the darkened room to the window. He raised the thick shade, allowing in a brilliant flood of morning sunlight.

"That hurts my eyes!" complained John while clapping both hands to his face.

"I expect," admitted Joe, "but I think we've all had enough darkness to last us a spell."

He came over and stood at the foot of the bed and stared down at the morose and sickly patient. In proper light, he could

219

now tell that John had lost a good twenty pounds and he had been skinny to start with. The man was simply shriveling up and dying. Joe was now going to either cure or kill him.

"You killed Tom Larkin."

It was not a question or even an accusation. It was a simple statement of fact with absolutely no inflection in the voice. Martin sat up sharply. He started to speak, but Joe waved him to silence. Both men turned to face Carter who now sat with mouth open and lips trembling, his ashen face somehow even pastier than before. Dead eyes had suddenly come imploringly to life. Joe eased himself onto the bed beside the sickened man.

"I, I…."

He couldn't finish. John Carter buried his face in his hands and wept noisily. Joe sighed, toyed with his cane and waited patiently for the flood of tears to run its course. It took nearly thirty minutes. Once, Reverend Watson stuck his head inside to investigate the racket, but Joe waved imperiously for him to leave. At long last the choking and gurgling began to taper off, some of the unbearable weight having been removed from a deeply troubled conscience.

"I, I never killed anybody before!" he blubbered.

That much was already obvious.

"Do you want to tell me how it happened?" pressed Joe gently.

Carter's mouth opened, but no words came out.

"Maybe it would be easier if I sketched it out, then you can fill in the gaps," suggested Joe. "I don't think there will be many."

Martin gazed at Joe with wonder. Carter merely nodded weakly.

"You came in from the field for some reason," began Joe. "It was a little past three. You found out Billy had been there and had just left. You got your shotgun and followed him. You meant to kill him. Or maybe you didn't. Most likely you didn't really know what you meant to do.

"But you didn't find Billy," continued Joe. "That's because he cut around and slipped into the house from the opposite side so his pa wouldn't see him. But you come straight on and found Tom workin' on his fence. You talked, then you argued. No, knowin' Tom, maybe you skipped the talkin' part and went straight to the arguin' stage."

Carter's lips wrinkled in an aborted smile. "He denied Billy was there."

"Sure. Tom was a proudful man. He didn't think Billy would dare come sneakin' back after bein' throwed off the place. I expect Tom called you a liar and a few more things besides."

Carter nodded confirmation.

"But you didn't kill him for that. Instead, you tried to leave."

"I, I realized it was a mistake to go there. I didn't want to kill anyone, not even Billy. I just wanted to go home and, and…."

"Pray?"

Carter nodded again. "Wantin' to do a sin is just as bad as really doin' it."

But turning away, giving up so easily had been the critical mistake. Such a show of weakness was almost guaranteed to incite Larkin to a frenzy of contempt and rage. It was like waving a red flag in front of an Andalusian fighting bull.

"Larkin wouldn't drop it," resumed Joe. "He followed you, likely cussin' ever' step of the way." That explained Larkin being drawn away from the fence. "At some point he said somethin', I think I can guess what, and you turned around again."

Joe paused a moment. "That's when you killed him."

Carter started to speak, stopped abruptly and then dropped his face into his hands, nodding between the stifled sobs.

"I don't understand any of this!" complained Martin. "Why would you want to kill Billy, Mister Carter?"

"Charley needs to know, John," urged Joe. "But we'll keep that part out of the official records."

"You, you know?" stammered Carter. Joe nodded. Carter shrugged helplessly. "I can't stop you from tellin' whoever you like."

Joe put a hand on the man's shoulder. "John, it goes no further."

Well, not much further, he silently added. Carter ignored the sympathetic gesture and stared down at the wrinkled sheets. Joe turned to Martin.

"John's daughter, Sally, is carryin' Billy's child."

Carter looked up suddenly. "He got her drunk!" he exclaimed, wanting the full story known. Sally deserved that much. "He got her drunk and, and…."

"All right, John," interrupted Joe. "We can guess the rest." He turned back to Martin. "That's the real reason Sally was sent to her aunt in Oklahoma."

He paused a moment. "John, let me ask you one more thing on this matter. When Billy came by that day, he tried to get Elaine to go with him, didn't he?"

Carter nodded weakly. "She had sense enough not to go after what happened with Sally."

A good thing, thought Joe, or more bodies might have turned up in Burnham that afternoon. "I want to know more about the argument, John. What did you two say to each other? I want exact words if you can recall 'em." This would be of critical importance in distinguishing between manslaughter and self-defense.

"He said that Billy wasn't there and that I was a liar."

"I know that part. What else?"

"He wanted to know why I was lookin' for Billy." The face went into the hands again. "Like a fool, I told him! Oh God, I never should have told him! I, I was so mad I didn't know what I was sayin'!"

"What did Tom say then?" prompted Joe.

"He laughed!" John looked up again. "He stood there and just laughed in my face!"

"You've got great forbearance, John," replied Joe. "Most men would have killed him right then. What else did he say?"

"He told me the child, he called it a brat, couldn't inherit no Larkin property 'cause it was a bastard. Anyway, Billy had been disowned. He said I was wastin' my time tryin' to gouge him. I didn't pay no mind to that 'cause I didn't want none of his property noway. Most of it's been got by foul means; whiskey, stealin'. The man had a black heart and a blacker soul."

"Nobody would ever dispute that, John. What happened then?"

"I started to leave. I was sick at heart for tellin' off on Sally. I, I just wanted to get away from there, away from that evil man."

"John, what did he say to make you turn on him again?" asked Joe quietly.

Carter dropped his eyes again. "He called Sally a whore," he answered almost in a whisper. He choked back a sob. "She ain't no whore, Joe! My little girl ain't no whore!"

"I know she's not, John. What happened when you turned around?" But he already knew. Larkin died.

"He, he stopped followin' just for a second," mumbled John, trying to recall again that terrible moment. "He was still carryin' that axe of his. I, I guess he thought I was goin' to shoot him 'cause he raised it back over his shoulder and come runnin' at me."

223

Carter suddenly reached up and grabbed Joe by the shoulders. "I wasn't goin' to shoot him, Joe! I swear to God I wasn't! But, but…."

"But when he attacked, you had no choice."

Carter released Joe's shoulders and flopped back onto the bed. "I didn't know what I was doin'!" he moaned. "Somethin' just come over me. It was like the gun had a mind of its own. The next thing I knowed, Tom was layin' there dead."

He covered his face again and shuddered. "Ever' time I go to sleep I see it all again; Tom layin' there and, and all that blood." He began sobbing again.

Joe waited a moment before continuing. "You turned him over?"

Carter nodded. That explained Tom's neat position on his back.

"Then you went home. Did you tell your wife?"

"She guessed when they found the body. I told her ever'thing then." He looked up in alarm "Will she have to go to jail, too? Oh God, who'll take care of our other younguns?"

"No, John, she won't have to go to jail," reassured Joe.

Carter sighed his thanks. "Maybe I oughta just shoot myself and put an end to this whole nasty business."

"No!" The exclamation was so sharp that both Carter and Martin jumped.

"You'll do no such thing, John! It wouldn't help Sally at all; it'd just make things worse. She's feelin' bad enough as it is. How do you think she'd take it if her daddy just up and killed hisself?"

"I, I never thought of that."

"John, there's still a chance, a small chance, of settlin' this without a lot of fuss. But I've got to have you alive to do it. The sheriff's tryin' to railroad an innocent man, John, and I can't let that happen; I just can't. And you can't either, John. In your heart, you know you can't let an innocent man be convicted for somethin' you did."

He nodded weakly. "What do I have to do, Joe?"

"We have to have a confession, John, and it has to be on paper."

Carter looked up uncertainly.

"Charlie is gonna write it all up. Now, he's real good at this kind of thing, John. He's even been to college. It's gonna tell how you killed Tom and about him takin' after you with his axe. It was self-defense, John, and that's what the statement's gonna say.

"But we're gonna leave out why you went lookin' for Billy, just that you did. It will say you wasn't lookin' for Tom at all. Then you'll have to sign it, John. Me, Charlie and Reverend Watson will also sign as witnesses."

"Do I have to, Joe?"

He nodded. "We really need it, John, else I wouldn't ask this of you."

"All right, Joe," he sighed. "I'll sign it."

Joe arose from the bed. "Charlie, did you bring pen and paper like I asked?"

"Got it right here."

"Call me when you get it done."

He started to leave, but Martin called to him. "Joe?" He turned back. "Just tell me one thing. How did you figure out it was Mister Carter?"

"A guess, but not a very wild one. I got curious about Sally not writin' to Jimmy. It didn't figure. I didn't think it could be over that easy. They had been too close. So I wrote to an old army buddy who lives near Sallisaw and asked him to nose around. Got his answer in the mail on Saturday. Spent all night puttin' two and two together 'til I finally come up with four."

JON R. JOHNSON

Martin smiled faintly. "I suppose you realize this is going to ruin Sheriff Faulkner's whole day."

"Oh, I think it's gonna ruin a heck of a lot more than his day, Charlie." He closed the door behind him.

Mrs. Carter was on the sofa and Reverend Watson had pulled up a chair so he could face her directly. The woman's tear streaked face was mute testimony that she had been crying. Watson was holding her hands in his and both had their eyes tightly closed as he quietly recited an impassioned prayer. Joe paused respectfully in the doorway until an emphatic amen sounded. He then hobbled into the room.

"Are you gonna arrest him?" asked the woman meekly.

"Not for the moment, Mrs. Carter. Anyway, he's too sick to take anywhere." He glanced at Watson. "She told you?" He nodded. "I don't think any of this should go any farther, Preacher," he suggested.

"What Mrs. Carter told me is strictly confidential!" flared Watson, angry that his discretion should be questioned. "I will not repeat it to you nor will I testify in court!"

"That's good, Preacher, that's good," soothed Joe. He hobbled to the wall and took down the shotgun from its pegs. "Mrs. Carter, I'll need to keep this for the time bein'. You'll get it back when all this is settled."

"You, you may keep it. I don't think I want it in the house anymore. I been thinkin' of just throwin' it out."

Joe nodded understanding. "Maam, are there any other guns in the house? I seem to recall John havin' a little .32 revolver."

"It won't shoot," she informed. "Somethin's broke inside it. It hasn't worked in years."

"Would you get it for me anyway, please?"

She arose and went into another room. Watson looked at Joe with curiosity. "Why do you want a broken gun? John certainly didn't carry it that day."

226

"Broken guns can be fixed. I just don't want John to be able to get his hands on any kind of weapon."

"You, you don't think...."

"I just don't want to take any chances."

Mrs. Carter returned with the revolver and Joe slipped it into a pocket. "Preacher, I'd appreciate it if you'd stay here the rest of the day or at least 'til I get back from Fort Smith. That may not be 'til tonight sometime."

"Well...." He stopped. "Of course," he agreed.

Watson had a regular job at the Franklin Mine. Few congregations were large enough to support a full-time minister and Burnham certainly did not rank among that elite category. This would mean missing a whole day of work and the consequent awkward explanation to his boss. But the Carters desperately needed his help on this trying day. Priorities were priorities.

"I'll speak to Mister Wellman," volunteered Joe. "I'm sure he will understand." A prominent member of the community with a secret mistress could be very understanding indeed.

Joe turned back to Mrs. Carter. "John has lost a great deal of weight," he remarked.

"He can't keep anything down."

"Well, you may have better luck now. Start with somethin' easy on the belly, some chicken soup maybe. Then some soft vegetables, no seasonin' of any kind. By tonight I want him able to take a proper meal, but don't let him overdo it."

"I'll try."

Martin called from the bedroom. "Excuse me," said Joe before hurrying away.

He squinted down at the document, a terse, one page account in Martin's small, neat handwriting. "This is real good, Charlie," he complimented. "It says what needs to be said and leaves out what ain't nobody's business." He scribbled his own name in the proper place and handed it back. "Go have Watson sign it and make sure he puts down his title, too. A preacher's John Hancock will add a little punch, don't you think?"

He turned to Carter. "John, Reverend Watson is gonna want to talk to you and likely do a whole heap of prayin', too. He knows ever'thing, John, but you don't have to worry on that account. The Devil hisself couldn't pry a peep out of him.

"And John," continued Joe, "you just got to eat somethin'. Don't force it. Take as much time as you need, but get some vittles in you and make sure they stay down."

Joe paused a moment. "John, I don't want to raise false hopes, but there's still a chance this could all work out a whole lot better than you expect. I should know one way or another by tonight." He reached down and shook the frail, bony hand.

He nodded to Watson on the way out, pausing only long enough to retrieve the shotgun. Once on the porch, he casually pulled down the quarantine sign. Martin looked at him questioningly.

"A guilty conscious ain't contagious," explained Joe. Then he muttered, "But there's times I think maybe it ought to be."

He turned and gazed out across the highway at Washburn Mountain looming mute and majestic in the August morning sunlight. The scrub timber was already turning brown, the foliage thinning and shriveling from the summer heat. It was somewhat like a giant reptile shedding its skin, as though the mountain itself were a living thing; slow, ponderous and utterly disinterested in human doings. Martin followed his gaze.

"What is it?" asked Charlie.

"Just thinkin'." He looked at Martin and smiled. "You know, if mountains could talk, I expect they could tell some stories."

"I suppose."

Joe looked away again. "Just think what that mountain has seen. Giant lizards, saber toothed tigers, things only winos see today after too much muscatel. All of 'em livin' breedin', fightin' and dyin', not knowin' nothin' about humankind or carin'. Maybe ever' million years or so a flood comes along and washes ever'thing away and it all has to start over from scratch."

"You think the world is that old?" asked Martin

Joe stared quietly a moment and then nodded. "Somethin' like that mountain just has to be that old."

Martin smiled without answering.

"Indians," spoke Joe.

"Pardon?"

"Then came the Indians. A long time before us white folks. They hunted and fished, had younguns and killed other Indians that talked different. I reckon their affairs were about as crazy as ours."

Martin shrugged. "All people are basically alike."

Joe nodded. "People are just like that mountain there. They hide most ever'thing. All you see is the surface. You can never really know what's deep down inside."

"You managed to see inside John Carter fairly well."

Joe smiled thinly. "Did I?" He shook his head. "Only a little, Charlie. We only saw a little of what's in there." He sighed loudly. "Maybe it's better that way. Maybe what's inside all of us is so black and rotten we couldn't stand to look at it."

"You don't really believe that."

"I don't know what I believe, Charlie. Sometimes it seems there's a hell of a lot more cussedness in this world than goodness. And even what goodness there is sometimes seems a bit out of plumb."

Joe took his eyes from the mountain and turned to face Martin again. "I do know one thing. John Carter is about as decent a man as you're ever likely to run across. He kills someone like Larkin in self-defense and his conscious almost kills him over it. Larkin killed two men I know of and I don't expect he ever lost a minute's sleep over it. Somethin's wrong with that, Charlie."

"I don't have the answer, Joe." He stepped off the porch to crank up the Ford.

"The answer's inside the mountain," muttered Joe. He hobbled down the steps and got into the car. As Martin piled in beside him, Joe said, "I want to see Laura before we leave. We'll need those first two statements you took."

Martin looked at him questioningly. "What do you think is going to happen, Joe?"

He smiled faintly. "A small earthquake. But it may be enough to crack open a mountain or two."

*****

Again, Wayne Saunders's secretary brought out the regulation smile as she gazed up from her desk at the two lawmen. "Do you have an appointment, or dare I ask?"

"No appointment," confirmed Joe.

"I will inform him of the potential riot," she replied caustically while arising from her desk.

"No riot today," corrected Joe. She hesitated with the unspoken question in her eyes. "An earthquake this time, and it's really gonna happen."

The bafflement showed on her face as she stepped to the inner door to announce the visitors. The muffled permission to enter came almost immediately.

Saunders leaned back leisurely in his chair and surveyed the two lawmen. After Joe had been thoroughly inspected, it was Martin's turn.

"Well, Deputy," he drawled at last, "I am pleased to find you dressed in a suitable shirt on this occasion." Martin shifted uncomfortably.

"Constable Potts, have you any progress to report? I presume this concerns the Larkin case."

"Yes, sir, it's about all wrapped up. Deputy Martin broke the whole thing wide open just this mornin'."

"What?" yelped Martin. Joe elbowed him in the ribs.

"Indeed!" The prosecutor's piercing blue eyes fastened on the deputy.

"Charlie, why don't you show Mister Saunders those first two statements you took last week?"

Martin handed over the two statements from Mrs. Larkin and Wanda Neely. Saunders placed the two documents side by side on his desk, laced his fingers under his chin and devoted all his attention to the words. He looked up after a time that seemed wholly insufficient to have read them.

"Very interesting. I assumed you had some such documents, but they say little more than what you told me at our last meeting, Potts. By themselves, they are of little significance."

"I realize that, sir. Charlie, show him the statement you took this mornin'."

This document took the prosecutor much longer than the first two. That was because he read it from beginning to end four times. At last, he sighed and looked up, his cold blue eyes revealing only the faintest sign of fire.

"Well, this certainly casts a different light on things. I presume, Deputy Martin, that you have this John Carter in custody."

"Uh, no, sir," he stammered.

Saunders raised ominous eyebrows. "Why not?"

Martin glanced nervously toward Joe for assistance, but discovered for once that he was completely on his own. "He's very sick, sir. He's been bedridden since the day Larkin died."

"You hesitate to call it murder?"

"Yes, sir. I believe he killed Larkin in self-defense."

Saunders shifted his eyes to Joe. "There seems little need to ask, but I suppose, Constable Potts, that you concur in this opinion?"

"Yes, sir. In fact, we have the axe Larkin carried that day. Some of the shot went all the way through him and spattered the blade with blood. The only way that could have happened was if he had it drawed back to use as a weapon."

"I see, I see," muttered Saunders. He glanced back down at the statement. "The one thing that is still unclear to me is the reason Carter went in search of young Larkin in the first place. Is this to remain a deep, dark mystery, Deputy Martin?"

"It's, uh, a delicate matter, sir."

The blue eyes stabbed again. "Humor me!" he snapped. Then he added sarcastically, "You will find, Deputy, that I am just dripping with delicacy."

Charley glanced nervously at Joe who nodded slightly. "Billy seduced Carter's oldest daughter and then attempted to seduce the younger one right in his own home." He paused a moment. "The older daughter is pregnant, sir."

"I see." Saunders smiled crookedly. "Then it is entirely possible that Mister Carter had nothing more in mind than a shotgun wedding." This was probably as close as he would ever come to making a joke.

The prosecutor drummed his fingers on his desk. "Ironic, isn't it? Larkin despised his son, yet he died because of him." He scribbled something on a piece of paper.

"Clearly," he continued, "we no longer have any case against Mister Prentiss. Here is authorization to release both him and young Larkin. Deputy, attend to it, please. Potts, you stay here. I'm not finished with you yet."

"Charlie, wait a minute!" called Joe. The deputy paused at the door as Joe turned back to Saunders. "If I might suggest, sir, only Billy should be released right now. Prentiss should be held at least an extra hour. We've just solved one killin'. We don't want another on our hands. Billy ought to have a head start in case Prentiss ain't in a forgivin' mood."

"Good thinking," confirmed Saunders. "Deputy, just release Larkin for right now."

"And Charlie," added Joe, "hold him downstairs. I want a word with him before he gets gone from here."

Martin nodded and stepped out the door.

"Now," demanded Saunders, "what's all this hogwash about that deputy breaking this case?"

"It will look good on his record, sir. Anyway, he had about as much to do with clearin' this up as anybody. And he put his job on the line to buck Faulkner."

"Yes, Faulkner's little scheme is still a loose end, isn't it? Call in my secretary." Joe did so. She soon appeared, regulation smile and all. Saunders handed her a scribbled note. "Type that up immediately."

Taking the note, she started for the door, glanced down at the paper and froze in her tracks. "Sir?" she asked, turning back.

"You are not seeing things," he assured her. "Sheriff Faulkner is retiring for reasons of health." She went out. "He will retire or he will have no health," muttered the prosecutor under his breath.

"What about John Carter, sir?" asked Joe.

"There will have to be a hearing, of course." He sighed. "As you and the deputy have pointed out, this seems a reasonably clear case of self-defense. Anything you can do to make it even clearer will be greatly appreciated. I presume there will be no shortage of character witnesses regarding both Carter and Larkin?"

"No shortage at all, sir," assured Joe.

"I prefer not to even have a trial. It could prove difficult to keep our former sheriff's little conspiracy out of it. Therefore, I anticipate a hearing that will be a mere formality. Is that what you were hoping to hear, Potts?"

"Yes, sir," he answered honestly. "Sir, what about Mister Carter's oldest daughter?"

Saunders shook his head slightly. "There is no need to mention that matter again. The two men argued and that is all that is necessary for the public record."

Saunders took out a bottle of Napoleon brandy and filled two snifters. "I owe you, Potts. I took your advice and covered my ass on this one. But had it blown up in Faulkner's face, a lot of manure would still have landed on me."

Joe accepted the glass. "You don't owe me anything, sir. I owed you. Now we're even."

"You owed me?"

"Yes, sir. You let me take the Neely kids and put 'em in a decent home."

Saunders toyed with his glass. "I know you're a world class snoop, Potts. How much do you know about me?"

"Not much," he admitted. "I know you come from Tennessee, and one of the reasons you left was because you're family is not, ah, what might be called socially prominent." He paused. "That's why I thought you might be agreeable to movin' those younguns."

Saunders smiled bitterly. "If you know that much, then you also know that Saunders is not my real name."

"Yes, sir."

"May I ask what you intend to do with this information?"

"Nothing."

"Nothing?"

"No, sir, nothing at all. A man can't help what his kinfolk might be. If he thinks he can do better for hisself by startin' fresh, then he ought to have the chance. I'd never hold somethin' like that over a man's head."

Saunders refilled their snifters.

"Any thoughts on Faulkner's successor, sir?" Joe suddenly asked.

Saunders was startled by the shift in conversation. "We have an under-sheriff."

"Another Willie Don only not quite as smart."

Saunders smiled thinly. "You have a nominee?"

"Yes, sir. Charlie Martin would make a dandy sheriff."

Saunders shook his head doubtfully. "He has little experience."

"Experience comes with time," countered Joe. "Character is either somethin' you have or don't have."

"Character plays a surprisingly small role in politics."

"Then maybe it's time to give it a chance." Joe paused. "Sir, suppose for a minute, just suppose there hadn't been someone like you keepin' Faulkner in line the last few years. What do you think this county would have been like?"

Saunders shuddered visibly. "I hate to even think about it."

"Mister Saunders, you'll be goin' to Little Rock after the next election. Wouldn't it be nice to have your home front covered by somebody who ain't gonna be a constant embarrassment by runnin' cons and framin' people? Wouldn't you breathe a little easier in your new job if there was somebody back here runnin' the county's police business the way it's supposed to be run?"

Saunders took a delicate sip, the proper kind of sip for expensive French brandy. "Your point is well taken. I will speak to the appropriate people concerning Faulkner's replacement." He glanced at Joe and raised a questioning eyebrow. "I presume you will always be available to him for consultation."

"I'm willin' to help him out any way I can."

"Very well, but you are to inform young Martin that torn shirts are not acceptable attire for our new sheriff."

"I'll be sure to tell him, sir."

The secretary returned with Faulkner's typewritten resignation. Saunders carefully inspected the document. He then shoved it into a coat pocket and stood up.

"Prentiss is your friend, is he not?"

"We grew up together."

"I am going down the hall and settle Faulkner's hash for good. Would you care to come along?"

"Wouldn't miss it for the world, sir."

Saunders gathered up all of Martin's documents and departed so quickly that Joe was left choking on his brandy. He still hadn't caught up when the prosecutor barged into the sheriff's office without pausing for the nicety of knocking or announcing himself. Another drunken poker game was in session with the same contestants as during Joe's last visit.

He noted sardonically that Willie Don had a new window glass. Too bad. It would soon have to be replaced yet again.

"Will you gentlemen please excuse us?" intoned Saunders in a voice that made it abundantly clear that this was more than just a polite request. "I have business to discuss with the sheriff."

Joe arrived just in time to get trampled by the stampede out of Faulkner's office. In the wake of the mad rush, at least a half a dozen aces were scattered across the floor along with a disproportionate number of other honor cards. There had to have been some interesting games conducted there, thought Joe.

Faulkner shifted the cheap cigar from one side of his mouth to the other as though this had some sinister significance. "What's this all about, Saunders?" he demanded with more belligerence than he actually felt.

Saunders proceeded to read aloud the statements from Mrs. Larkin and Wanda Neely. He did this rather than let Faulkner read them himself for he did not intend to allow the sheriff to get his hands on the documents even for a second. Faulkner tried to protest several times, but Saunders ignored him and kept on reading until he reached the end. Faulkner, seeing his interruptions ignored, fell silent until the prosecutor finished and put the two documents back into his pocket.

"Them's damned lies!" growled Faulkner when he finally had a chance to speak.

Saunders also ignored this remark and proceeded to read John Carter's confession. The bluster immediately vanished from the sheriff. His mouth flopped open and the cheap stogie dropped to the floor. When he finished, Saunders calmly placed this document back into his pocket with the other two.

"Pick up that cigar before it burns a hole in the rug!" was the first thing he said. Faulkner finally made his trembling fingers accomplish the task.

"Sheriff Faulkner, I believe it was last Thursday that I specifically asked if you were attempting to frame Mister Prentiss. You assured me that you were not."

"I, I can explain, sir."

Saunders shook his head. "No, you may not explain. What you will do is sign this." He slapped the resignation on the sheriff's desk.

Faulkner's eyes almost popped out when he saw what it was. "I, I can't sign this!" he protested.

"You will sign it, Faulkner, or you will be inside Tucker State Prison before the month is out. And considering the usual fate of lawmen who are imprisoned, you will very likely be in your grave shortly thereafter."

"Please, sir!" he squeaked. "You gotta give me another chance!"

"You lied to me, Faulkner. You lied to me and you tried to use me. No man uses me, Faulkner. In another age, we would settle this down by the river with dueling pistols. At the moment, I sincerely regret that civilization has progressed beyond that point because, quite frankly, the prospect appeals to me."

A puppy dog whine escaped from Willie Don's throat.

"If that document is not signed within thirty seconds, I will return to my office and begin criminal proceedings against you."

Faulkner fumbled wildly for a pen. Saunders retrieved the signed document, inspected it closely and then placed it in the same bulging pocket containing the statements.

Even Joe was astonished by what happened next. But he was not nearly as surprised as the former sheriff. Willie Don's eyes almost popped out and he probably ruined a perfectly good pair of Fruit-of-the-Looms. Saunders snatched him by the lapels of his white suit and dragged him halfway across the desk, scattering poker chips and playing cards. Faulkner twitched a couple of times, but there was no shaking that vice-like grip.

"Not one word about any of this, Faulkner," intoned Saunders threateningly. "Not now, not ever. I will not have your clumsy frame coming back to haunt me. There is one thing you better understand. I may wear a suit now, but I come from hill people and I have learned how to use a knife to kill a man a little at a time. So don't piss on my parade or you will be dead, fat man Willie."

Still holding Faulkner with one hand, Saunders reached out with the other and snatched off the badge of office, leaving an ugly, gaping hole in the beautiful white coat. Then with just one hand, he literally threw Willie Don back across the desk, tumbling him onto the floor in a mushy pile.

"Gather your personal effects!"

Faulkner looked around wildly for a box to pack his things, could not find one and so began cramming items into his pockets. Then he started to open the bottom left drawer where he kept his precious Scotch supply.

"No!" barked Saunders. "That liquor is contraband. You will leave it here." He turned to Joe. "Constable Potts, will you be so good as to dispose of it for me?"

"Be glad to, sir." He gave Faulkner a wink.

"Do you have everything, Faulkner?" demanded Saunders impatiently.

"I, I think so, sir."

"Then waddle your fat ass out of my courthouse!"

Willie Don waddled in record time.

Saunders watched him go. He then turned and flipped the badge to Joe. There was still a strip of Willie Don's white coat on it. "Give that to Deputy Martin and inform him he is to be in this office at eight o'clock sharp in the morning. There will be some papers to be signed and he will have to be sworn in."

Joe looked at him questioningly. "Will there be any problems with his appointment, sir?"

Saunders smiled acidly. "I know where every body in this county is buried, Potts. That is why certain people always try to be nice to me. Why, you'd be astonished now nice some people try to be."

"No, sir," corrected Joe." I don't think I'd be astonished at all."

Saunders turned and walked out of the office.

Joe examined the heavy badge, shiny and un-battered. It had not seen hard use but had been used hard. He laid it against his chest alongside the beaten and tarnished constable star. He chuckled lightly and slipped the badge into a pocket.

Seating himself behind the desk, he swept off the remains of the poker game and sniffed the contents of the large jug. Pushing it aside, he reached into the lower left desk and inspected the 'contraband' to be destroyed. There were six bottles of Scotch, each one a different brand. All but one, a fifth of Johnny Walker, had been opened. The situation seemed to call for virginal whiskey, so he took out the Johnny Walker and broke the seal. After filling a large tumbler, he picked up the telephone set from the floor and placed it on the desk before him.

"Hello, operator, would you get me the Goldman Hotel, please?"

There followed a brief wait.

"Hello, Goldman Hotel? Is Willis Cox still checked in there? He is? Would you call him to the telephone, please?"

Half the tumbler was emptied while he waited.

"Hello, Willis? Joe Potts here. I was hopin' you was still in town. You got your checkbook with you?"

There was a pause while Cox spoke.

"That's right, Willis. The Larkin case is now solved. Or it will be once a hearin' can be scheduled. It was self-defense. There won't even be a trial. What? A man named John Carter."

Cox spoke again.

"Just a silly quarrel, Willis. I won't tell you what it was about except to say it didn't concern you boys in any way at all."

There was another long pause.

"That's right; I still want it to go to the preacher man. Oh, Willis, one more thing. We're gonna have us a new sheriff startin' tomorrow mornin'. Willie Don Faulkner just resigned for reasons of health.

"What's that, Willis? Yes, I expect you would like to know the details. Sorry, you'll just have to wonder about it. By the way, there's a couple of things you might like to know about the new man. He can't be bought and he can't be scared.

"What? No, this ain't a warnin' to get out of town by sundown. But come to think of it, Willis, that might not be bad advice. And Willis, next you're gonna be down Burnham way, give me a little notice. I'll fix you a nice big chicken dinner."

He broke the connection.

Joe came down the courthouse steps carrying a sack of clinking bottles. Martin was waiting for him on the first floor with Billy in tow. The younger Larkin was a frail man in his early twenties with a thick black shock of dirty, unkempt hair. His build, his face, his very manner bespoke weakness of both body and character. It was little wonder his father had despised him so. In a properly foul mood, Tom might even have killed him. How much grief would have been prevented had he done so? Joe wondered. But how much more grief might have been caused? Who was to say?

Billy stood fidgeting and looking about nervously for he had learned the horrible truth that Jackie Prentiss was to be released rather than executed. As he looked into the terrified face, Joe almost felt sorry for him. He quickly and brutally crushed that perverse emotion. Billy had already ruined several lives and would do so again if given the opportunity. Such people never felt any remorse, only terror of consequences. The greatest of all evils was to pity such a creature. It was like defending a killer disease.

"A fine mess you've got yourself in, Billy," remarked Joe solemnly.

"I want to see Sheriff Faulkner!"

"Sorry, Billy. He ain't the sheriff no more. He just resigned."

Martin raised his eyebrows at this.

"My God!" hissed Billy. "What am I gonna do?"

"Go somewhere far away," suggested Joe.

"He shook his head. "I can't! I'm startin' to get a good operation goin' over in Moffett."

"Not anymore. They know about your daddy bein' a big Klan mogul."

"Christ! How did they find out about that?"

"I told 'em."

"Damn, Joe!" he whined. "What're you tryin' to do to me?"

"Get rid of you, Billy. And keep you alive, too. Not that I really give a tinker's damn about you. But if you stay around here, some miner or darkie is gonna kill you one of these days, and then we'll have to send a good man to the pen for stompin' on a rat. That just ain't right, Billy, and I don't want to see it happen."

Joe checked his watch. "In twenty minutes there's a freight train leavin' for Oklahoma City. I think you oughta be on it, Billy, 'cause in thirty minutes we're cuttin' Prentiss loose."

Billy's eyes got very big. "My God, Joe, I ain't got a cent on me!"

"Then you're apt to get a few wrinkles in your belly over the next few days. But you still got your life, Billy, and that's a hell of lot more'n you deserve." He checked his watch again. "Eighteen minutes. You're wastin' time, Billy, and you just ain't got much to waste."

Billy took a couple of steps backward. He glanced at Martin, hoping for some kind of support from that direction. He saw only icy contempt. With a guttural moan, he whirled and bolted away in the direction of the railroad yard a half a mile to the north.

"That Neely girl is going to be disappointed," remarked Martin.

"Sometimes disappointment is better than gettin' what you want." Joe shrugged. "Hell, she was never gonna get Billy noway."

Then he brightened. "I got a message for you from Mister Saunders. You're to be in Faulkner's old office at eight sharp in the mornin', and you damn well better not be wearin' a torn shirt. He wants you lookin' proper for your swearin' in."

"My what?"

Joe smiled, pulled out the badge and tossed it to him. "Congratulations, Charlie, you just moved up in the world. You're gonna be our new sheriff."

"But, but...."

"Close your mouth, Charlie, or you'll get a fly in it. Come on, I'll explain it all while you drive me home."

*****

It was late and Joe was tired, very tired. He gazed with dismay at the piles of dirty dishes scattered across the table; three, maybe four days worth. They would have to be washed sometime. He shrugged. Tomorrow was soon enough. Belly full and eyes heavy, he heaved himself up and limped into the bedroom.

His foot was hurting again. Maybe there would be more rain. He would enjoy spending a day just lying in bed, sipping some of Faulkner's fine whiskey and listening to the gentle murmur of water from heaven. He pulled off the constable badge and stared at it, a cheap, battered piece of tin lying there in his palm. Then he dropped it into a drawer and closed it.

Just before he dozed off, it struck him that he had forgotten to quiz Billy about what had become of Tom's dogs. He would have to ask around about them.

END

CPSIA information can be obtained at www.ICGtesting.com
Printed in the USA
LVOW100928200912

299548LV00007B/70/P